Five interesting things about Kate Lace:

1. When I left school I joined the army instead of going to university – there were 500 men to every woman when I joined up – yesss.

2. While I was there I discovered that there were more sports than hockey and lacrosse and learnt to glide, rock climb, pot hole, sail and ski. I also discovered that I wasn't much good at any of them but I had a lot of fun.

3. I met my husband in the army. We've been married for donkey's years. (I was a child bride.)

4. Since I got married I have moved house 17 times. We now live in our own house and have done for quite a while so we know what is growing in the garden. Also, our children can remember what their address is.

5. I captained the Romantic Novelists' Association team on University Challenge the Professionals in 2005. We got to the grand finals so I got to meet Jeremy Paxman three times.

By Kate Lace

The Chalet Girl
The Movie Girl
The Trophy Girl
The Love Boat

Moonlighting

Kate Lace

6/10

little
black
dress

First published in 2010
by LITTLE BLACK DRESS
An imprint of HEADLINE PUBLISHING GROUP

A LITTLE BLACK DRESS paperback

1

Cataloguing in Publication Data is available from the British Library

ISBN 978 0 7553 4793 3

Typeset in Transit511BT by Avon DataSet Ltd,
Bidford-on-Avon, Warwickshire

Printed and bound in Great Britain by
Clays Ltd, St Ives plc

Headline's policy is to use papers that are natural, renewable and
recyclable products and made from wood grown in sustainable forests.
The logging and manufacturing processes are expected to conform to the
environmental regulations of the country of origin.

HEADLINE PUBLISHING GROUP
An Hachette UK Company
338 Euston Road
London NW1 3BH

www.littleblackdressbooks.com
www.headline.co.uk
www.hachette.co.uk

To my fellow members of the Romantic Novelists' Association in this its 50th glorious year, for the friendship, support and encouragement they have shown to me and each other. What a wonderful gang of writers they are!

Acknowledgements

I would like to thank Lacey and Seraia, who are both very classy and highly paid pole-dancers. They gave me lots of ideas and tips about what their work entails from the clothes to the moves, from the hours to the pay, and every other aspect you could imagine. I am incredibly grateful. In order to make Shoq a truly fictional establishment – which it is – I did alter certain details. If, in doing this, I have made any errors, then it is entirely my fault.

Jess Dryden kept her life compartmentalised. It was easier that way. Her sister, Abby, didn't know that she was a Special Constable in addition to temping in a succession of London offices, and the Metropolitan Police didn't have a clue that she'd originally trained as a dancer. It wasn't lying – absolutely not. It was just being economical with the truth.

Why did she do it? Well, she kept the stuff about the Met Police away from her sister as Abby had very strong views on absolutely everything, including her belief that anyone who had anything to do with any profession which made its staff wear a uniform (and that probably even went for the check-out girls at Tesco) was just one step away from enlisting into a fascist organisation and becoming a modern-day Brown Shirt. And Jess hadn't told the Met she was a dancer – or had hoped to be one – because she just knew it'd lead to jokes and leg-pulling and demands that she should join the Am-Dram Society or 'do a turn' at the Christmas Social. No, thanks. They didn't know about her past because it just made life easier.

It wouldn't have been as bad if it were only the truth that Jess had to be economical with; the trouble was, she had to be economical with everything. Despite living in a really grotty bedsit not far from Wormwood Scrubs – the men's prison in the west London Borough of Hammersmith, known locally as 'the Scrubs' – her earnings didn't quite cover rent, food and heating. And the situation was getting worse. So that was why she phoned Abby to ask her about their gran's house in the hills behind Marlow above the Thames Valley.

'What exactly do you mean?' said Abby tartly. 'You want me to ask the tenants if they need a housekeeper?'

'Yes, I mean exactly that. Gran's house is big, it has that huge attic which no one uses, and I could clean, do the gardening and generally look after whoever is renting it at the moment and live there for free in exchange. I can't afford to live in London on what I earn, and if I move further out, what I save in rent I'm going to lose on train fares. Abby, I'm skint, and I need to find somewhere I can live for almost free – or better still, completely free. I'm going to look for a better paid job, but until I land it, I really need some help. So how about it? Please, Abby? It's only till I get sorted out.'

There was silence.

'Look, I'm in a hole and I need digging out,' Jess went on. 'If you had space I'd ask if I could move in with you for a while.'

Jess heard a snort down the phone. 'You know that's impossible.'

'Yes, and I said "*if* you had space" and you don't – I know that.' Crikey, thought Jess, there was barely enough space for Abby and her husband Gavin in their tiny terrace in Fordingham, a minute market town ten miles from High Wycombe; there certainly wasn't any room for her too. 'But Gran's house is huge. I thought you said it was four blokes sharing it at the mo. So that's one in each bedroom, which leaves two bedrooms and the attic. I mean, how much room do these guys want?'

'Come off it, Abby, it's not as easy as that. They pay

rent so it's going to look bloody odd if we let you live there for nothing.'

'What's odd? I've got a half-share in that place. I know we agreed that we'd save all the rent money till we've got enough to modernise it and then sell it for a decent amount, but frankly, right now I'd far rather get half the rent. I need the money and if I can't have it, then at least let me live there. If I could live rent free, then the extra for my season ticket into London from the country would be easily affordable. Besides, I said I'd be a housekeeper so I'd hardly be freeloading, would I? All I'm asking is that you ask them.'

'I'll talk to Gavin.'

Jess bit her lip to stop herself from saying, 'Whoopee!' in the sort of sarky tone of voice that would have had her sister slamming down the receiver harder than Wile E Coyote hit the ground after falling off a cliff. Why did Abby always have to ask Gavin? thought Jess. Didn't she have a mind of her own? Besides, Gran had left the house to Abby and her – not to Abby, *Gavin* and her. Still, it wouldn't do to rile her sister, so she just said, 'Fine, please do that.'

'I'll ring you in a day or two. Let you know.'

'Good. Thanks.'

Jess disconnected the call and slumped back into the tatty armchair in her grotty room. Why did she always feel fed up when she'd just spoken to her sister?

Actually, Jess knew full well why. It was because Abby always treated her as if she was second-rate, a disappointment – a failure and not terribly bright. Obviously, being her big sister, Abby never quite said as much, but Jess could tell. It was implicit in everything Abby said that Jess was the one who had never quite lived up to their mother's expectations, who had never quite got the grades, never achieved her potential. However, Jess couldn't see why being a committed Green Party activist, conservationist, champion of animal rights and all-round tree-hugger gave Abby the high ground – but she was over four years her senior so Jess had learned not to argue. Besides, Abby had a quicker wit and a sharper tongue and always bested Jess in an argument so it was a waste of time to try.

There was also the hard fact, which Jess knew in her heart, that she *was* a bit of a failure. Since the age of six she'd spent twelve years training to be a professional dancer, only to fail to get beyond parts in the chorus of her local rep. She'd been good, very accomplished technically, but she didn't have that special quality that turned a good dancer into a really talented one. She'd auditioned for dozens of shows but had never made a break-through. At eighteen, when she'd failed to get into a performing arts college she'd given up the struggle and learned to type and use a computer instead.

It was while she was typing that she'd decided that an office job was going to kill her emotionally. She felt she had to do something that involved activity, being with other people who had a bit of a spark, doing some sort of good – anything but sitting behind a desk. And there was still a part of her that wanted to dress up – to play a role. Somehow the idea of joining the police seemed to tick all these boxes.

She'd been excited about the prospect when she'd told Abby. She should have known her sister would be horrified (obviously joining the Met was just one rung down from becoming an SS stormtrooper) and then, when the Met hadn't wanted her as a proper copper because they'd been on a recruiting drive for males from ethnic minorities and a white female didn't fill the bill, Abby hadn't bothered to disguise her *schadenfreude*. There was no way now that Jess was going to tell Abby she'd decided to get in through the back door by working as a Special.

And if she didn't hurry up and get down to the station she wasn't going to be working as a Special for much longer.

Wearily Jess hauled herself out of her chair, took her glasses off and popped in her contacts, then went to get her coat. It was a triumph of her willpower over her exhaustion that she forced herself out of the front door and back onto the cold pavement. The four hours of sleep that she'd grabbed after coming back from work were not really enough to keep her going through the night shift, but she told herself that as tomorrow was Saturday she could sleep as long as she liked, once she came off duty in the morning. Just eight hours of pounding the beat, being visible to the public, sweeping up drunks and stopping fights – then she could sleep all day. Besides, if she slept all day she wouldn't be tempted to eat – handy as there was no food in the fridge – and on her mealbreak at the station she could tuck into a huge fry-up for under a fiver. One of those tonight, and another tomorrow, would see her through the whole weekend and she wouldn't be using her own gas to cook for herself at home. It had to be cheaper, she told herself.

Jess locked the peeling door behind her, walked down her street to the main road and the brightly lit shops that she could rarely afford to do more than gaze at. God, being poor was grinding. She hated it; making do and mending, always having to think about every last penny, never having money for small luxuries.

It would be so much easier if she was like her sister and cared nothing for luxuries. Abby and Gavin despised such things – or at least Abby did; there wasn't much proof that Gav did, what with his job working for a software company with his laptop, nice suits and swanky company car. Which, in Jess's opinion made him a two-faced creep: preaching one thing and doing another.

Abby might have her faults but at least she was consistent.

Gavin had seemed to be totally committed to Green issues when he and Abby had been courting, but now they had been married for almost four years he seemed little more than lukewarm about the plight of the planet. It was like he'd been out to impress her and now he couldn't be bothered. OK, they were the only people Jess knew who used rainwater to flush their loo, plus they had a solar panel on their roof to provide hot water and Abby grew almost all their own veg, but Gav flew when he travelled abroad on business – even if it was only to Paris – and drove to work each day rather than travel on public transport.

Gav's lapses might have been offset by Abby's zealous recycling and by the way she only bought second-hand books, clothes and furniture, but Jess didn't think Gav gave a fig about his carbon footprint any more. And although she did agree with Abby about the state of the planet and the awfulness of conspicuous consumerism, it was the way Abby banged on about it *all the time* that got up her nose. She knew that Abby's sentiments were admirable and she did respect her sister's commitment to the cause – but it would be nice if, just occasionally, Abby could worry about her little sister instead of the planet. Abby could, if she wanted, buy new clothes or the odd luxury, which was more than Jess could. Maybe, Jess thought, if she could choose between ethical and extravagant she would choose ethical, like her sister, but it was the lack of choice she hated and the inability to splurge on something new and expensive.

Which made her wonder, not for the first time, why on earth she moonlighted from the day job as a volunteer police officer. Dumb, she knew. Well, not *dumb* that she did her bit for the community, but *dumb* that she chose to do it in a way that didn't help out her finances at the same time. But she had to keep telling herself that it was all part of her cunning plan to join the Met as a proper, full-time copper. Her track record as a Special would surely stand her in good stead, the next time she put in her application.

Of course, being a Special also injected a bit of excitement into her otherwise mundane life. There was nothing glamorous about being a temp, and at the moment she was temping for a company that imported wholesale plumbing supplies from the Far East. Dealing all day with invoices and orders for ballcocks, cisterns, washers and taps left her feeling brain-dead with boredom by the time she got the bus home.

It took Jess a good thirty minutes to walk a couple of miles to her police station which was between Kensington High Street and Earl's Court. There were buses and tubes but walking was free. She arrived just before ten o'clock and greeted her co-workers and fellow police officers, then made her way through to the locker room and began to get ready to go on duty. As Jess slipped into her stab vest and buckled on her belt kit, she was thankful that she'd found something to do that she really enjoyed, now she'd come to terms with the fact that she was never going to make it as a professional dancer – an ambition she'd had since the age of six when she'd seen *Cats* and fallen in love with the idea of wearing costumes and make-up and *performing*.

'Dancing's for sissies,' Abby had said disparagingly when Jess, on the train journey home from the show, had confided her dream in a whisper to her older sister. But Jess's mum had been more supportive and had found the money for her to go to stage school to learn ballet, tap, modern and jazz dancing. Abby had been offered the same opportunity, but had muttered deprecating things about it being a 'waste of money' and 'only for losers' and had loftily said that she'd rather boil her own head than learn to prance around like a twit like Jess. But there was something about the way she had spoken which made Jess wonder if Abby hadn't painted herself into a corner. Perhaps she was jealous of Jess and her new skill, and had felt that she'd cut her own nose off to spite her face. But as her sister was the sort who would never admit she was wrong or mistaken, it had been pointless to approach the matter.

And even more pointless, thought Jess, wishing for what would never happen now. She wasn't ever going to be a dancer and that was that. And working as a Special mightn't be glamorous but it certainly gave her a buzz – and besides, there was another bonus: Matt.

Matt Green was a proper copper who was also, in Jess's opinion, the sexiest thing on two legs. Sadly, their paths didn't seem to cross that often since their shift patterns rarely seemed to coincide, and even when they did, they didn't seem to get to work with each other. However, there was always the chance that she might get lucky the next time she was on duty. Whenever she saw him, Jess felt her innards go wobbly, her skin go tingly and her heart race. And no wonder, given his intense blue eyes, slightly olive skin tone and dark wavy hair. He looked fantastic in his uniform, although Jess had a private fantasy about what he might look like out of it, which did nothing for her equilibrium or her blood pressure. The one time they had had to work together she'd spent the entire night either burbling incoherently or in a clammy state of embarrassment at her inability to string a sentence together in recognisable English. Yet despite his unfortunate effect on her she still longed for a repeat experience. But not tonight, she noted sadly, as she read the roster sheet. Bum. Maybe Saturday she'd get lucky.

2

Jess was sound asleep on Saturday morning, after a hard night of breaking up two fights, which had resulted in five arrests for disorderly conduct and assault and then the mountain of paperwork the arrests had engendered . . . when her mobile hauled her back into consciousness. Bleary-eyed she checked out the caller ID – her sister's home number – before she hit the button to answer it.

'Hi, Abby,' she mumbled, still fuzzy with sleep.

'It's Gavin.'

'Oh.' She snapped awake. Gavin never phoned her. Was something wrong?

'Just a quick call,' which sounded reassuring. 'I've got an idea for a job for you that might earn you more than typing. A mate of mine told me about it. It would save us the hassle of having you live in your gran's house.'

What?! *Save us the hassle of having you live in your gran's house?* That woke Jess up even more and she could feel her blood pressure hurtling upwards. Any second now it might burst out of the top of her head like lava out of an erupting volcano. She was livid. However, before she had time to form a coherent response and tell Gavin exactly what she thought of his last statement, he carried on.

'There's a job as a dancer going. Good money too.'

That stopped Jess in her tracks. 'A dancer?' But almost more surprising than the possible job opportunity was the fact that it was her brother-in-law passing on the information. Gavin? Trying to help her? Jess felt stunned. Gav and she had never got on and neither of them made a secret about their feelings for the other.

'There's this joint in London and they're looking for girls to dance for the punters.'

Jess's heart sank. *That* sort of dancing, she should have guessed. It was probably the only sort of dancing Gav knew about. 'Forget it, I'm not interested.'

'Hear me out, Jess. It's good money and you don't have to take all your clothes off.'

She sniffed disbelievingly. 'Really.' All the places she'd ever heard of where the girls danced 'for the punters', that was exactly what they had to do.

'No, they don't. This is a class joint. Honest. I hear that some girls earn up to a grand a night. I'll email you the details.'

That was a shitload of money. Maybe she owed it to herself just to take a look at the job on offer; after all, just looking wouldn't put her under some sort of obligation to do anything about it. But a grand a night . . . Blimey, a couple of nights a week doing that and she could clear her debts, move into a decent flat and pay off her overdraft in less time than it would take to say, 'Get your kit off.'

Jess checked that Gavin had her email address and disconnected the call. As she put her phone back on the bedside table she thought about the possible job. Exotic dancing, or whatever this club was going to call it, certainly wasn't what she'd foreseen as a career path when she'd first slipped on a pair of ballet shoes. Her vision of curtain calls for some West End show had long since crumbled, but until quite recently she'd hoped she might get some chorus work in a provincial theatre. Working in some seedy club in London was not what she wanted, but could she afford to turn it down? And whatever Gavin said, she was sure that for *that* sort of money she would be required to do more than just dance. No way would it be possible to be that highly paid and not be expected to provide extras. The thought made Jess shudder.

Besides, what would her mother say if she were still alive?

Jess thought she knew.

A couple of hours later, curiosity had got the better of Jess and she was round the corner from her flat at an internet café and logging onto her email. She found the one from Gavin amidst the plethora of spam offering her enlargement procedures for bits of her body she didn't possess, pills of dubious origin and assurances that she'd been bequeathed large sums of money from bizarre relatives and well-wishers in far-flung corners of Africa.

The email gave her the club's website that Gav promised would tell her all she needed to know about getting an audition, which he also promised was just a formality. Although how he knew was something that worried Jess. 'But don't tell Abby I put you on to this,' he'd added. Like she was going to. She could just hear the sort of scathing comments Abby was bound to come out with. 'Slut' was a word that would feature large in them – or possibly 'slapper'. But dancing on a podium didn't necessarily mean that you were just a heartbeat away from prostitution – although, considering the thoughts that Jess had already had about that sort of club, the punters and the dancers, there was a chance that it *might* be a possibility. However, her conversation with Gav had roused her curiosity and while she was on the internet there was no harm in checking out the website, was there?

She cut and pasted the web link and hit the return key. As she waited for it to load she pushed her glasses up her nose and took herself back to the couple of foreign holidays they'd had with their mum (before she had got ill and Abby had discovered the Green Party and Animal Rights and had decided that having fun was wrong), when she and Abby had strolled along a Mediterranean beach in their skimpy bikinis that had hardly hidden anything at all and had tried to pretend they were ignoring the approving glances and whistles of the local males. In fact, looking back, Jess was now sure that Abby had been quite provocative in the way she'd swung her hips and stuck her chest out but, being only about ten or eleven at the time, Jess hadn't been worldly wise enough to appreciate quite what her older sister was up to.

Abby had lapped up the attention, the lustful looks and the occasional wolf whistles – although she'd denied it hotly later. Was that so very different or more acceptable than dancing in a club? No doubt Abby would think so – she would say that on a beach, wearing almost nothing, she was freeing her body, or being liberated. Just as she would say that dancing in a club was a subjugation of the female spirit to the lewd desires of the male psyche, or some such wordy bollocks.

Not that Jess felt she was capable of dancing in a revealing costume in front of a load of tanked-up and testosterone-laden men but if she did, well, the way she looked at it, it was more about earning cash with her god-given talents than being some sort of sex slave or being subjugated – assuming she wasn't actually required to be some sort of sex slave or be subjugated. In which case she would stand entirely corrected and Abby would be proved right. Actually, thought Jess with a wry smile, if she was a sex slave she'd probably have to *lie* corrected; she didn't think she'd be on her feet much.

The website loaded and Jess was surprised to see that the club – Shoq – was really quite sophisticated as she clicked through the various pictures and files. The décor was ornate but not over the top, the lighting was pretty decent from what she could see, there was no hint of rooms to rent by the hour and their restaurant offered a very sophisticated menu. Improbable though it seemed, maybe Gav hadn't been lying about what the girls there were required to do. And the girls, although heavily made-up, didn't look like they were on the game or any-thing really sleazy. Actually, Jess thought, some of them looked very classy.

So, given the quality of the dancers, Jess decided that even if she wanted a job there she probably wouldn't get one. How could she, Jess-from-the-sticks, short-sighted, world-class failure, temp typist and part-time flat-footed copper, possibly fit into that world? Sadly she closed down the web page and put the job opportunity to the back of her mind. Living for free and doing housekeeping in lieu of rent would be much more her thing.

Except that, according to Gav, it would be a *hassle* if she moved into her gran's old house. Why would it put anyone out to have her living in the attic? It wasn't as if the house wasn't big enough to accommodate another person. It was just typical of the couple's ability to make her feel as if she was a complete waste of space.

She sighed as she thought about the happy times she and Abby had spent in the house when Gran still lived there, when Mum had still been alive, when Abby had been just her big sister and hadn't taken on the role of being her moral guardian and her superior in every way.

And they *had* had happy times there. She tried to recall if it had ever rained. It must have done, but in her memories, when their mum had taken Abby and her there on holiday, the two of them always seemed to be playing in the garden, or lounging on the swingseat on the big back lawn reading books, or scrambling up the old apple tree by the garage. Maybe it had rained on the days she and Abby had played shrieking games of hide-and-seek over the house, or when they'd made toast in front of the sitting-room fire, scorching their knuckles along with the slices of bread. Accurate or not, her early memories of time spent at the house were filled with joy and laughter.

That had changed when Mum had been taken ill when Jess was eleven and Abby fifteen and they'd moved away from their house in Manchester to live with Gran permanently. The games of hide-and-seek were replaced with more grown-up games of doctors and nurses – only they weren't make-believe as they'd had to help their grandmother cope with a seriously ill patient. Jess couldn't remember any happiness in those last, dark months, just the constant trips up- and downstairs to see if Mum wanted anything, to help her take her pills, to carry up trays of food or glasses of water. There was the endless laundering of her bedding, the doctor's visits, the whispered conversations between him and Gran, her mother in and out of hospital, the agony of watching that vibrant laughing woman fade to a gaunt shadow.

Of course they'd realised that their mum might die, but it was still a terrible shock when it happened. Other people had got better from cancer – you read about it all the time. They had their radiotherapy, their chemo, they were poorly, they lost their hair – but then they turned a corner and they got better.

Only their mum didn't.

Jess blinked away the tears that sprang, even now, into her eyes and let herself back into her flat.

Hanging her coat up, she told herself to get a grip and that she was being unfair on Abby. No wonder Abby was as she was; she'd had a tough time too and then to cap it all, she'd had to take over responsibility for Jess when Gran died just as she left university. Not much fun for her to suddenly have to look after a teenaged sister, a house and everything that went with it and put her career plans on hold. Maybe that was why she was always so prickly and difficult.

3

Matt Green looked at the roster for the Saturday night shift on the station wall. He felt a small buzz of pleasure seeing that Jess was on the same shift as him. She was, without a doubt, the fittest policewoman he'd ever encountered, with her flawless skin, big grey eyes and gamine hairstyle that emphasised her cheekbones, and wonderful wide smile. In fact, she was such a looker he'd wondered, the first time he'd clapped eyes on her, whether she might be some sort of Strippergram sent to the police station as a send-up for one of the real policemen. The uniform usually made even pretty girls look utter frumps, but Jess's slim figure and yard-long legs made her look like sex-on-a-stick, even wearing a stab vest, which turned most other PCs into Humpty Dumpty lookalikes.

However, as she only ever worked Friday and Saturday nights and his shift pattern was quite erratic, it wasn't often that they were on duty together. He wondered if they would be rostered together on the beat. He really hoped so. It had happened once before and he'd found her easy humour and unflappability a real bonus. Added to which, she'd aroused his curiosity. Okay, he knew she was a Special so she had a day job, but even taking that into consideration she didn't look like a part-time police officer. No, that wasn't quite right; it wasn't that she didn't *look* like one – obviously she didn't, with her cover-girl looks – but she didn't move like one either. Which was why he'd asked her, as they'd paced along their beat the last time they'd been together, what her day job was.

'I'm a temp, a typist.'

'Oh.'

'You sound disappointed.'

'No, not at all.' Matt had shrugged. 'I mean, someone's got to do it.'

'And sadly, I got the short straw.'

'Don't you like your job?'

Jess was noncommittal. 'As you say, someone's got to do it.'

He'd been about to pry gently into her background, but at that moment their conversation had been interrupted by a shout on the radio, and most of the rest of the evening and night had seen them racing from one incident to another or completing the reams of paperwork that resulted.

Matt rather hoped that sometime soon he'd get the chance to find out more about the intriguing Jess. Maybe tonight would be his lucky night.

No, not 'lucky' like that, he told himself sternly. Although he wouldn't complain if it did turn out that way. Frankly, he'd just be thrilled if she gave him a second look because he felt she was so out of his league as to be unattainable.

It obviously *was* his lucky day – or rather shift – as he found out that he and Jess were being sent out on patrol together. Having been given their briefing, they returned to the locker room to collect their Hi-Vis jackets, their belt kit and their caps.

'Long time no see,' said Matt, trying to sound casual but friendly as they walked through the station corridors towards the front door. He didn't want his feeling of total pleasure at being rostered with her to become too obvious, because there was no way she was going to be interested in him.

'Yeah. A month?'

'About that.' Actually it was almost six weeks, but to say that might make him sound a bit like a stalker. 'So what have you been getting up to since then?'

'The usual. Eat, sleep, work – not necessarily in that order.'

'Lots of excitement then.'

Jess smiled at him. 'Adrenalin all the way. What about you?'

Matt shrugged. 'Oh, a couple of court appearances—'

'What were you up for?' She said it so deadpan that for a second Matt nearly took the bait.

'Ha ha. Anyway, it beat pounding the street in the pissing rain all day or filling in forms. Sitting around in court for six hours, drinking tea, reading the paper and waiting to be called is a fine way of earning a living in my humble opinion.'

'As a taxpayer I ought to object.'

'But I'm a taxpayer too and I definitely approve.'

The pair went out of the station, onto the busy main road. The cars swished over the damp tarmac, their headlights sweeping through the dark night.

'Roll on summer and longer evenings,' said Jess, suppressing a shiver.

'Warm evenings bring the scumbags out onto the streets. There's a lot more trouble on the beat when the weather is nice.'

Jess knew Matt was right but all the same it would be nice to tramp along the pavements without rain trickling down the back of your neck. They paced along in silence for a few seconds, their steady footfalls in perfect step.

'So what made you want to become a Special?' asked Matt.

Jess answered glibly, 'To annoy my sister.'

'Why? Has she got something against coppers?'

'Not coppers specifically – more anything that represents the Establishment. She's quite a political creature but her politics are a bit wacky.'

'Tell me about her.'

So Jess did. She kept it light-hearted and told Matt about her sister chaining herself to lorries exporting veal calves and refusing to buy anything tested on animals, about her recycling rainwater and about the solar panels on the roof and about her diet that largely consisted of chickpeas and lentils.

'So she has her own wind farm too,' Matt commented.

For a second Jess stared at him nonplussed and then, to Matt's relief, she gave a snort of laughter.

'So tell me about you,' said Jess, looking up at him.

'Not much to tell,' Matt said. 'Left school, joined the Met and I'm still here.' He was scanning the tax discs in the windscreens of parked cars as they walked along the pavement.

'A career copper.'

'Pretty much. I want to take my sergeant's exams in a year or so, but they're no pushover. I'll have to study like crazy for them, and the thought of that's a bit daunting.'

'I know what you mean. I'm not much of a one for exams either.'

'So what are you a one for? Oh, got one.'

'Got one what?'

'Lawbreaker. And I bet this vehicle isn't insured either.' He radioed in for a PNC check, gave the registration and then waited for the answer.

'No insurance, no MOT and no tax,' crackled a voice back over the airwaves. Matt replied with the location of the car and the radio operator promised that a tow truck would be sent out to take the car off the street pronto.

'Feeling better now?' said Jess as they resumed their beat.

'The owner's breaking the law. And supposing he has an accident, or mows someone down.'

Jess put her hands up. 'I'm not complaining. It was just a throwaway comment.'

'Sorry. I shouldn't have been so quick to climb on a soapbox.'

'Hey, no worries.'

'I just don't like to see illegal cars on the road. And besides, nabbing one is bound to help fill some Home Office quota or other.'

They strode on at the regulation pace that seemed almost leisurely but which was designed to allow police officers to keep pounding the beat for hours at a time without getting exhausted. Matt turned off the main road and Jess followed him into a side street, flanked by lock-up garages. They tried the handle of each one they passed, making sure all was secure before heading into the housing estate the garages served. Lights from some uncurtained windows painted rectangles of green on the black grass, music blared from a couple of flats but the streets were deserted and, if there was any lawbreaking going on, it was happening behind closed doors.

It was one of those inner-city estates which exist cheek-by-jowl with some of London's most upmarket postcodes. Two roads over was the back of Kensington Palace Gardens, and it amazed Jess that some opportunist developer hadn't managed to evict the population, level the site and stick some seriously swanky apartments there instead. Obviously the local council had a duty to provide affordable housing for their less well-off residents, but it hadn't prevented exactly the same scenario happening in loads of other places, usually with the connivance of the rich neighbours who were only too happy to see the sink estate and its problems disappear.

'Let's check out the Windmill,' said Matt.

'Okay.' If this estate merited the adjective 'sink' then the Windmill was the plughole. Actually, thought Jess, it was the U-bend below the plughole.

Matt glanced at her. 'Not nervous, are you?' The Windmill was a huge pub at the far end of the estate, a renowned hang-out for under-aged drinkers, smalltime drug dealers and most of the area's lowlifes. It was the sort of place most self-respecting women of Jess's age and upbringing wouldn't go near.

Jess slapped on a bright smile. 'No,' she said. 'Bring it on.' She hoped he couldn't tell it was all an act. She knew she had her night-stick and her stab vest, and she had a big strong policeman beside her to protect her – and over and above all that she had been trained to cope with aggressive and difficult situations. But the training was one thing and knowingly walking into a potentially hazardous area was something else entirely. She put her shoulders back and told herself that they could always call for back-up if things got nasty. She then tried telling herself they almost certainly wouldn't. However, she checked her vest was fastened to the neck and that her night-stick was handy.

They could hear the ruckus that the pub was kicking up from a hundred yards away. There was the low frequency thumping of a boom-box playing from a car in the car park and the squeal of tyres as that car or another burned rubber. Shouts and yells were audible above the two other sounds but there didn't seem to be anything sinister behind the raised voices; the voices were just loud, not raised in anger.

As they approached, the whiff of cigarette smoke

drifted towards them. A ghetto of smokers were gathered under the shelter of a big rectangular umbrella that had been fitted with downward pointing heaters suspended under the canopy.

'Your sister would go ape looking at all that heat being used to warm the sky,' observed Matt.

'She certainly would. Mind you, I think much the same too. If you're not warm enough, put a coat on.'

'Or go indoors. This is Britain not California.'

'You've noticed too.'

'I'm not called Sherlock by my admiring public for nothing!'

As they approached the pub a series of catcalls and defamatory remarks echoed towards them.

'Ignore it,' said Matt quietly.

'I have every intention of.' Jess said it with a confidence and a bravado she didn't feel. They wandered closer and a couple of the group shot them a look and slid off sideways into the shadows.

'They looked guilty,' said Jess. 'I wonder what they're up to.'

'Probably a bit of minor drug dealing – skunk or E. But we're just going to walk quietly past and say good evening and not give them any hassle. We're here simply to remind them that we're around and about, that's all.'

'Good,' said Jess, although she wasn't sure whether she was glad they weren't going to give this group any hassle, or whether she was glad that the crime that was possibly being committed was only a minor one, or glad that they were just going to walk right on by.

Matt eyeballed a couple of the gang as they strolled past and wished them a good evening. A grudging greeting came back in reply. It was only when they were about ten yards beyond the pub that Jess realised she had been holding her breath. She exhaled.

'That sort are all bravado and no balls,' said Matt.

Just like me, thought Jess, who hadn't felt at all at ease at the prospect of a confrontation. On the other hand, the presence of Matt had been deeply reassuring. She was sure she'd have felt even more edgy if she'd been in the same situation with some of the other police officers at the station. There were some people who you definitely wanted by your side if things got sticky and Matt was one of them. She glanced up at him as they tramped off the estate and back towards the main road. And *sooo* good-looking too. She reckoned she was quite lucky to be spending the night with him again. The trouble was, pounding the streets with such a hunk wasn't her idea of a dream date. She sighed. Maybe one day . . .

S imon Fellows sat opposite Matt Green in the canteen and swivelled round to see what it was that Matt was staring at so intently. When he saw the object of Matt's attention, he grinned broadly.

'Well, I'd give her one,' he said in a low voice.

Matt turned his head and said, in accordance with Met Police equality awareness procedures, 'That's a sexist remark and I feel I ought to challenge you on that.' Actually, he'd have challenged Simon over that remark even if it hadn't been in direct contradiction of Met Police policy. Sometimes, despite the fact that he'd known Simon since their training course and they were friends, Simon's macho, swaggering attitude could hit a really off-key note. And this was one of them.

Simon snorted. 'Yeah right. Cut the PC crap. You're only saying that because you don't fancy any competition from me.'

Actually, thought Matt, he was 'only saying it' because he found it quite offensive, but didn't think he could be bothered to explain this to Simon, who was a lost cause in that respect. Besides, he didn't want his friend to know how much Jess fascinated him. On the way back to the station for their mealbreak, Matt had tried to get Jess to talk about herself again but her answers had been evasive and perfunctory. Did it mean she disliked him, or was it just that she didn't want work colleagues to know about her private life? Whatever, the way she protected her privacy just made her all the more attractive in his view. Not that he was going to let anyone, least of all Simon, get the smallest hint – because if he did, he could be sure that his interest in Jess would be the butt of locker-room jokes for days to come.

'She's a fox, I agree,' he conceded, because Simon would really smell a rat if he said otherwise, 'but it doesn't mean I fancy her. And besides, what would your fiancée say if she knew you were ogling Jess?'

'Sal doesn't mind me window-shopping. There's no harm in looking, now is there? And don't change the subject. Admit it, you do fancy her.'

Matt shook his head.

'Then you're the only bloke for a mile around who doesn't. I mean, look at those legs. What wouldn't a red-blooded bloke give to have those wrapped around him?' And with that, Simon cleared his tray off the table and went outside for a smoke.

As much as Matt despised the opinion Simon had just voiced, it would be hypocritical to deny that he'd had a similar fantasy himself, although hearing Simon say it out loud was disturbing. He didn't like to think that Jess was the object of other people's lewd thoughts. He wanted to protect her from them – though, realistically, how could he? He didn't question the irony that although he fancied her deeply, he didn't want anyone else to.

Matt studied her surreptitiously via her reflection in the window with the black night behind turning into an effective mirror. As he watched, Jess gathered up her plate and tea cup, stood up from the table and walked across the canteen to the trolley, already laden with dirty crockery. He noticed, watching her from a distance, rather than from his previous position of being alongside her, that she moved beautifully – planting each footstep very precisely in direct line with the previous one, as if she was walking a tightrope. The effect was extraordinarily graceful and caused her hips to sway most attractively. Matt, looking at her, thought this side effect of the way she placed her feet was entirely accidental and that Jess was unaware of the seductive power of her sinuous walk. In fact, he thought, she looked like a cat-walk model. Maybe that was it! Maybe she did that in her spare time. He could almost see her, dressed to the nines in some designer gown, sweeping along a runway. He'd ask her if he was right when they went back out on the beat.

They walked out of the station in silence when their mealbreak was over; Matt using the opportunity to work out how to formulate his question.

'So,' he said eventually, 'I was wondering if you'd ever done any modelling, only your face seems familiar somehow.'

Jess stopped in her tracks and stared at him, completely nonplussed. 'Me – a model? You must be joking. What on earth gives you that impression?'

There was no way Matt was going to admit to having studied her across the canteen. Christ, how much of a stalker would that make him seem? He bluffed on. 'As I said, I just thought I'd seen you somewhere before.'

'Perhaps you managed to recognise me from the last time we were on the beat together.' Jess raised an eyebrow in amusement before she continued pacing again.

'I should have said that I feel I've seen you somewhere else. Maybe in a picture,' he added lamely. This wasn't going as he'd planned. He sounded like a real headcase. Not good.

'So now you're telling me that you think you've seen my mugshot. What, on *Crimewatch*?' she offered.

'No,' protested Matt. He gave up. 'Never mind.'

Jess gave a quiet little laugh. 'I'm intrigued, because the only pictures I've noticed you looking at are the ones around the station of "Britain's most wanted". It could be I'm a criminal mastermind who has infiltrated the Met Police for my own nefarious ends.'

It was Matt's turn to laugh. Anyone who looked less like a criminal mastermind than Jess was hard to imagine.

'I know – I'm a hooker or a shoplifter and you've nicked me in the past.'

Matt wished he'd never started on this tack of conversation. 'Forget it. I was wrong.'

To Matt's relief, Jess let the subject drop. However, he didn't think she was going to give him any more details about herself. If anything, she'd put an even greater distance between them. Bum.

Jess didn't waken till mid-afternoon on Sunday. Working two night shifts after a full week's work wasn't the most restful way of spending a weekend, although what she missed out on sleep she generally felt she gained in experience, camaraderie and a host of other ways. And, of course, this weekend she'd had the wonderful bonus of time spent with the delectable Matt. God, he was gorgeous. Although what had that weird conversation about seeing her picture been about? Or had it been a chat-up line? If so, chat-up lines didn't come much lamer. As if she could ever have been a model! He was definitely someone who should have gone to Specsavers.

Even so, Jess felt a little frisson of lust zip through her insides as she thought about Matt. What she wouldn't give to get up really close and personal with him, rather than just tramping along some grubby streets beside him. But how likely was that? He was a hunk, and her sister had always told her that men didn't like girls who wore glasses – and besides that, she was too skinny to be fanciable. Abby had always been the one with the looks and the curves; Jess the one with the braces and the glasses, although at least the braces were now a thing of the past. But even though her teeth were now straight, none of her other faults could be addressed without the help of surgery. Abby had told her in no uncertain terms that her mouth was too wide and her eyes too far apart and besides, Abby had said, it was a well-known fact that no one liked grey eyes. So, that was it – she was officially plain. There was no way Matt Green would give her a second look.

Besides, he was such a fit guy he was bound to have a girlfriend stashed away in the background. Nope, she didn't stand a chance.

She yawned, stretched and looked at her watch. Too late to go to the nearby cyber café and get her emails; she decided to have a bath instead. Jumping out of bed she glanced out of the window and changed her mind. The bright sunshine made even the crappy bit of Shepherd's Bush that she lived in look halfway decent. She'd go for a nice run and then she'd have a bath. After that, she'd have a relaxing evening in front of the box with a glass of wine or two, and then she might have a fighting chance of getting a relatively decent night's sleep before she went back to work on Monday.

Decision made, she pulled on her joggers, a T-shirt, socks and trainers, limbered up a bit by doing some stretches and a few minutes later she was pounding down the streets. Jess had no clear idea where she was headed but when she saw a road sign pointing to 'West End' she let her feet head that way. Maybe she'd jog into Hyde Park, at the Kensington Palace gate, run through it, out again at Marble Arch and then head back along the Bayswater Road towards Shepherd's Bush.

She'd always been fit, her dancing had seen to that, and she'd had the self-discipline to keep it up since then. Being in the police helped, since they expected a certain level of fitness from their constables. Being too unfit or overweight to catch a felon running away wouldn't go down a storm with the brass. Jess's mind cleared to a virtual blank as her feet thudded rhythmically on the pavement while she covered first yards and then miles. She barely noticed her surroundings as her route took her from mostly suburban housing estates towards a small industrial complex then along a main road that boasted B&Bs and cheap hotels rather than flats or houses, and then bright lights into the smart squares and avenues and the brighter lights and bigger shops of the edges of the West End. This bit of London, from Notting Hill through to Kensington she knew fairly well; it was part of the beat she often patrolled when she was on duty, although mostly her beat took her off the main roads to the more residential areas tucked away behind the thoroughfares. The area cars cruised amongst the bright lights, while the foot patrols were down the side roads making sure people slept safe in their beds – or that was the theory.

She was jogging on the spot, waiting for the traffic-lights to change, when her eye fell upon an unlit neon sign – *Shoq*.

Shoq? It certainly was that. That was the night-club slimy Gav had said she ought to try out for. She'd never noticed it before, but then she'd never heard of it before Gav had mentioned it. She reckoned she'd only noticed it now because the name rang a bell. Her feet stilled as she stared, transfixed by it, until the lights changed. Then, as if she was being pulled by some hidden magnet, she walked across the pavement to examine the billboards that decorated the exterior. Glossy pictures of the same sort of classy girls who had featured on the website were posted in the showcases. Jess studied them intently. There was no suggestion that there was total nudity on offer – or anything else for that matter. Maybe the club didn't offer 'extras'. She was so engrossed she didn't notice the man standing beside her, studying her equally hard.

'Fancy a go?'

Jess jumped and spun round. A middle-aged man was standing a little too close for comfort. Nice suit, slicked-down hair, loud tie was her instant impression and then, over and above the good clothes, she thought he looked a bit smooth, a little smarmy. She couldn't put her finger on it but he was the sort of bloke she wouldn't want to share a taxi with.

'You scared me,' she said as she recovered her composure.

The bloke looked at her blandly and repeated his question. Then said that he'd audition her there and then if she wanted. 'I'm always on the lookout for new talent,' he added.

'Do I look like the sort of girl who'd work here?' retorted Jess, still feeling edgy.

'Frankly, yes. You've got the figure and the face – what else do you think you need?' He looked her up and down.

Jess felt her jaw sag slightly. Did she really look like someone who wanted to earn her living as an exotic dancer? She couldn't think of an answer but crossed her arms defensively across her T-shirted chest.

'Shame,' said the stranger. 'Even with that crap tracksuit on I can see you could be cut out for it. Never mind.' He turned away.

Quite what possessed Jess to yell, 'Hang on a moment,' she didn't know. Possibly some brash alter ego took her over. Or maybe her subconscious was telling her she needed the money.

'Does that mean you *do* want a go?'

'Now?' Jess still felt as if she'd been possessed by some other bolder, more reckless person.

'Why not?' He fumbled in his pockets and withdrew a large bunch of keys which he used to deal with the array of locks that secured the double doors.

'Do you open on a Sunday?' Jess enquired.

'Nah. Just coming in to do some admin. Miles.'

'Miles of what?'

'No, I'm Miles. It's me name.'

'Oh. Jess.'

'Jess? Nice name.' Miles swung one of the doors open and gestured for her to precede him. As she entered the building, he flicked on a light. 'Hang about,' he said as he dived off to one side.

Jess paused and took stock of her surroundings. A staircase led down from a fairly spacious lobby. To her right was a desk behind which were racks for coats. The walls were black, as were the carpets. Ahead and over the stairs was an enormous mirror in a heavy gilded frame, tilted forward to reflect anyone entering the building. But that was it on this level; just an entrance area. Obviously, all the action took place downstairs. She looked up into the mirror and saw herself, her face pink with the exertion of her run and her eyes even greyer and wider than usual, and realised that the expression in them was one of anxiety. In fact, she looked scared rigid, as well she might. What on earth was she doing, going into an empty building with a completely strange man? A man she'd already judged to be not entirely trustworthy. No one knew where she was or was expecting her back. If anything happened . . . What was she thinking of ?!

'I'm sorry,' she said, stepping away from the top of the stairs and heading back towards the door.

'Hey!' Miles, who was fiddling in a cupboard, spotted her dash for freedom. 'Where do you think *you're* going?'

Jess froze. 'I . . . I'm . . . I've changed my mind,' she said, trying to control the shake in her voice which mirrored the sudden onset of the shakes in her knees.

'Why? Do you think I've got evil plans? That I'm going to jump on you as soon as I get you downstairs?'

'Well, I . . .' Jess suddenly felt rather foolish. Were her fears so obvious?

Mile gestured to a CCTV camera in a corner. 'These have movement-sensitive switches. They turn on as soon as anyone enters the building. We've got them all over the place – they protect us and our clients. We can't afford to have anyone making false allegations about what goes on here; it'd be too easy for one of the dancers to accuse a customer of inappropriate behaviour or vice versa. So unless you think I want to spend some time in nick for being stupid enough to make a pass at a potential employee and getting caught in glorious Technicolor, I would suggest you're probably pretty safe.'

'Oh.'

' "Oh" indeed.' Miles sighed. 'So, now I've switched the alarms off so we don't have the fuzz thinking there's a break-in, and the cameras are monitoring me to make sure your virginity is safe, do you want to have a try-out?' He sounded almost bored at the prospect of conducting an audition. Obviously, having a young woman put on a private show was nothing unusual for him.

Jess felt more than slightly foolish, and irrationally angry that he thought she might still be a virgin, but was surprised, given her implied accusation, that Miles still wanted anything to do with her, let alone consider offering her a job.

'Well . . .'

'Up to you, doll. But I'm a busy man and I haven't got all afternoon. Yes or no.'

Jess made up her mind. 'Yes.'

5

Jeez, why on earth had she said that? But too late now, Miles was already heading for the basement and expecting her to follow, so she did. He ran down the shallow, black-carpeted stairs and into a huge dark void with Jess hard on his heels. He hit another bank of switches and lights flicked on around the huge subterranean space – uplighters, downlighters, spots, chandeliers, the works. But all cleverly done, all quite subtle and in the right place so that corners were softly illuminated, focal points highlighted and this huge, windowless room was made to look . . . cosy. Bizarre though it seemed, given the size, the mirrors and the uniformly black décor, the place really did look genuinely cosy – and inviting. Whoever had designed Shoq had put a lot of thought into it and possibly, even more money. She also noted the pictures that decorated the walls. Jess didn't know much about art but even she thought that they had a touch of class, and judging by the visible brush-strokes on the one nearest her, they were originals.

In pride of place in the centre, and lit by several spotlights, were three, waist-high podiums each with a shiny chrome pole stretching up to the ceiling. Around them were numerous tables with comfy padded chairs – all upholstered in black. A vast bar stretched the complete length of a wall, with mirrors behind it and huge arrays of bottles and glasses all lit to glint enticingly. At right angles to the bar was a smoky mirrored wall and then on the other two walls were alcoves with tables surrounded by cushioned banquettes. Each alcove looked quite private, although they would all get a view of the room, and each one was lit by several uplighters that managed to make these areas look faintly exotic, quite luxurious but somehow, not tacky. And then Jess noticed that each alcove had its own pole in the centre of the table.

Well, thought Jess, maybe that was the closest she would be expected to get to any of the clients. If that was it, she'd be able to cope, as long as they didn't paw her or expect her to sit on their laps. The thought of some dirty old man touching her up made her feel quite queasy, although she reckoned in a place like this it would have to be a *rich* dirty old man. Did that make it better? Jess answered her own question in a nano-second. No.

'Okay,' said Miles indicating one of the podiums. 'Hop up. Done this before?' Jess shook her head. 'Well, I've got to go to the office and download some stuff onto my laptop. You have a twirl about, or whatever you want to do; have a practice, get a feel for it. I'll be back in a few minutes and you can show me some moves. If I think you've got what it takes, we can train you up. I'm not expecting perfection; we can teach you to dance the way our customers expect. What I *am* expecting is for you to be fanciable. Alluring. Hot.'

Jess nodded and stared at the pole. Blimey, what sort of 'moves' was she expected to do? And 'hot'. She didn't think she could do hot. She swallowed.

Miles smiled at her. 'Just think of the pole as a bloke you fancy. Get up close to it, wrap yourself around it. Try to turn it on. Music?'

'What?' Jess was trying to work out how you turned on ten foot of chrome-plated scaffolding pole.

'Music?'

'Oh, yes please.'

'Right, I'll put some on from my office. I'll come back and have a look at you in about five. Okay?'

Miles walked to the back of the club, to the huge smoked-glass mirror that covered the whole rear wall. He opened a door concealed at one end and disappeared, leaving Jess alone. Despite being on her own she still felt incredibly self-conscious as she made her way over to one of the podiums and climbed up the three steps. She sat on the edge, toed off her trainers and then examined the circular stage she was to perform on. It was quite big, she noticed; plenty of room for her to move around and not to make a complete arse of herself by falling off. A song from the Killers began to play and Jess stood up and let her body start to move to the music. Dancing she could do – but dancing with a ten-foot pole? Well, she could give it a shot. And anyway, there was no one to see her make a fool of herself while she worked out what to do.

She grabbed the chrome and used it to support her while she leaned back and allowed her spine to arch, her head almost touching the floor. As she pulled herself upright she swung her body sensuously in time to the beat. Then she placed both hands on the pole and wrapped her left leg around it so the crook of her knee held it firmly, then she leaned back again. She put her hands on the floor behind her, then released the pole, pushed her body so her weight was over her shoulders, kicked slightly with her right foot which was still on the ground, went up into a handstand and then brought her feet back down again and stood up. She swung round so she could watch her moves in the huge mirror. Despite her chunky jogging bottoms she could see that she looked quite sexy dancing with this length of metal.

Forgetting the incongruity of what she was doing, with

no audience and dressed completely inappropriately, she gave herself up to the music. She pirouetted and strutted, she straddled the pole, slid up and down it and generally writhed around it, wondering if this was what a serpent felt like, sliding through branches in a jungle. The music changed to something slower and more seductive, and Jess altered her dance to a more balletic style. She was so utterly engrossed in what she was doing that she didn't notice Miles re-enter the main bar. In fact, the first time she caught sight of him was when she spun round and saw him sitting at a table about ten feet from her. She stopped, mid-move.

'You've done this before,' he said.

'Never,' she said, panting slightly. 'I did train as a dancer though.'

Miles nodded. 'It shows – you're good. What have you got under your jogging bottoms?'

Jess was horrified. What business was it of his? 'I beg your pardon?'

'I want to see what your legs are like. Can't see nothing with those shit-awful trousers on.'

'Oh.'

'So can I see your legs?'

Jess felt the colour rush into her face and she tried to remember just exactly what knickers she had on. Were they some antique pair that had gone grey and tatty from too many trips through the washing machine? Or had she put a thong on this morning? Oh God, please let her be wearing something decent – and clean.

'Well, can I? Look, love, if you're going to be shy this is the wrong business for you to be in so you might as well sling your hook right now.'

Jess remembered what Gav had said about the money. A grand a night. Knowing him, he'd probably exaggerated but even if it was only half – or a quarter – that amount, it wasn't to be sneezed at. Anyway, this bloke had probably seen it all before, even thongs and grubby pants. Jess put her hands on the elastic of her tracksuit bottoms and slid them down, glancing at her undies as she did so. Phew, her newish pink ones; clean and respectable. There was a God after all. She stepped out of her trousers and tried not to feel too hideously embarrassed by Miles staring at her lower half.

'Okay,' he said after a few seconds. 'Do some more moves for me.'

Jess bent to retrieve her trousers.

'Leave those. I want to see you perform properly.'

Jess swallowed and thought about the money again as she began to move. She'd probably let people see more when she'd been on the beach. Bikinis didn't leave much to the imagination. After a few bars, she began to forget about Miles and her knickers and dance properly to the music, feeling the beat flow through her, letting her feet respond to the melody. The track stopped and there was silence. Jess grabbed her trousers and hurriedly pulled them on.

'When can you start?'

'Oh.' After a life of being rejected following an audition, this wasn't what she expected. 'Sorry?'

'I'm hiring you. Seriously, you're great. We're going to have to get you some dresses made and you'll have to learn some moves. I'll ask Carrie to call you and tell you how things work here: the rules, the hours, what we expect from you and what you can expect from us. Carrie looks after the dancers for me so she'll be your point of contact from here on in. So when can you start?'

Jess bit her lip. 'Soon, I suppose. It's just, well, I've got a day job and . . .'

'Sack it.'

'I don't know that I can,' Jess said.

'What? You're locked into some sort of contract, is that it? Okay, I'm patient. I can wait till you've worked your notice out.'

Jess shook her head. 'It's not that. I don't know if I can afford to give it up.'

Miles let out a bellow of laughter. 'So what's the day job? Robbing banks?'

'No, I temp.'

'Trust me, you can afford to give it up.'

Jess plucked up a last dreg of courage. How did he know? She might get paid quite a decent amount, enough so that she wouldn't have to moonlight as well, which was what she thought she might have to do. She hadn't considered giving up the day job completely. 'So what's the salary here?'

'We don't pay salaries, you get tips.'

'Tips?' She was horrified. She'd worked as a waitress, she knew exactly how lousy tips could be. Tips weren't going to pay the rent. Huh! A grand! What a joke. She'd be lucky to make enough to feed herself, let alone cover any of her bills. And with only tips on offer she didn't think that moonlighting was an option. She couldn't risk being taken off the employment agency's books because she was too knackered to work and upset the regulars she temped for. No, this was an opportunity she'd have to pass up. And next time she saw Gav she'd tell him his mate was talking out of his arse. A grand a night. Pah!

She sat down on the edge of the podium and began to shove her feet back into her shoes. The sooner she got out of this dive the happier she'd be. The sleazeball had just wanted a cheap thrill, a private show and she'd fallen for it. She finished tying her laces and stood up. 'Right,' she said, trying to sound casual. 'It's been an experience, but if I only get tips then I can't possibly afford to work for you. I need a job that pays me properly.'

'So what's your definition of properly?' Miles seemed to be laughing at her.

'Fifteen hundred a month.'

'You could earn that in a week here – easy. Possibly in a night if you're good enough.'

Jess sat down on the edge of the podium. 'A week?'

'A week. My best girls can earn two hundred and fifty an hour, easy. And in case you're wondering, there's no funny business involved either. This is a respectable joint. Of course, you probably won't make that to start with, but stick with me, kid, and . . .' He let the sentence and the implication hang in the air.

Maybe Miles wasn't such a sleazeball after all.

Abby stood by the kitchen sink, washing up their supper dishes. No un-ecofriendly dishwasher for her, no thank you. In front of her the old sash window which gave a view onto their garden had sheets of plastic taped over the frames to provide some rudimentary secondary 'glazing' till they could afford to have the house properly double-glazed (but only as a strategy against fuel inefficiency), and the kitchen behind her was hardly state-of-the-art as most of the fixtures and fittings were the ones from the seventies that had been there when they bought the house in Fordingham in that pretty corner of the South-East where Oxfordshire, Buckinghamshire and Berkshire come together. It suited Abby; the last thing she wanted, she said, was somewhere that had had money spent on wasteful consumerist trappings like fitted kitchens and power showers. Gav professed he didn't mind either, although Abby had noticed that in the last few years – since they'd got married – he'd been a little less enthusiastic about Green issues. Of course, she knew that this was because he now had to earn enough to support his wife as well as himself, and this left him little

time for campaigning. To make up for this she threw herself even more enthusiastically into the cause; the windowsill bore witness to this with a row of environmentally-
friendly cleaning products lined up along it.

'You know,' she called over her shoulder to Gav who
was in the other room of their tiny terrace, 'I've been
thinking. Having Jess live in Gran's house wouldn't be
such a bad thing. It isn't as if it would cost us anything.'

'No,' replied Gav flatly. 'I'm dead against it and you
know that.'

Abby wished she understood why he was so anti the
idea. What harm could Jess possibly do, living in the attic
of that huge house?

'But she wouldn't be doing any harm.'

'I don't think the tenants would like it. It's a blokes'
house and she'd cramp their style.'

'Jess wouldn't get in their way.'

'Of course she would. She'd have to share the
bathroom and the kitchen, and you know what it's like
when there's a woman about – they always want to be
tidying up or bitching if there's beer in the fridge or not
being able to spend four hours in the bath.'

'But Jess wouldn't be like that. Couldn't we at least ask
them?'

'No.' Then Gavin seemed to change tack. 'Look, we
actually rent the house to the company that employs
them. We can't go putting other people in there willy-
nilly. It just wouldn't be fair. It's probably a breach of the
tenancy agreement.'

'Oh. I hadn't thought of it like that.' Actually, Abby
now realised that she had no idea that the tenancy
agreement was with their tenants' employer. Hell, she
didn't even know they were all employed by the same
outfit. In fact, she suddenly realised she knew very little
about the tenants, full-stop.

Not that it mattered. Gav had handled everything to do with letting the house when she and Jess had inherited it. They'd all agreed that it was too big to keep on, too expensive to run, and that the only way they could share the inheritance fairly was to sell the place. Then Gav had said that to get a decent price for it they had to do it up first – which was indubitably true – and as neither she nor Jess had the sort of money it was going to take, they ought to let it out and save the rent till they had enough to pay for the modernisation. He'd said he knew someone in the estate agency business so they'd let him take care of everything. It seemed the obvious solution. Which was fine – except Abby currently didn't have a clue about what was happening with the house, how much rent it had earned them, how close they were to being able to sort it out, nothing. And the house had been let out now for a couple of years. She wondered about asking Gav if she could have a look at the paperwork. It made sense for her to have a grasp of what was happening, didn't it?

'Tea?' offered Gavin, coming through into the kitchen as Abby tipped the dirty washing-up water down the sink.

Abby was so surprised at Gav's offer – he rarely set foot in the kitchen – that she forgot her concerns about the running of her inheritance. Instead she made her mind up to ring Jess and tell her sister that her plan for rent-free living was a no go. Jess wouldn't like it but Abby knew she'd find it far easier to upset her own sister than her husband. Gavin had a filthy temper and he was tough to live with when he was in a mood. If Jess got in a strop Abby wouldn't have to suffer the consequences like she would with Gav.

6

'Sorry, Jess, but there it is.'

'It doesn't matter,' said Jess honestly. Now her new job was about to start she felt much more relaxed about the matter of her rent. She'd had a phone call from Carrie the day after Miles had offered her the job, and the woman had confirmed Miles's estimate of her earnings potential. Jess now not only didn't need to live rent-free but was actively considering finding a nicer and therefore more expensive place to live. 'In fact, I was going to ring you myself soon to tell you that I've got a new job and that my finances are rather healthier than they were last time we spoke.'

'So what are you doing now? Still temping?'

Jess was prepared for this moment. Pole-dancing wasn't going to be the answer of choice to give her sister. 'I've got a position working for a bloke in the entertainment industry. I start next week.'

'Oh? What sort of entertainment – books, films, theatre?'

'More sort of cabaret acts.'

'Sounds a bit tacky.'

Typical bloody Abby, thought Jess. She hasn't got a clue what my new job is about but she takes the opportunity to sneer at it anyway. Always looking down on anything I do, always trying to belittle me. 'Maybe,' she said tightly, 'but the pay's good.'

'Pay isn't everything,' sniffed Abby. 'There's no shame in being poor.'

'Says you. I'm the one who's on the breadline.'

'Don't exaggerate so, Jess.'

It was all very well for Abby to be so superior when she was, in effect, a kept woman. She and Gav might live in a small house but that was because Abby insisted that their Green credentials would be compromised if they moved into anything larger. And they didn't go on holiday – well, not ones to exotic locations, for the same reason, although Gav often seemed to have to jet around the world on business, which apparently didn't count. Abby tended to buy clothes from charity shops – recycling being everything – and she only rode a bike, although Gav was happy to get to work in his company car – something else which didn't seem to count – so quite what they spent their money on defeated Jess. Not that it was any of her business, of course, but she couldn't help but be curious. They weren't loaded but they must be comfortably off, although Abby always behaved and looked as though she never had a brass farthing. Did Gav keep her short? Was her fixation against buying anything new just a cover for that? Jess, if she was honest, didn't really care. She had enough problems of her own without worrying about her sister's finances.

And if she didn't have time to worry about Abby's finances, she had still less time to talk to her sister. She had an appointment over at Shoq, with Carrie. She'd been told to get herself over to the club several hours before it was due to open at nine to get fitted for some frocks, meet some of the other dancers and learn some moves using the pole. As she hadn't finished her office job until five it was going to be a scramble to get changed, grab a snack and get back up to the West End by six-thirty. A chat with Abby had been the last thing Jess had needed with such a crowded timetable. With a firmness and speed that startled them both, Jess finished the conversation then turned her attention to getting ready for her first encounter with her future co-workers.

She popped a couple of slices of bread into her toaster, threw herself into the shower and was out of it and dried again before her toast had had a chance to cool completely. She munched on it while she unpacked the new undies she'd treated herself to in her lunch-hour. She suspected she would be sharing a dressing room with the other dancers and there was no way she was going to risk being embarrassed by her pants ever again.

She slipped them on between mouthfuls and admired the bra-and-knicker set briefly in her mirror before covering them up with leggings and a pullover. When Carrie had phoned, Jess had asked what she ought to wear and had been assured that it didn't matter as she would be found a suitable outfit from stock when she turned up. Jess had to admit that she was just a little apprehensive as to what this suitable outfit was going to be like. She was, however, told to bring pretty shoes that she could also dance in. That was a bit more of a problem until she remembered a pair of green strappy sandals that lurked at the back of her wardrobe. She hoped they would do as, frankly, she had nothing much else.

She needn't have worried about either the shoes or the outfit. Carrie, a stunning blonde of nearly six foot and who couldn't have weighed more than ten stone, met Jess at the entrance to the club and swept her off to the dressing room.

Jess was intrigued to discover that the smoked looking-glass at the far end of the bar was in fact a two-way mirror and behind it ran a corridor that gave access to the dancers' dressing room. A similar smoked-glass window with a door in it flanked one side of the passage, and Jess guessed that not only was this another two-way mirror but that there were rooms or offices behind it so a view could be had into the main area of the club from them. She wondered whether, before her audition, Miles had watched her dancing when she thought he'd been busy in his office. It gave her a faintly creepy feeling that he'd spied on her – or might have done.

Carrie led her into the big room where the dancers changed.

'Normally it's pretty crowded in here. If you're still here around nine, when things start to get really busy, you'll see what I mean.'

Jess took in the room; along one wall was a long counter strewn with hair-driers and straighteners, bags of cottonwool balls, boxes of tissues, bottles of cleanser and nail-polish remover, brushes, combs and all sorts. Above it were a dozen mirrors, each surrounded by lights, just like she was used to from her few sallies into the theatrical world when she'd landed one of her rare roles in the chorus line. Opposite this huge, communal dressing-table was a bank of built-in wardrobes, each with a name, neatly typed on a label, on the door.

'Here's yours,' said Carrie, pulling open a door halfway along. She reached onto the shelf above the empty rail and picked off a key which she handed to Jess. 'Try not to lose it.'

Jess thanked her and stashed it carefully in her bag.

'Now let's get you kitted out. Size eight?' Jess nodded as Carried moved to the end of the room and threw open another cupboard. It was full of sumptuous dresses covered in sequins or beads or embroidery. All beautiful, all individual and all, Jess had no doubt, fantastically expensive. 'This is where the girls put the frocks they've done with. Often someone else will buy one – you'd be surprised how the same dress can look totally different on another dancer.'

Jess was a little confused. 'How come they can sell their dresses? Doesn't Shoq own them?'

'No, the girls buy their own. They each have about a dozen at any one time so they can create a whole mass of different looks. We get them made for them, of course.'

Jess felt a cold wave of disappointment. A dozen frocks, all made-to-measure – how much was that going to cost? Suddenly her first week's – even her first month's wages – seemed to have been swallowed up in an expense she hadn't foreseen. She put any tentative plans for moving on the back-burner.

Carrie was busy flicking through the hangers. 'Here's one. This should do you.' She glanced at the label. 'And Chantelle only seems to want twenty quid for it.' She ran her eye over it. 'Ah, here's the reason.' She pushed the dress at Jess. 'Look, a tiny split in the seam. You could fix that in a trice. Try it on.'

'But why doesn't Chantelle fix it?'

'Got bored with it, I expect.'

'Twenty quid doesn't seem enough for such a lovely dress, even with that repair that needs doing.'

'Honey, if that's what she wants then I wouldn't argue. It only cost her a hundred in the first place.'

Now Jess was completely lost. 'How do you know?'

'That's the flat rate for all our dresses.'

'What?' Jess pulled out a fabulous cream affair with a scooped, plunging neck, heavy and intricate gold beading round the waist and a full, though very short, skirt. 'Even this one?'

'Even that one.'

'Blimey.'

'Now hurry up and get changed. We won't have long

before the punters arrive and I need to teach you some moves.'

'Okay,' said Carrie, 'now do that again but this time, undo the fastening at the neck and jiggle your tits as you slide the top of your dress down.'

Jess tried to look nonchalant as she carried out her mentor's instructions. Getting her tits out and jiggling them in public – okay, it was only Carrie watching at the moment so it wasn't exactly public – was going to be a step into the unknown as far as Jess was concerned. Even as her hands went up to release the fastening on the halterneck she could feel her face flaring with embarrassment. Goodness, she felt prudish; in the dressing room, when she'd changed into the dress, Carrie had seen most of her that anyone could see at any one time, but suddenly, in this big room where anyone might walk past, it was terribly different.

'You got a problem, honey?' asked Carrie, not unkindly. 'You haven't stripped in public before, have you?'

'Is it that obvious?'

Carried nodded. 'Just don't think about it. You've got a beautiful body and the men who see it are just going to admire it like a work of art. They can't touch you, the bouncers see to that. You don't care who sees your arms or your legs, now do you? So what's so different about your tits?'

Jess wanted to answer, 'Just about everything,' but she knew that Carrie was right. She'd been programmed from birth to cover up although she'd watched enough TV documentaries about tribes in odd corners of the world to know that in many cultures women's breasts were no sexier than their cheekbones or their bare feet. But now it was *her* tits about to get displayed and all of a sudden her ingrained social mores were screaming that she was Doing Wrong.

'Okay,' said Carrie. 'I'll turn around. Will that help?'

Jess nodded and as Carrie turned her face away, she pulled down her top. The beaded waistband held the lower part of her dress up and Jess tried to ignore the freed fabric which was swishing about as she 'jiggled' as per instructions and danced.

'You look great,' called Carrie.

How . . . ? Jess felt her face flame again and then she sighed. This place was all mirrors. Just because Carrie had turned away didn't mean she couldn't still see everything that was taking place on the podium. Duh! And Miles was right: if she was going to get embarrassed about taking her clothes off, she was in the wrong job. It was only her top, after all. Her knickers, like all the dancers' knickers, would stay put. Gav had been right about one thing: totally nudity was not required. Thank goodness. Jess squared her shoulders, relaxed and threw herself into her dance.

Then the doors opened and half a dozen blokes wandered in. Shit, the club had opened and these were customers. Jess felt a surge of embarrassment pulse through her, so strong she nearly froze completely. But if she did, she could forget trying to work here. She forced herself to carry on till Carrie said she could return to the dressing room.

'You did well,' said Carrie, as they walked down the concealed corridor. 'You're going to be a hit, I can see that.'

'Really? You think so?' Jess was still feeling shaky with shame at being seen almost naked by total strangers.

'Do I think so? You heard the reaction from those early clients.' Carrie smiled when she saw that Jess was still wracked with uncertainty. 'Look, it takes everyone a while to get used to performing like this in public. Miles said you trained to be a dancer.'

'Yeah, but I never really made it. A couple of chorus-line roles, that's all.'

'Never mind, you look great on the podium. Now, come back to the dressing room and we'll work out a rota for you.'

'A rota?'

'Yeah, the days we'd like you to work.'

'Oh.'

'I take it you'll be available anytime? Miles said you've got a day job but you'll be giving that up. Am I right?'

'Sort of.'

Carrie shot her a glance. 'Sort of?'

'I've got commitments.'

Carrie held the door to the dressing room open and Jess passed through.

'What sort of commitments?'

'Commitments.'

Carrie narrowed her eyes. 'So just when *can* you work?'

'Any time except Friday and Saturday evenings.'

'Our busiest evenings.'

Jess shrugged. 'Is that going to be a huge problem?'

'Not necessarily. I mean, sweetie, as far as this place is concerned you're freelance, but this job pays best at the weekends. Your commitments really have to be important to give up on the sort of pay-packet you would take home then. But it's up to you. If it were me . . . well, I'd take Friday and Saturday and sack the rest of the week.'

Jess simply shrugged. Telling Carrie that she worked as a Special Constable at weekends was hardly going to be greeted with joy and a fanfare of trumpets.

'So that's when your boyfriend expects to see you, is that it?'

'Something like that.'

Carrie stared at her as if she was going to press for

further details and then changed her mind. 'Well, whatever. The only nose getting cut off here, sweetie, is yours. If you don't want to work those days you'll end up earning less than the average. But if that's okay with you . . . who am I to argue?'

'How's the new girl?' asked Miles when Carrie entered his office half an hour later. He took a slurp of water.

'Okay. Very naïve and very private though.'

'Is that going to be a problem?'

'Probably not. The other girls may not warm to her if she's stand-offish, but I don't think she'll be any trouble.'

'No?'

'It's probably just that she's got hang-ups.'

'Gav didn't tell me about the hang-ups.'

'Gav?'

'No one you know.'

Carrie shrugged. She didn't care about Miles's private life. His friends and his association with the girl he'd just recruited were none of her business.

7

Matt looked at Simon across the littered canteen table. 'A stag night? You're having a stag night? Blimey, when's the wedding? I didn't realise Sally was this close to getting the shackles on you.'

'Listen, the only shackles Sal's going to get on me are the ones we bought in Ann Summers.'

Matt held his hand up. 'Sorry, mate, but there are some images that are too strong even for the likes of me. And the scenario of you, naked and handcuffed to a bed is going to put me off my nosh for a week.'

'Come off it, you're jealous.'

Matt thought about Sally momentarily. And no, he wasn't jealous. Good luck to Si and all that, but Sal wasn't Matt's type at all; too loud, too full on, too full of herself. It was as if she didn't have a volume control or an off switch. In Matt's view, a little of Sal went a very long way, but he couldn't say that. It would be unkind – true, but unkind. He decided lying was a much better option.

'Sal's a lovely girl but, as she's only ever had eyes for you, I've had to move on, accept there's only one man for her and it's you.' He stared at his friend and kept his face resolutely straight.

Simon grinned and said, 'We can't all have what it takes to attract such a babe.'

Matt continued to keep his expression deadpan; he

mustn't look relieved, that would upset his mate. 'You haven't answered my question. When's the wedding?'

Simon told him.

'Bloody hell, that's not long.'

'We brought it forward. Sal's up the duff and her mum is really old-fashioned. We thought it better this way.'

'Sal's up the duff and this is the first I've heard about it? But I'm your best mate.'

Si looked embarrassed. 'I know, and I'm sorry, but we really felt we ought to break it to Sal's mum first and Sal said she couldn't do it over the phone and she wanted me there – and you know what it's like getting time off together and . . .' Si shrugged. 'So it all took a while and, well, I'm telling you now, aren't I?'

'I suppose,' said Matt grudgingly. 'Sally's going to have her work cut out organising a wedding so quickly. I know women who've taken the best part of a year over it.'

'We're not going for a big do. Sal has been married before and so this time she said she'd be happy with a register office and a knees-up after.'

'Lucky escape for you, if you ask me. I know some poor saps who are still paying for the weddings after the decree nisi has come through.'

'What are you implying? You don't think Sally and I will stay the course?'

'No, nothing like that obviously,' said Matt hastily. 'Just that weddings can cost more than the down payment on a house and paying them off can take for ever. Maybe it's because I'm a bloke but I just can't see the sense in throwing thousands and thousands of pounds at one. Total waste, if you ask me. But a stag night? Well, that's obviously money well spent.' Matt laughed and Simon joined in. 'So what have you got planned?'

'We thought we'd start off at the Red Lion for a few drinks – you know, get a few warmers in the bank, get people on a roll – then go to the Balti House on the High Street for a slap-up meal and to line the old stomach. Then my bruv, Colin, says he's got a surprise sorted – on him.'

'Cool,' said Matt. 'Quite an itinerary. What's the surprise?'

'Well, if I knew that it wouldn't be one, would it, you moron. Duh. Anyway, you up for it?'

'I'll have to check what shift I'm on but I should think it won't be a problem. Even if I am rostered I could always take a day's leave to make sure. There's no way I'm going to miss your stag party.'

'Good man, make sure you don't. This is going to be one to remember.'

'I had a phone call from Jess last night,' said Abby to Gav as she passed him a mug of tea and a plate of buttered toast and pulled her dressing gown tighter around her against the cold. The house had central heating but Abby disapproved of it and kept its use to a bare minimum.

'Oh yeah? I hope she isn't still going on about moving into your gran's house.' Gav put his plate and mug down and straightened his tie, screwing up his eyes against the low, early-morning sun as it slanted through the kitchen window behind Abby's head.

'No. She's got a new job. She said it pays well enough for her to give up on the idea.'

'Really? That's good. What's she going to be doing?'

'She says she's got a job with a bloke who has something to do with cabaret.'

'Cabaret?' said Gav indistinctly through a mouthful of half-chewed toast and marmalade.

'That's what she said.'

Gav looked a bit confused, muttered, 'Cabaret?' again, and then carried on munching. 'So what have you got planned for today?' he asked Abby after he'd swallowed.

'The Amnesty office in town want people to stuff envelopes for a mailshot so I said I'd help with that. And I want to get the spuds into the big bed at the end of the garden. That'll take most of the morning, I would think, so I promised Amnesty I'd go over in the afternoon. Why?'

'No reason. Just asking.'

'Just one thing though, Jess talking about the house made me wonder,' said Abby. 'You know we're saving the rent money for renovations? Well, I was wondering how much we'd got. I mean, are we getting anywhere close to being able to make a start on getting some quotes for the work?'

'Oh, I wouldn't think so,' said Gav airily. 'That house is going to take a bucket of cash to put right. As you know, last time any money was spent on it, Britain still had a King on the throne and most of the world map was coloured pink.'

'Hardly,' said Abby, 'but it is a bit dated.'

'Look, I haven't time to discuss this now. I'll be late for work.' He pushed his plate away and downed the rest of this tea. 'But trust me, it'll be quite a while before we'll have got enough stashed to even think about sorting that dump out. And remember, while we're doing that, it'll have to stand empty so we'll need a cushion of rent to pay stuff like the council tax for as long as it takes.' He stood up and dropped a kiss on his wife's forehead. 'I'm as keen as you to get going on that house, but while we've got tenants who don't care that the kitchen looks like one Wilma Flintstone chucked out, then I suggest we don't rock the boat. If we upset them and they go, we may not find anyone else to take on that wreck and want to pay good money for the privilege.'

After he'd left, Abby realised that she still didn't have a clue how much they'd managed to save. Obviously 'not enough', was the answer but even so, she'd like to know how big or small the amount was.

Gav got into his car and drove for about ten minutes before stopping at the side of the road and pulling out his mobile phone. His thumb moved over a couple of buttons, he scrolled down and then hit the call button. The phone rang at the other end and then an answer-phone message cut in.

'Hello, this is Miles. I can't take your call right now. Please leave a message after the tone.'

Gav shook his head in exasperation. Of course Miles wouldn't be answering his phone right now; he'd be dead to the world in bed after a hard night at the club.

'Miles, it's Gav. Did you give Jess that job? Ring me. I'm confused. She's got a job which pays and the heat is off the house, but it doesn't sound as if she's working for you. Call me when you can.'

Gav ended the call, chucked his phone on the passenger seat and drove off towards Reading and the software company. He was sure that Jess had to be work-ing for Miles, but what Abby said didn't make sense. A cabaret act? That didn't sound like she was pole-dancing – but then Jess wasn't going to tell her big sister the truth, now was she? Maybe she'd said cabaret so she was only telling a little white lie to Abby. Or perhaps Abby had got hold of the wrong end of the stick – or pole. Jeez, he hoped Jess had got that job with Miles. He needed to make sure she had something that paid her a decent wage and stopped her bleating once and for all about moving into the house. And if her new job wasn't with Miles and wasn't paying her a big enough screw to keep her living in London, his set-up with Miles might still be in jeopardy. Damn.

He was barely concentrating on his driving as he

made his way to work. He was functioning on autopilot as he turned the steering wheel, changed gears and threaded his way along the roads to his destination. He went over and over his brief conversation with his wife to try to figure out if Jess had taken the bait and had gone for the job at Shoq. Surely if Jess had done as he'd told her and emailed Miles, asking for an audition, Miles would have contacted him to tell him the result? He was brought out of his reverie by a blast on a car horn: the set of lights he was at were now showing green. Hurriedly he slipped the car into gear and sped away, just as his phone rang. He checked the road ahead before reaching out to the passenger seat and picking it up.

He pressed the button to answer the call and simultaneously tucked it under his ear.

'You'll have to be quick,' he said without preamble. 'I'm driving.'

'You rang,' said Miles.

'I'll call you back in five. I'm just getting to the car park.' Gav hung up, manoeuvred his car through the entrance to the company car park and into his slot. Then he picked up his phone, redialled Miles.

'Right, I'm legal now and I can talk.'

'Good.'

'So did Jess get the job?'

'Better than that, she's got the job but thinks it's kind of accidental.'

'How come?'

Miles explained to Gavin about his encounter with Jess outside Shoq. 'When she said what her name was, I had a job keeping my face straight, I can tell you. But there was no mention of you and I don't think she connected me with the "mate" who told you I might be recruiting so she really does think she was just dragged in off the street.'

'That's great, and even better that you're now her employer.'

'Yes. And you're right, she's good. She's got the face, the figure and the skills. She's a bit of a cold fish apparently, very closed up but I don't care as long as it doesn't cause trouble in the dressing room.'

'But what about the punters? Aren't they going to mind if she's a bit . . . aloof?'

'Doubt it. Most of them just want to drink and get off on their fantasies about pulling one of the dancers – which very few of them have a cat in hell's chance of doing. Nah, the guys just like to drool; they're not too fussy about scintillating conversation.'

'And you're absolutely certain she doesn't think there's a connection between you and me?' Gavin persisted.

'Not unless you told her. Which you didn't, did you?' There was a steely note in Miles's voice which Gavin picked up on, even over a less than perfect mobile connection.

'No, no,' he replied hastily. 'She doesn't know I know you. And she won't, I promise.'

'Then we'll keep it that way, won't we.'

Jess sat in front of the big mirror and tried for the umpteenth time to get her contact lenses in.

'Got something in your eye, honey?' asked Carrie as she slinked past in a lime-green lamé dress that was slit to the hip. 'Can I get it out?'

Jess screwed up her left eye to try to stop it watering and ruining her make-up. 'It's just a contact not behaving itself,' she mumbled. 'If I can't get it in next shot I'll leave it out.'

'Will that be a problem?'

'I can see well enough to get to the podium and climb on it. The punters'll be a bit of a blur but that won't matter.'

'Okay, if you're sure. Only you need to hurry up, sweetie. You're due to do your set next.'

Jess knew. It was partly because she'd rushed getting her lenses in that she was making such a mess of it. 'Hell,' she said, dumping the little circle of plastic back in its pot. 'I'll do without them tonight.' Swiftly she ran the corner of a tissue under her eyes to repair her liner, then swept her mascara brush over her lashes a couple more times and leaned back in her chair to survey the effect. As all she saw was a fuzzy blur, she had to assume she hadn't made a complete pig's ear of her finishing touches as she slipped into a skimpy claret-red wrap dress with a plunging neckline.

'Jess to podium two,' called a voice over the Tannoy in the dressing room.

'On my way,' she muttered as she thrust her feet into a pair of matching shoes.

She opened the door and sashayed along the corridor behind the two-way mirror. From the indistinct blur, the club seemed rammed. The last couple of Thursdays that she'd worked had been pretty busy, but this looked exceptional. Never mind, the tips would be good; she could sleep all day on Friday and then go out on the beat again Friday night, as fresh as a daisy having had a proper eight-hour kip. And if she got to bed around four tonight, she might even feel up to a bit of flat-hunting in the afternoon before her shift at the station.

She wove through the tables, picking her way carefully in the dim light, which didn't help her already challenged eyesight, till she got to the podium, then walked sexily up the three steps and onto the circular stage. As she grasped the shiny pole, the opening bars to the chosen music for her set blared out and partially drowned the raucous hubbub of booming male voices. Jess began to sway to the music, using the pole to support her as she gyrated and writhed sinuously. The racket slowly subsided as Jess's dancing began to attract the attention of the men and they found they would rather watch her than engage in banter with their mates. She could make out a sea of attentive but indistinct faces turned towards her as she danced and pirouetted, but nothing was the least bit clear.

Maybe this was the way to perform, she thought. All cocooned inside a soft-focus sphere where she was protected from the punters' lascivious leers and slack-jawed lust. The music throbbed and crescendoed as Jess slid up and down the pole, twirling, caressing, thrusting. The beat was insistent as she moved her body as sexily as she knew how, cocking her leg around the metal like she was wrapping herself around a lover, twining herself and contorting her joints in a way that she knew was provocative and suggestive. Pouting, she toed off her red shoes, then she began to undo the sash that held her wrap dress closed. Slowly, seductively she eased the dress open and let it fall. She did a few more twirls and kicks to the closing bars of the music and then took a bow. Whoops and wolf whistles accompanied the huge appreciative roar of applause that filled the silence left by the music. Jess blew the customers a kiss then gathered up her dress and shoes and slid back through the packed club to the safety of the mirrored door to the dressing room.

'It was noisy out there,' she commented to a fellow dancer, Laura, who was brushing body glitter over her shoulders.

'There's a stag night in,' said Laura. 'A load of pumped-up, drunken blokes all egging each other on. If I were you, I'd steer clear of their table. Carrie's already warned the bouncers to keep an eye on them.'

'Troublemakers?'

'Not especially, just pissed and excitable. I'm surprised you didn't notice them when you were doing your set.'

'I wouldn't have noticed a herd of elephants doing a conga line around the club. I didn't have my lenses in and without those I'm as blind as a bat with an eye-shade on.'

Laura laughed. 'Well, wish me luck. I'm on next. And sadly I've got twenty-twenty vision so I shan't be spared anything.'

As Laura left, Jess hung her dress back up in her wardrobe and got out another outfit – this time a shimmering, silver number that barely skimmed her crotch.

When the dressmaker had fitted her for it, Jess had asked for the hem to be lengthened by several inches, but both the maker and Carrie had told her 'no way'. And Carrie had also told her that if she fake-tanned her skin and slipped on some seriously high heels, she'd look red-hot. Jess had done as she'd been told but even now, when she peered at herself in the dressing-room mirror, she still didn't think she looked anything out of the ordinary. Abby's endless taunts about her being too skinny and her lack of looks had done just too much damage to her self-confidence for it to be easily repaired. Jess simply had no idea that she'd blossomed into a beauty.

Realising that she didn't have to continue to endure the world in a haze, she got out her contacts and tried again with them. With no clock ticking and feeling quite relaxed they slipped into her eyes at the first attempt. She glanced at her reflection again. Shit, this dress was short. Frankly, she had longer vests! Twitching down the hem fruitlessly and making several mental notes not to bend over, unless she wanted to give everyone a good look at her thong, she made her way back into the main show room.

Her job was to entertain the guests but, until a table paid for her company exclusively, she could hang around the bar and talk to some of the punters there. She crossed her fingers that the stag party didn't ask for her. Judging by what Laura said, they were going to be a handful.

Jess strolled across the black carpet towards the bar. Every evening there were always a few blokes in the club on their own who needed a warm smile and a friendly word and just a hint of encouragement to buy some expensive wine for a pretty girl – which was how Miles made a great deal of his money – that and the 10 per cent he kept back from all the girls' tips. There weren't many guys standing on their own there. A couple were obviously waiting to be served and were flashing wads of notes about in the hope that their cash might attract the busy barmen's attention. There was a group of men deep in conversation; Jess reckoned they didn't look like they wanted interrupting. As she sized up the blokes, standing at intervals down the length of polished black marble, she didn't think that any of them seemed to be crying out for company. Although she could welcome a break, if she wasn't dancing or entertaining, she wasn't earning. She just had to hope that someone would want to pay her for her company soon.

Jess hitched herself as decorously as she could onto a black velvet-covered barstool. The fabric against her bare thigh was as prickly as a five o'clock shadow, but she ignored the discomfort and smiled serenely at the room in general and hoped she didn't look like some sort of demented pixie on its toadstool. 'Come on, guys,' she muttered to herself. 'Don't some of you want to buy my company?'

'This doesn't look like a typing job,' said a voice she recognised instantly.

Jess jumped – literally – and almost fell off her stool. A strong hand held onto her elbow and steadied her.

'Matt!' Shit, what was he doing, creeping up on her like that? And what was he even doing *here*?

'Sorry, didn't mean to make you jump. But you're not the only one suffering from shock here. I have to confess to feeling quite gobsmacked. Who'd have thought that Jess the Special Constable could be quite so special in other ways?'

Jess felt her face flame up and for some reason she felt unbelievably guilty; as if she'd been caught with her hand in the till at the station canteen or something equally criminal and unforgivable. And it didn't make it any easier that one of her co-workers now knew exactly what she looked like in her knickers. Somehow displaying (almost) her all, in front of complete strangers, was something she could blank out of her mind, but undressing in front of a colleague – well, that was another thing entirely.

'You know, I always knew there was something about you that set you apart from the standard sort of girl who wants to be a Special. I didn't have you down as a stripper, though.'

'I'm not a stripper,' mumbled Jess.

Matt looked at her. 'Sorry, but didn't I just watch you take your clothes off to music, in front of an audience?'

Jess nodded, feeling unaccountably ashamed.

'So why did you tell me you were a temp?' asked Matt, looking completely bemused.

'Because I was, till a couple of weeks ago.' She swallowed. She'd been found out – and by Matt of all people.

'And then you suddenly decided to go into this business.'

'Yes. Well, no . . . I mean, it's complicated. But the reason I changed jobs was to earn some decent money. I'm sick of being on the breadline, of going to bed because it's the only way I can keep warm, of choosing between eating or heating, or clothes and a roof. And now I can actually pay for a taxi home when I finish here and not care about the expense.' Jess suddenly pulled herself up. Why was she justifying herself to Matt like this? She said more strongly, 'Not that it's any business of yours.'

It was Matt's turn to colour. 'You're right, your spare time is your own affair. I didn't mean to pry. I'm sorry.'

'No, I'm sorry,' Jess said. 'I shouldn't have unloaded on you. Although,' she added with a smile, 'I'd prefer it if you called me a dancer, not a stripper.'

'Yes, totally, I can see that.'

Jess's smile broadened.

Matt smiled back. 'And I can see that you are. Honestly. You were fantastic on that podium – even before you took . . .' He stumbled to a stop. 'You were fantastic,' he finished lamely. 'Can I buy you a drink?'

'It's okay.' Jess glanced round. It wouldn't be well received if Miles knew that she was actively discouraging a client from spending money at the bar.

'But I'd like to. Really. What's your poison?'

Jess knew she ought to ask for champagne but she couldn't bring herself to fleece a friend, especially given what the prices were. 'Actually, I'm really thirsty – all that dancing. What I'd love is an orange juice and lemonade.' She hitched herself on board the stool again.

Matt ordered her drink and a pint of bitter for himself.

'So what brought you here tonight?' asked Jess as she sipped.

'A stag do. Simon's.'

Jess's eyes widened in horror. 'What? The whole shift is here?'

'Quite a few,' nodded Matt. 'I think Simon invited most of them.'

'So they've all seen me . . .'

'Relax. Most of the guys are so pissed they can't even focus on the guy sitting next to them, and even the ones that are still fairly sober weren't really paying attention to the dancing. Besides,' Matt smiled at her, 'can I say you don't look a bit like you do in uniform?'

Ain't that the truth, thought Jess. Navy-blue serge, stab vest and an unbecoming hat compared to a few wisps of silk jersey, fake tan, heels, and half an inch of slap – hmmm, not really on the same fashion wavelength.

'But you recognised me.'

'I'm not pissed for a start. This is only about the second drink I've had all evening. I got dicked for the early turn tomorrow so I've got to be back on duty at seven. I didn't think the shift sergeant would appreciate me rolling in reeking of stale booze.'

'That's bad planning.'

'Not really. I'm rostered again for Saturday night after that.' Matt gazed at Jess. 'Which I think is rather *good* planning. Planning I arranged even before I knew what you looked like in civvies.'

Jess gazed back and felt her ribs tighten and her breathing go all funny. Ohmigod, he'd sorted his shifts out to work with her. She was lost for words. Fit Matt had arranged things to be with her.

'You are working tomorrow night, aren't you?' asked Matt.

Jess nodded, not trusting herself to speak.

'Only I did wonder, when I saw you doing your thing, whether you might have jacked in the Met.'

'No, no, I love being a Special. I really *am* just doing this for the money.'

'So you're not a closet exhibitionist.'

'Of course not.' Jess took another sip of her drink. 'And if your mates haven't realised what I do, I'd really prefer it if you don't spread the word around.' She looked at him imploringly as she thought about the comments she was liable to get if they knew. 'Show us your tits' would be the least of them.

Matt tapped his nose. 'Your secret is safe with me.' His glance slid behind Jess. 'And if you want it to stay that way, I suggest you make yourself scarce. I think Simon is just about to join us.'

Jess slid off her stool again, and keeping her back to the stag party and Simon, she strolled as casually as she could towards the other end of the room, making a private vow to keep as far away as possible from Simon's group for the rest of the night. As she departed she heard Simon complain that Matt was being a party-pooper. She didn't hear Matt's response as the music racked up in volume to accompany Laura's turn on the podium.

'Who was that you were talking to?' asked Tom, one of the bouncers, as Jess leaned against the far end of the enormous bar. 'I thought he was getting a bit heavy with you for a while.'

'It was cool,' said Jess. 'Honestly.'

Tom looked at her, worry still written all over his face. His job was to see there was no trouble in the club and if there was, he got the blame. He rolled his shoulders in a way that drew attention to his muscle-bound neck, and although he had the clean, shiny face of a schoolboy he had the body of a prize-fighter.

'Didn't look like it.'

'It was just someone I know a bit.' Jess almost said, 'Someone I know from work,' but managed to bite her tongue in time. As far as everyone at Shoq was concerned, she'd been a temp and had given it up. She didn't want anyone prying into her private life and so she'd made a decision not to mention anything about it, past or present. 'I just wasn't expecting to see him here.'

'Tricky,' said Tom sympathetically. 'I mean, I can imagine that you don't want . . .' His voice trailed off.

'That I don't want the world to know what I do for a living,' finished Jess helpfully. Tom was all right but not the sharpest knife in the drawer.

The big man shrugged. 'I don't mean you ought to be ashamed of what you do.'

'It's all right,' said Jess with a smile. 'I can't say I'm exactly proud, myself. I don't think this is what my mother saw me doing when she bought me my first pair of ballet shoes. Now, if I was in the buff but strutting about in a modern dance production at the London Coliseum – well, that would be a whole other issue. It might be no less titillating to the men in the audience, but if you're starkers for the sake of Art the middle classes don't think of it as stripping.'

Now Matt had mentioned the 'S' word Jess was trying to face up to the fact that that was how people saw her – a stripper.

'I don't think of you as a stripper,' said Tom. 'You're too classy to be called that.'

Jess gave him a full-on, genuine smile. 'Thanks, Tom. You're sweet.' She saw Tom blush – which, given that he was built like the proverbial masonry khazi – was both touching and incongruous. 'Aren't we *all* classy girls?' she added, pretending she hadn't noticed Tom's embarrassment.

He nodded. 'But you . . . You're . . .' He stopped. 'You're not like the others.'

Why didn't he think she was like the others, she wondered. Was it because she'd trained professionally or because her policework made her different? Jess was just trying to work out how to respond when the sound of raised voices reached them, audible even above the music for Laura's set.

'Got to go,' said Tom, putting on a surprising turn of speed for someone of his size. Jess watched as he got to the seat of the problem, almost before anyone else in the club was aware there was one. It seemed that one of Simon's friends had taken exception to something and was squaring up for an altercation. Jess couldn't see or hear what it was about but the bloke was busy pushing up his sleeves and generally looking like he wanted a fight. Tom put his hand on the man's shoulder and stood squarely in front of him. Jess could see the situation calming, the whole incident getting defused. She had no idea what Tom had said or done but whatever it was, it had worked. He might not be university material but he was good at peacekeeping.

Jess glanced at her watch. Nearly two. Only a couple more hours and she could go home. She wasn't scheduled to do any more dancing, unless someone asked for her to perform privately. It would be nice if they did. A private dance in one of the booths was worth a couple of hundred quid but she was the newbie and most of the regulars who frequented the club – and, from what Jess had observed so far, most of the members did seem to be regulars – had their favourites that they liked to ask.

'Jess.' Carrie appeared by her side. 'There's a group of men on Table Nine who would like you to spend some time with them. They've booked you for an hour.'

For a second Jess felt sick. Hell, which was Table Nine? She still hadn't got a handle on the table-numbering system in the club and had a sinking feeling that it might be Simon's. Dear God, had someone other than Matt recognised her and was making some sort of sick joke, or was it just some ghastly coincidence?

Carrie looked at her, a small frown creasing her perfect forehead. 'Problem?'

Jess licked her lips, her mouth suddenly dry. 'Er, Table Nine?'

'That one, sweetie.' Carrie indicated a table about ten feet from Jess – nowhere near Simon and Matt's. And every man around the table a stranger. All faces Jess had never seen before in her life. Phew.

'Fine,' she said brightly to cover up her momentary wobble and now felt happy to spend an hour of her time feigning an interest in this group of guys; what they did for a living, how big their bank balances were, how long their yachts were and pretending that she was not only impressed but that she liked them too. It was talking crap, as Laura had once so succinctly put it. But Jess didn't care. She could talk crap with the best of them if it was going to net her several hundred pounds, which was what these guys paid Miles for the pleasure of her company. Although it was several hundred pounds, less Miles's cut by the time the cash got to her. Still, not bad for an hour's work.

Jess slapped on a smile and slinked her way across to the table. Apart from anything else, her shoes were killing her and the chance to sit down for an hour was very welcome.

'What's the new girl like?' Miles asked, swilling a large cognac around in a cut-glass brandy bubble. He lounged in his expensive leather swivel chair, feet up on his desk, looking through the mirrors onto the main room. He knew Carrie didn't miss anything going on in the girls' lives. He didn't know if she did it by tuning into the dressing-room gossip or by just keeping her eyes open, but however her intelligence system worked it was impressive.

Carrie sat so she didn't impede his view. 'She's okay. Settling in well, the other girls like her, the punters too. Yeah, no problems.'

'Good.'

'She doesn't chatter though, very quiet.'

'Does it matter?'

'No, but it just makes her different. You know, the other girls, they chat, gossip, swap stuff, but Jess . . . I don't know. And then,' Carrie paused, 'she's just different from the rest of the girls in other ways too. They get excited when a celeb comes in and they love the glamour and the clothes. But Jess looks as if she finds it all a bit silly, like it's beneath her.'

'Well, there's no law against someone not being into all that shit,' Miles grunted. And knowing what he did about her background, she probably *did* think it was a bit silly. Her sister had no doubt brainwashed her into thinking the entire world was about to end in a cloud of toxic gas or drown under melting ice-caps, so schmoozing a few celebs was hardly important in the bigger picture. But he wasn't going to tell Carrie what he knew.

Miles's attention shifted to the main show room of the club. It was almost empty now, the last of the clients preparing to go home. A handful of girls still decorated the booths and were entertaining the die-hards but most of their colleagues had called it a night.

'Tom handled that incident well tonight,' remarked Carrie. 'It could have turned ugly.'

Miles returned his gaze to her. 'Yeah. Especially as they were all coppers.'

Carrie sat bolt upright. 'You're kidding.'

'Straight up. Laura told me.'

'You'd have thought they would have behaved better than they did then.'

'It was only one guy causing trouble. Drunk as a lord, but Tom coped.'

Carrie leaned her elbows on the arms of her chair and pressed her fingers together under her chin. 'I thought at one stage that Jess and one of that group were going to have a bit of a scene. There was definitely something going on between them. I wondered if I was going to have to get involved.'

'Stuff like that happens,' said Miles, taking a swig of

brandy. 'You'd have sorted it, you always do. You sure I can't get you a drink?'

'No, thanks. Empty calories, Miles, empty calories.' She thought about the incident she'd witnessed again. 'I don't know. There was something about the pair of them, I swear to God. It was like they knew each other.'

'So what?'

Carrie shrugged. 'Jess and a copper? I don't fancy the idea of our girls being chummy with the filth.' She paused for a moment. 'You don't think she's got some sort of record and that's why he recognised her – and why I thought something was going to kick off between them?'

'Nah, she's not the sort. Jess wouldn't say boo to a goose. Maybe she's neighbours with this guy, or maybe they were at school together. London's a big place – there are bound to be people in the Smoke that she knows, so why shouldn't she run into acquaintances?'

Even so, despite the fact that Miles had outwardly dismissed any connection between Jess and a member of the police stag party, inside he wasn't so sanguine. Miles didn't like the idea that Jess might have friends in the police any more than Carrie did. It was a worry, however casual her relationship with the guy might be. He'd have to ask Gav what he knew about that. Which gave him a momentary prick of annoyance. Bloody Gav's relations giving him headaches. But then again, if he didn't have Gav he wouldn't have access to that house. Maybe he'd have to find a way of getting the house and losing Gav's lame wife and sister-in-law. Actually, if he could find a way to make the house his, he could lose Gav as well. Now that was a thought.

'You're very quiet,' said Matt, as he and Jess paced the streets near the Windmill pub yet again.

'Nothing much to say,' said Jess. Actually, she had quite a lot she wanted to say, but as most of it referred to their previous encounter she wasn't quite sure how to broach the subject.

'I didn't see you to say goodbye, last night.'

Well, if Matt was going to talk about Shoq she could hardly avoid the issue. 'No. I, er, was booked by a table to entertain them just after we spoke.'

Matt looked at her, his eyebrows up by his hairline. 'Entertain?'

'They pay to have a girl or two to talk to them, to sit at their table, laugh at their crap jokes, be nice, encourage them to buy drinks. Didn't you have Laura at your table for a bit?'

Matt nodded. 'I thought she just joined us because she felt like it.'

'Trust me, nothing in Shoq comes for free, least of all us girls. Well, you can talk to the girls standing at the bar for nothing but they generally expect you to buy them a drink at the very least, preferably the overpriced champagne.'

'Judging what I paid for drinks, champagne wasn't the only thing that was overpriced. And talking of drinks,' Matt stopped and looked at Jess. 'I don't suppose there's a chance you'd come out with me one evening? I really want to say sorry for giving you such a fright last night, but I was so shattered to see you . . . dancing . . . I'm afraid I didn't think. I'd like to make it up to you.'

Jess almost stopped dead in the street as she felt her insides do flick-flaks. Shit, Matt was asking her out for a drink! She'd fantasised about the moment he might invite her out on a date but she'd never thought that her dream would turn into reality. She risked a quick glance at Matt and saw that he looked really nervous and uncertain.

Blimey, was he worried she was going to turn him down? Taking a deep breath, she raised what she hoped was a nonchalant eyebrow, as if she was offered dates from hunky blokes on a daily basis.

'Oh,' she said. Oh? What sort of response was that? For God's sake, couldn't she come up with something a little more articulate? If that was the best she could do, she'd probably blown it. No bloke was going to feel encouraged if all he got was 'oh'.

'Maybe I shouldn't have asked. I'm sorry, forget it.'

Yup, totally blown it. Her heart carried on falling past her navel and down towards her shiny, black, issue lace-ups. She was going to have to work bloody hard to drag this disaster back from the brink. 'No, no.' Oh God, she thought, please let me get things right now. Brain, engage with tongue! 'I mean, what I mean to say is, I'm just . . . well, I mean, now you know that I'm a stripper, I wouldn't have thought . . .' Jess tailed off. Her brain had obviously disobeyed orders.

'You're not a stripper, you're a dancer. You said so yourself.'

'Yes, but I think we both know we're splitting hairs here.'

Matt carried on walking, not looking at her. 'You haven't answered my question.'

Jess cast her eyes skywards as she mouthed the words 'Thank You.' Perhaps God had listened even if her brain hadn't. Don't fuck up your second chance, she told herself sternly. Carefully she said, 'I'd like to very much. You tell me when you're free and I'll book a night off from the club.'

Matt sat at the back of the briefing room, listening to the sergeant with one ear but letting his mind wander around the gritty question of where he could take Jess on a date. Obviously, it had to be somewhere pretty special when she was used to working in such a swanky venue on a daily basis. He didn't think the Red Lion, the local for those members of the station who liked a swift half when they came off shift, was going to cut the mustard.

'So we know the area round the Windmill estate is being flooded with skunk,' said the sergeant.

Drugs on the Windmill, thought Matt cynically. Hold the front page.

'And we've had intelligence that it's all home-grown. This stuff isn't being imported and there's a big operation on to find the source. Any of you in that area should be aware that drug-related crime is at an all-time high, and that if you suspect anyone of dealing then we want them nicked – and when we bring in the dealers we're going to lean on them to find out who their suppliers are.'

Goody, thought Matt, although if the brass wanted to bring in the dealers the easiest way would be to send in several coachloads of coppers and round up the entire estate. There might be some families on it who didn't supplement their benefits by dealing in illegal substances, but precious few, surely. You only had to look at the number of Beemers and Mercs parked to know that there had to be something other than the fortnightly Giro going into the housekeeping accounts.

'These local dealers may only be small fry,' continued the sergeant, 'but someone knows where this stuff is coming from. Someone is bound to have a weak point; it's just a question of finding the person who is more scared of the law than the Mob, or the Triads or whoever is growing the stuff in the first place. Questions?'

Matt was tempted to ask if anyone had a bright idea as to where he could take Jess for a night out, but decided against it. It wouldn't be a good career move. He'd think of somewhere. As the briefing room emptied, Matt applied his brain to the little he knew about Jess and tried to work out the sort of place that might appeal to her.

Jess didn't know that places like the Golden Crown still existed in the capital. It looked more like somewhere she'd find out in the sticks, and the roaring fire that was toasting her toes was a complete bonus. Matt sat beside her on the saggy old sofa and smiled nervously.

'All right?' he asked.

'Better than all right. This is bliss.' Outside, the weather was diabolical; rain lashed against the window, driven by gusting winds, so the rustic interior seemed even cosier. Jess sipped her wine.

'I was afraid it might be a bit old-fashioned.'

'Well it is, but I like old-fashioned. It reminds me of a pub near my gran's old house. My sis and I used to go there with our mum and Gran sometimes for Sunday lunch. But it's probably all changed. Abby and I haven't been there for ages.'

'So why did you stop going?'

'Mum died,' said Jess.

'Oh my God, I'm so sorry. I didn't know.' Matt looked stricken.

Jess smiled sadly at him. 'It's okay. Anyway, how would you know? I mean,' she shrugged, 'I haven't put notices around the station telling people.'

Matt gave her a lopsided smile. 'No, but even so.'

'It was a while back. History and I'm over it.' Which was a lie but it would make Matt feel less uncomfortable. She decided to change the subject. 'What about you? How was your childhood?'

As Matt told her about his rumbustious upbringing in a London suburb in a house full of boys with a father who encouraged tree-climbing, chemistry experiments and hadn't, apparently, heard of health and safety, Jess sipped her wine and warmed her feet. 'I think my mum was on first-name terms with most of the nurses at our local A and E by the time we were all at secondary school. And I swear we had our own cubicle there.'

Jess was laughing by this time. 'Now I know you're exaggerating.'

'I'm not. Cub's honour. In one year we had two broken wrists, a cut that required stitches, two missing front teeth—'

'Well, I had that,' interrupted Jess. 'All kids lose their front teeth.'

'Courtesy of a baseball bat?'

'Um, no.'

'Right, two missing front teeth and several emergency tetanus jabs. But, in mitigation, it was between four of us.'

'I thought you said you had two brothers?'

'I did. Dad needed a jab when he put a garden fork into his foot and he also broke a wrist showing us the right way to walk on stilts.'

'Your poor mother.'

'I know. Funnily enough, the only time I really saw

her lose it was when Dad suggested a mountaineering holiday.'

Jess giggled. 'He didn't! You didn't go?'

'No. Actually I'm making that bit up. He wouldn't have dared – and if you met my mum you'd see why. Although he did buy a chainsaw.'

Jess's eyes widened. 'Oh my God. What on earth happened with that?'

'Mum took it back to the shop the next day. Dad never even had the chance to get it out of its box.' Matt sounded rather sad.

Jess laughed, however, took another sip of her drink and stared at the flames licking round the logs in the grate. She was having a great time. Matt was easy company; he made her giggle, he was interesting, he was attentive.

'Can I get you another one?' His voice broke into her thoughts.

'Best not. If I have any more I'll end up rat-faced.'

'Not if we have something to eat. I hear the food here is very good.'

Jess hesitated. A drink was quite a casual date, food put it into a slightly higher league. But if they went Dutch, well, then it would be two friends sharing a meal. And although the idea of this date morphing into something a little more serious was attractive, Jess wasn't sure she was ready for things to happen quite so quickly. On the other hand, Matt was incredibly fit and she could afford a meal out, which made a very pleasant change from her circumstances of just a few weeks ago. So why not live a bit, she told herself. Oh, to hell with it, she would.

'That's a great idea. Blotting paper.' She smiled at him as he reached for the menus propped up on a nearby table. She'd address the matter of the bill and any advancement in their relationship if and when it arose. But as she perused the list of food on offer she found herself distracted by the idea of her relationship with Matt advancing. She risked a glance at him and decided it was quite a yummy thought.

It had been a perfect date, Jess decided. Matt had been wonderful – everything a girl could want. And having been in a total relationship desert for over a year, to have had such a great evening with a man had made her feel All Woman. She smiled to herself as she remembered that Matt had managed to feel *all* of this particular woman too. She really had just meant 'coffee' when she'd invited him back to her new flat but, well . . . One thing had led to another and then that had led to a bit of the other. And a very nice 'bit of the other' it had been too.

And, as she rolled over and wondered if she had the energy to go for an action-replay, she could swear she could smell toast and coffee. She opened her eyes just as Matt walked into her bedroom carrying a tray and wearing nothing but a smile.

Breakfast in bed *and* blinding sex. This man was perfect.

'So, tell me more about your childhood,' said Matt as they munched their toast, propped up against the pillows. 'I mean, if you don't mind. I don't want to pry into anything that'll upset you.'

'The only really painful thing was Mum dying,' Jess told him. 'Up to the moment when she got taken ill, me and my sister Abby had a great life – idyllic really. Dad pushed off when I was tiny. I've no memory of him at all and Abby can only remember a couple of things because he wasn't about much even then. After he'd gone it was just me and her and Mum and Gran. We spent a lot of our holidays at Gran's house in the Chilterns between

Marlow and Wycombe. It was in the middle of the country and it had a huge garden so Abby and I just ran wild. It was lovely.'

'I bet.'

'And the house was wonderful for kids; it had an attic and a cellar so there were endless places to play hide and seek, and Gran wasn't house-proud so she didn't care if we made a den under the dining-room table or got all the dressing-up clothes out. Looking back, she was incredibly tolerant.'

'She sounds it.'

'The house is mine now.'

'Really? Cool.'

Jess nodded and chomped on her toast. 'Well, mine and Abby's,' she said stickily, through butter and thick marmalade.

'So why don't you live there? I mean,' Matt glanced around Jess's new flat, 'this is nice but it's hardly palatial.'

'If you'd seen where I lived until last month you'd think this was Buckingham Palace,' responded Jess, grinning. And compared to the scuzzy bedsit it certainly was; this flat was light, modern, nicely appointed even if it was still pretty small. But Jess had reasoned that all she needed was a bedroom, a living room and a bathroom – and this place provided all of those plus a balcony besides. The blond wood floor, pale walls and neutral furnishings meant she'd been able to brighten the place up with a few cushions and pictures at minimal cost, and the added bonus was that it was remarkably easy to keep clean and tidy.

'But if you've got this wonderful house in the country . . .' Matt persisted.

'Yes, it *is* a wonderful house, but it's also in need of repair and neither Abby nor I have the cash – yet. So we rent it out, save the money we get from that and one day, we'll be able to give the place a proper make-over.'

'And then what?'

'Well, the plan was we'd sell it and split the money, but now . . .'

'Now?'

'Well, I've got this idea that if I keep dancing for a few years and don't spend too much of my earnings, I might be able to buy Abby's half off her.' Jess paused and her brow furrowed.

'So what's the problem? There obviously is one.'

'This is going to sound mean but I've got this feeling that Abby won't want me to have the house. There's no way she could ever buy me out, but that doesn't mean she'd be happy if I bought her out.'

'So she'd rather see the house go to a stranger?'

Jess shrugged. 'I think so, yes.'

'Have you talked to her about it?'

'You've not met Abby.'

'So that's a "no" then.'

Jess nodded.

Matt slurped his coffee and took another bite of his toast. 'Tell you what, how do you fancy a trip out to the country?'

Jess looked perplexed. 'I don't understand.'

'We both get in my car,' said Matt slowly and carefully, 'and we go to a place where the city ends and there are big wide-open spaces and lots of plants and animals.'

His deadpan delivery made Jess giggle and she almost choked on her toast. When she recovered she asked Matt why he would want to go to the place where the city ended.

'Because I'd like to see this house you lived in, and we can then take ourselves out to lunch at that nice pub you were telling me about last night. We could go today, if you haven't any other plans. I'm not on duty again till tomorrow.'

Outside, the sun was shining out of a flawless blue sky, the previous day's storm having blown itself out, and there was a real promise that spring was about to burst upon the world again.

'The woods round Gran's house always look lovely at this time of year. A bit early for the bluebells but still glorious. And it would be great to see if the old pub is still serving bacon butties like they used to.' Jess smiled at Matt. 'As you're going to be doing the driving I'll do lunch.'

'Sounds like a plan.' Matt put his plate and mug back on the tray and pushed the duvet back. 'In which case, I shall whiz home, shower and change and pick you up in about an hour.'

'How about,' said Jess, pulling the duvet back into place, and smiling provocatively, 'you and I set out a little later and indulge in a spot of exercise first – just to burn off breakfast and to make sure we have room for lunch?' She arched an eyebrow.

Matt slid down, back under the duvet. 'Sounds like an even better plan.'

11

'What do you mean, he looked like a copper?' asked Gav into his mobile.

The voice at the other end became agitated. 'Look, Gav, I've seen enough of 'em in my life to know what I'm talking about and there was definitely a fucking plod snooping round the house.'

'Calm down. When?'

'Lunchtime.'

'And what did he do?'

'He and this bird came up the drive from the road. She was pointing things out to him and he was just looking.'

'Just looking. And then?'

'Then they fucked off. But I swear he was plain-clothes.'

'And the girl?'

'Slim, brunette, attractive. She was a girl, what else can I say?'

'Did they see you?'

'No.'

'Sure?'

'Certain. I was in the attic and they didn't really look up at the roof. Besides, I kept back from the window.'

There was a pause while Gavin thought about what Paul was telling him. 'Okay, I'll ring Miles and tell him, but I don't think you've got anything to worry about. I reckon it was just a couple out for a stroll. Nothing sinister, nothing to get all worked up about.'

'But he was a copper, I tell you.'

'So what? Even police officers go out for walks and have girlfriends.'

There was a snort of disgust down the phone. Gavin wasn't sure if Paul was repelled by the idea of policemen dating or polluting the countryside with their presence or both. Gavin finished reassuring him and then rang off.

He dithered for a second or two and then flicked open his mobile again and rang Miles as he had promised. He cut straight to the chase.

'I've just had a phone call from Paul at the house. He thinks he saw the filth snooping round.' Down the line he heard a splutter followed by the sound of choking. He let Miles recover before he added, 'Of course, Paul doesn't know for certain it was the police – he just said he thought the bloke looked like a copper.'

'And just what was this "copper" doing?'

Gavin told Miles as much as he knew which, now he was repeating it, didn't seem to be very much at all.

'So it could all be a lot of fuss about nothing,' concluded Miles as Gav finished.

'Yeah, but Paul doesn't get spooked easily.'

'No.' There was silence down the line and then Miles said, 'Does your sister-in-law know any coppers?'

Gav was flummoxed. 'I don't think so. Why?'

'She was chatting to one at the club the other night. There was a stag party in – mostly police – and she seemed to know one of them.'

'Sorry,' said Gav, trying to sound casual but inwardly seething that his bloody sister-in-law was coming to the attention of Miles for all the wrong reasons, 'but isn't that what the girls are employed to do at your place? Chat up the punters and get them to drop loads of cash?'

'Yeah. Maybe I'm getting as flaky as Paul. Forget it.'

Gav let out a sigh of relief as he put the phone down. He didn't want Jess upsetting Miles. When Miles was upset things had a habit of turning very nasty, and Gav couldn't be sure who might be on the receiving end of any unpleasantness. He didn't care if it was Jess who had a rough time, but he cared very much about his own skin – and the last thing he wanted was that silly bitch messing things up.

How had Paul described the girl with the policeman? Slim, brunette, attractive . . . obviously that could cover a huge chunk of the population, but why did Jess now spring to mind? Yes, she was all those things but more worrying was the throwaway comment by Miles that she might know a copper. Did she? He was uneasily aware that he knew next to nothing about Jess. Okay, he knew she was a dancer and he knew where she worked. But her address, her friends? Zilch. Did she have a boyfriend? Not a clue. And he didn't think Abby was much wiser.

It wasn't beyond the bounds of possibility that Jess had had a look at the house. Paul had said the girl had been pointing things out. If Jess was showing a friend the place where she'd spent her childhood then it was exactly the sort of thing she could be expected to do. It didn't sound as though this random couple had been casing the joint. They hadn't tried to conceal themselves or anything. The more Gavin thought about Paul's description of the incident, the more he convinced himself that there wasn't anything to worry about. So why was he?

The problem with the bloody house stemmed from the fact that it wasn't his but belonged to the two girls. When he and Miles had gone into business together, the fact that the house didn't belong to them was part of its attraction. What was more innocent than the two girls letting the house to some tenants because they needed to earn enough money to do it up so they could maximise its potential? And with neither girl professing a head for business, it was perfectly natural for Gav to manage the property, the tenants, and everything about it. He and Miles had thought their plan was as safe as houses – till Jess had announced she wanted to live in the place. And now it might prove true that she was taking an interest in it yet again.

Which presented another problem. Gav really wanted to find out if it was Jess who had been round the place, and what's more he needed to know about her bloke. Christ, what would Miles say if he found out Jess really was involved with the filth? Could he get Abby to ask the right questions without either sister smelling a rat? And then he had an idea. Maybe Abby shouldn't ask the questions. Maybe Miles should.

Miles sauntered into the dressing room, seemingly oblivious to the fact that he'd caught about a dozen girls in various states of undress. For their part, the girls seemed just as unperturbed as him and carried on as though he wasn't there; hooking up bras, rolling on stockings, drying themselves after a shower. Jess, who'd never been a fan of communal changing rooms in sports centres and dress shops, tried to look as nonchalant as her fellow dancers but inwardly she found his presence quite creepy. It was as if he owned them, she thought. As if the dancers were his private harem. As she watched him in her mirror, Miles's gaze raked around the room and Jess dropped her eyes and pretended to fiddle with her mascara as he began to walk across the crowded room. Still not looking up, she sensed him approaching her and had to repress a shudder when her lowered eyes saw his polished brogues beside her chair.

She flicked on a smile and turned to face him. 'Miles,' she greeted him, with false sincerity.

'And how's the new girl?' Miles said.

'Fine.'

'The punters like you.'

'Do they?' She hadn't noticed. In fact, she hadn't even thought about it. As long as she got enough tips at the club each night to pay her rent, cover her late-night taxi fares and allow herself a few small luxuries, she didn't care. Any other money she earned was bunce which she shoved straight into savings.

'Yes, they do. If you've got a moment I'd like a word with you.' He paused. 'In my office.'

'Oh.'

Several girls around Jess looked at her, raised their eyebrows and exchanged significant glances.

Jess was reminded of a moment, years previously, when her Head Teacher had come to the door of her classroom and asked Jess to step outside to talk to her. Jess had been convinced she was about to be expelled or something equally dreadful, and she could vividly remember the feeling of sick dread which had seeped through her as she'd made her way between the desks. Even then, in her limited experience, you didn't get asked for a private word if that word was a good one. Private words were reserved for bad news or bollockings. She'd been proved right then as the Head had told her that her mother had been taken ill and Jess was needed at home.

Well, Jess reasoned as she followed Miles, whatever it was it couldn't be worse than that.

'Shut the door,' he said, as he plumped down into the big leather chair behind his desk. She pushed the door to, shutting out the thumping beat of the music and the babble of the clients' voices from the club. With the door closed his office became strangely quiet. Jess realised that nowhere else in the club enjoyed any sort of peace. His office must be pretty soundproof.

'Grab a chair, make yourself comfortable,' exhorted Miles, waving a hand at the pair in front of his desk.

Jess sat as primly as her skimpy frock would allow. Miles's relaxed demeanour was not reassuring her that this 'word' he wanted with her was just a casual chat.

'Happy here?' he shot at her.

'Er, yes.' Shouldn't she be? And from the gossip she'd gleaned in the dressing room, she hadn't so far had the impression that Miles was overly worried about the girls' welfare. So why was he taking this interest in her?

'Good, good. Glad to hear it.'

Jess sat quietly, waiting for Miles to speak again. If he wanted to have a chat – a *word* – with her she wasn't going to make it easy for him.

'You dance well,' he said.

'I trained professionally.'

'You said – it shows.'

'Thank you.'

'You ought to work at the weekends, you'd make a killing here on a Saturday.'

'Thanks, but no thanks.' So was this what the 'word' was about? Persuading her to work different days?

'You've got commitments, Carrie tells me.'

'Yes.' Or was Miles angling to find out what she did in her spare time? Did he know something, had he found something out? Jess's anxiety level rose.

There was a pause. 'Why don't you wriggle out of them?'

'I prefer not to.' Keep calm, offer no information, she told herself.

'Your choice.'

'I earn plenty working weekdays.'

Miles leaned forward and steepled his fingers. 'You know this is a young girls' game. You can't go on very long. Once you get past thirty, that's it, you're out of here. If you want my advice, you need to maximise what you earn while you can.'

'I don't plan on doing this for long. Just till I've earned enough to . . .' Jess stopped. Miles didn't need to know what she wanted the cash for, just like he didn't need to know how she spent Friday and Saturday nights.

'Go on.'

'Nothing. It doesn't matter.'

'A boob job?'

Despite herself, Jess smiled. She shook her head.

Miles shrugged. 'It's what a lot of the girls get done.'

Jess knew that was the truth – she'd seen the results in the dressing room, some more implausible and unlikely than others.

'So what is it then?'

She decided that it wouldn't do any harm to tell him. It was hardly an unusual ambition. 'I want to buy a house.'

'Very sensible. More sensible than a boob job. You can't go wrong with bricks and mortar. In my opinion,' he added. 'Not if you look at the long term. If you're going to go into property development it can very risky, unless you know what you're doing. And do you?'

'No, not at all. I've no ambitions to do any sort of development. I just want to buy somewhere to live in. A home.'

'Anywhere in mind?'

'The Chilterns. I grew up there.'

'Very nice. Not cheap though.'

Jess nodded. 'I know that.'

'Still,' continued Miles, 'if you play your cards right here you could earn enough to buy a little place there. Got your eye on anything?'

'Sort of. I already own half of it and I want to buy my sister out.'

'So only half as much cash to find.'

Jess nodded. Why was she telling Miles this? She'd made her mind up to keep schtum but somehow his interest was quite beguiling. Anyway, what did it matter? Her plans were hardly state secrets.

'So what sort of place is it?'

'Nice, with a huge garden but it's a bit rundown really. It'll need modernising at some stage. My sister and I were going to do it up when we could afford it and then flog it for mega-bucks, but now I'm on a decent wage – well, I can think about keeping it.'

'What does your sister say?'

'I haven't told her yet.'

'Is that wise?'

'I don't know. I think it's going to cause a row. Her husband didn't like the idea of me moving in there as an unpaid housekeeper when I was so broke I wasn't sure how I could afford to pay rent.'

'Well, you're not in that situation now.'

'No.'

'When was the last time you saw the house? I mean,' he added hastily, 'are you keeping an eye on it or letting the estate agent run it for you?'

'Actually, funnily enough I visited just the other day. I haven't been there for an age and it's just as I remembered it. The tenants have done nothing to alter it – which is reassuring.'

'They wouldn't though, would they, without your permission.'

'I suppose not.'

'So, even though you want to buy your dream house in the country, you don't want to work longer hours.'

Jess smiled. It seemed this conversation really was just about trying to make her reschedule her days off. 'That's about it.'

'So,' said Miles, leaning back in his chair again, 'your boyfriend must be pleased he gets you to himself at weekends.'

Somehow the conversation seemed to have come back to how she spent her weekends. Jess was on guard again. 'Well, seeing as I don't have a boyfriend, it doesn't really matter, does it?' she lied.

Miles's eyebrows shot up. 'I find it very hard to believe that a pretty girl like you doesn't have a whole load of men beating a path to your door,' he said silkily.

Eugh, she wanted to shudder and she suddenly remembered that Laura had once casually mentioned that 'Miles' was an anagram of 'slime'. At the time she'd thought that, although Miles could be a bit of a creep, Laura was being unduly harsh; he wasn't *that* bad. But now she found herself rapidly revising that opinion. How oily was his last comment!

'Believe what you like, it's the way it is,' she replied coolly, renewing her vow never to tell anyone, and least of all Miles, about her private life.

Miles gave her a long look, which Jess returned.

Suddenly he dropped his gaze and said, 'Well, I mustn't keep you. Shame I can't change your mind about the hours.'

'No.' Jess stood up and smoothed down the front of her short skirt. 'If that's all . . . ?'

But Miles already seemed to be involved in some paperwork so Jess just left and shut the door quietly behind her.

As soon as she had gone, Miles picked up the phone

and dialled Gavin's number. He needed to tell him about Jess's recent visit to the house – which meant she might have been the bird with the alleged copper in tow, and especially as she'd been chatting to one of them at that stag party. It was all very worrying.

'We ought to have your sister over one weekend soon,' said Gav from where he lounged in his arm-chair.

Abby nearly dropped the saucepan she was drying. 'I beg your pardon?' she said.

Gav repeated himself.

'Why?' asked Abby, still not quite sure her ears were working properly.

'She must be lonely all on her own in London. Besides, it's been an age since you two have met up.'

Abby put the saucepan down on the counter and folded the tea towel. 'Firstly,' she said slowly, 'how do we know she's all on her own? She might have loads of friends. And secondly, we haven't met up for an age because neither of us can be bothered to make the effort. We might be sisters, but that's all.'

'Exactly. You're sisters – you oughtn't to be strangers.'

Abby put the tea towel down beside the saucepan and walked into the sitting room. 'Are you all right, Gav? I mean, you've never given a monkey's about Jess before.' She frowned and narrowed her eyes. 'Why the sudden change of heart?'

'No reason.'

'Come off it.'

'Just something someone said at work, about losing

one of his relations,' lied Gavin, 'and how he'd always meant to say things and had never got round to it and how he now regretted it.'

'So?'

'So, I don't want you to ever feel the same way.'

Abby was taken aback by this rare display of thoughtfulness by Gav. She sat down on the spare armchair. 'But Jess and I have never been that close.'

'You must have been once.'

'But that was before . . .' She was going to say, 'Before I married you,' but thought the better of it.

'Well?'

'Well, nothing.'

Gav remained silent.

'Besides, I expect she has lots of friends in London and a weekend out in the country is the last thing she wants.'

'But maybe she hasn't and she's lonely.'

Abby sighed and remembered some weekends when she'd been at uni, when her flatmates had all gone home and she had been stuck there, without the cash to do anything or go anywhere, and how alone and bored she had felt. Maybe she was being too hard on Jess. Besides, Gav was right. Apart from some distant cousins, Jess was her only living relative.

'Maybe you're right,' she conceded. 'I'll ring and invite her over.'

'And ask her if she wants to bring anyone.'

'You've just said we're inviting her because she might be lonely – because she mightn't have any friends.'

'Well, you can hardly invite her and then withdraw it just because she *might* have a mate or two.'

'Yes, but—'

'But nothing. Besides, if Jess does have someone in her life, aren't you curious to know who it is?'

'Not really,' said Abby. 'And I can't see why you might be.'

'But supposing she's hitched up with someone truly dreadful? You wouldn't want that for her, would you?'

'So what if she has? That's her lookout.'

'Don't you feel the least bit responsible for her?'

'No, not any more, and I really don't understand your sudden concern over my sister. What's going on, Gavin?'

He coloured. 'There's no reason. None at all. Really.'

But Abby wasn't convinced. There was something odd about the way Gav was behaving and he certainly wasn't being level with her. There was a distinct aroma of rat around.

'Gav, I'm not stupid,' she said coldly. 'You want Jess to come and stay, you're worrying about her love-life and until very recently you never gave her a second thought. In fact, when she said she was in a bit of a financial fix and wanted us to help by letting her have the attic in the big house, you were dead against it. So what's changed?'

'Nothing,' he blustered. 'Nothing at all.'

But Abby was still left with the feeling that he was lying through his teeth. And why did he suddenly care about Jess?

Shit – that couldn't be it, could it? He *cared* about her. Gav and Jess? Then Abby saw sense. *No way, never.* Quite apart from the fact the two of them had never got on, when would they have had any opportunity to meet? So if it wasn't that, what the hell was it? Not that she could be bothered to pursue it further right now, she had other issues to occupy her time, like finishing the washing up and then drafting a leaflet about ethical farming. But if Jess did come and stay, and Abby was now quite keen that she did because it might be the way to discover just what the hell *was* going on, she was going to watch the pair of them like the proverbial hawk.

*

Jess sat by the window in her new flat and pondered her sister's invitation. She stared sightlessly at the glittering lights of London, at the white and red lights of the cars streaming along the busy road underneath, some six floors below, as she considered the unexpected summons. Abby wasn't one for spontaneity or generosity – nor, for that matter, altruism or thoughtfulness. Well, she was if it involved farm animals, the world's poor, lab-rats or one of her many other causes, but as Jess didn't fall into any of those categories she usually found herself out of luck when it came to her sister's goodwill.

However, it was true that they hadn't seen each other for an age and Abby had intimated that they ought to discuss Gran's house, so Jess knew she really ought to go. Added to which was the fact that she hadn't had a weekend off for months. Maybe it was time she had a break. Then again, if she was going to have a break, did she really want to spend her precious time off with Gav?

Jess considered her options. On balance she thought that a trip to the country would be nice, although she'd go alone despite the fact that Abby had asked her, rather insistently in Jess's opinion, if she wanted to bring a friend.

'What, no one?' she'd said when Jess had declined. 'All that time in a big city and you haven't met anyone?'

'I've met plenty of people,' retorted Jess evenly, 'just no one I want to spend a weekend with' . . . *at your house, with you and Gav,* she added silently. Matt and Abby under one roof? The idea was so far beyond scary it was almost farcical. Abby in the company of a police officer, but not in an armlock, being escorted away from a protest and shouting abuse at him. Nope, it wasn't an image Jess could get her head round. Although, she thought, Abby probably would start shouting abuse at Matt the minute she found out what he did for a living. No, this was another occasion where Jess was going to keep her life compartmentalised; Matt was going to stay in one and Abby in another.

'There must be someone. A girlfriend maybe.'

'Abby, if I come, I shall come to see you. We haven't seen each other for months, we'll have a lot to catch up on. If I brought a friend, he or she would probably only end up feeling left out.'

'So you *are* coming.'

'I expect so. I don't know. My weekends are . . . busy.'

'Doing what, for heaven's sakes? Surely you only work nine to five like the rest of the population.'

For a nano-second Jess had been tempted to tell Abby that she did indeed work nine to five – just round the other side of the clock. Let Abby put that in her pipe and smoke it. It would make a change from some of the substances Jess was pretty certain her sister had tried at uni.

So now she tapped her fingernails on the back of her mobile and weighed up the pros and cons of Abby's offer, at the same time trying to push to the back of her mind the niggling fact that Abby never did anything without good reason. Why was she inviting her over right now? Why, after several years, was it suddenly important that they discussed Gran's house?

There was only one way to find out. Jess decided she would call at the police station on her way to Shoq and ask if she could have the weekend off. If they said yes, she'd ring Abby and accept her offer. Having made her mind up, she grabbed her bag with her make-up, body spray and several sets of expensive lingerie, and went downstairs to hail a taxi.

As Jess stepped off the train at High Wycombe, Abby did a double-take. Jess? Blimey, talk about the ugly duckling turning into a swan. However, as Abby watched Jess walk towards her along the platform she could see there was nothing intrinsically different about her sister. She was just – it was hard to quantify – more *polished*.

Jess's hair was beautifully, and probably expensively, cut and it now bounced and shone like something out of a shampoo ad and, although she looked as though she wasn't wearing any make-up, Abby's feminine intuition knew full well that she was. And the glasses had gone. That made a difference, quite a big one. Was this now Jess's everyday look, Abby asked herself, or had she made a special effort and if so, why? The thought she'd briefly entertained before about Jess and Gav flashed into her head once more, but then she told herself not to be so bloody stupid. Whatever was going on, Abby was completely certain there wasn't a link between Jess and her husband.

Abby made her way towards her sister to meet her and hugged her warmly, inhaling a perfume she also recognised as being something classy and no doubt just as pricy as the hair-do.

'Let me take your bag,' she offered as she eyed up her sister's clothes. And they certainly hadn't come from a thrift shop like Jess's wardrobe had obviously done the last time they'd met. Abby was suddenly very conscious of her Doc Martens, tatty jeans and worn and stained sweat-top. She felt she'd gone from 'comfortably off' to 'poor relation' without missing a step.

'I can manage,' said Jess.

Abby noticed the wheeled case; brand new and a good make. Jess's new job obviously paid well. 'You're looking very fit,' she said, trying not to sound too surprised, and shocked by the little jab of envy she felt at her sister's trappings of success.

'So do you, Abby. Life treating you well?'

Abby nearly retorted with *not as well as it's treating you, apparently*, but managed to bite her tongue. 'Yes, fine,' she said, a little tightly. Her lifestyle – second-hand clothes, lack of car, everything re-used and re-cycled – was a personal decision, based upon her total belief that the planet was in danger and that being Green and not consuming was the only way to save it. The trouble was that underneath, she was still a woman and her basic, hard-wired female genes just occasionally transgressed and backslid, yearning for something pretty or frivolous. Mostly she could clamp this feeling down but today, Jess's great look, coupled with her innate sibling rivalry meant that it was a real struggle. She knew she should disapprove of Jess – so why did she feel so jealous?

'Gav well?' asked Jess, oblivious of her sister's turmoil.

'Yes.' Abby didn't trust herself to expand in case she let her feelings slip.

Their conversation, such as it was, stumbled even more when they reached the ticket barrier.

On the concourse outside the station Jess stopped and looked around. 'Isn't Gav meeting us?'

'No. I said we'd get the bus.'

Jess's eyes widened a fraction. Then she said, 'Sod that. Let's grab a cab.'

'Don't be ridiculous. It'll cost a fortune.'

'My treat.'

'I can't allow you to waste your money like that. Besides, think of the carbon footprint. No, we'll get the bus. It's not far to the stop.' Abby might secretly covet Jess's clothes but that was where it was going to stop. Clothes and hair were one thing – wasteful carbon emissions were something else.

Jess paused for a moment. 'Abby, I work long hours these days. I'm tired, thirsty and I want to stop travelling. The thought of an hour on some poxy bus is just more than flesh and blood can stand. Sorry as I am for the environment, I'm getting a taxi. If you don't want to share it with me you can give me the keys and I'll meet you at your house when the bus finally delivers you there.'

Abby was completely wrong-footed. Since when did Jess answer her back? Abby had always got her own way. It was a given. It's what happened to big sisters when they bossed around their younger siblings. She stared at Jess and Jess stared back. No, she absolutely wasn't going to give way. They were getting the bus.

'Keys, please,' Jess repeated after a pause. 'Or come with me. Your choice. But I'm not hanging around outside your house, waiting for you to pitch up. I'd rather go straight back to London, so make your mind up and do it quickly, please, because there'll be a train back any minute now.'

There was a steely tone in Jess's voice and a look in her eye that Abby knew meant Jess wasn't joking. Where had this assertiveness come from? Abby knew she was beaten. Meekly she fell in beside Jess as she strode over to the taxi rank and spoke to the driver through the open passenger window. He then instantly leaped out and opened the rear door for Jess as if she were royalty.

'I really don't approve,' said Abby as they settled into the back seat, Jess's case stowed in the boot by the eager and compliant cab driver. Abby thought sourly that no bloke had ever fawned over her like that. She decided it was rather degrading of Jess to allow it. Where was her sense of dignity?

'I'm so knackered I really don't care if you don't approve,' said Jess calmly. 'But I promise I'll be as Green as possible for the rest of the weekend. I won't waste electricity or leave the taps running while I clean my teeth, or throw recyclables in the general waste, promise.' Jess flashed Abby a warm smile. 'And it *is* good to see you, sis. Honest. I'm sorry I was cranky just now – being tired makes me bad-tempered.'

'It's okay. And you're right, coping with the bus and a suitcase wouldn't be easy.' They sat in silence for a while as the cab driver wove his way through the busy streets of Wycombe and then finally up the precipitous hill that led out of the steep-sided valley in which the town nestled. A few minutes later they drove over the M40 towards the rolling hills, meadows and beechwoods of the Chilterns.

'I ought to get out of London more often,' said Jess as she looked over the startlingly green countryside and wide blue sky, lambs gambolling by their mothers and red kites circling overhead.

'You should. Gav and I are always happy to put you up, you know that.'

Jess shot Abby a look.

'I know you and Gav have had your differences in the past but that's water under the bridge now.' Abby missed Jess's raised eyebrows of surprise. 'Anyway, we've both been looking forward to seeing you again so much. It's been months and months.'

'Over a year. The Christmas before last,' said Jess.

'Goodness, as long as that. Remind me what you did last Christmas?'

'I had to work Christmas Eve and it was too late to get a train to yours when I'd finished.'

'Oh yes. And Gav had a problem with the car and couldn't pick you up from your bedsit. Very unfortunate. Well, we must make it up to you now.'

Jess looked at her sister and wondered if she really had forgotten about the previous Christmas. Hell, it had only been a few months earlier, so how could she? Or maybe, because Abby and Gav hadn't had a totally miserable Christmas, like she had, with nothing much to celebrate and bugger all to eat because she'd been planning on going to Abby's, her sister had actually managed to erase the fact that Gav's car had had 'a problem' from her memory bank. He couldn't be bothered to drive fifty miles to get me, more like, thought Jess. Still, as Abby had said, it was water under the bridge now, something that had happened in the past and she must move on. All fine and dandy in theory but Jess still wasn't sure she would be forgiving Gav any time in the near future. He might be her brother-in-law and Abby might be married to him, but as far as Jess was concerned he was a sly, unpleasant git whom she'd disliked from the start and with good reason.

The first time she'd clapped eyes on Gav was when Abby had brought him home from uni; she was in her second year and seemed very grown-up and sophisticated to Jess, who was deep in the throes of GCSEs and still bound by school rules and uniform. Abby going to uni had left an enormous hole in Jess's life as Abby and she had come to depend on each other hugely since the death of their mother. Their gran had done her best by them, but Abby and Jess had grown inseparable as they'd comforted each other.

Although Abby was now a student she still came home for at least one weekend every month. Jess remembered how they used to sit at the table in the big kitchen, after Gran had gone to bed, Abby recounting tales of raves and demos, of drugs and debates, while Jess listened, rapt at this life which was a world away from her girls' school in High Wycombe, coursework and thinking a late night out was catching the last bus home. Abby and she had shared secrets and confidences and had told each other everything. And Jess had longed to meet Gavin after Abby had described him as being a sophisticated trendsetter who all the female students fancied. Jess could barely believe it when Abby told her that she'd been asked out on a date by him, and of course she was mad with curiosity and couldn't wait for Abby to bring him home.

But the day Gavin arrived Jess had suddenly found herself shut out of Abby's life. Her sister and Gav had raced off to the attic and pretty much ignored Jess and Gran for the entire weekend. And when the pair had made an appearance, very occasionally, Abby had been wide-eyed and distant, almost as if she were half-asleep, and hadn't been at all interested in anything Jess had to say to her. Now, Jess knew that Abby's bizarre demeanour had been drug-induced, which was probably one of the reasons why Abby thought Gavin was so sophisticated, but then her sheltered upbringing meant she hadn't a clue.

Gav hadn't been out of it like Abby though – quite the opposite. In fact, he'd been slightly sinister and spooky, Jess thought. She remembered finding him, early one morning, wandering around Gran's house, opening cupboards and doors, poking around in the corners and nooks, and when Jess had asked him why he was so interested in the place, and when she'd pressed him for answers he'd told her to mind her own fucking business and drawn his fist back which made her think he was about to hit her. Jess, brought up almost entirely by women and used to good manners and gentleness, was stunned and frightened. She knew the swearword, of course she did, but she'd never had it used against her in quite such a vicious and unprovoked way, nor by someone she thought was a friend of the family. Nor had she ever thought she was in danger of physical violence before. Hurt, confused and frightened, Jess had run to her room before Gav found out she was crying. If that had happened, the humiliation would have been the final straw.

After that, despite the fact that Gav became a permanent weekend feature at Gran's house, Jess developed strategies to keep out of his way as much as possible. She'd tried telling Abby what had happened but her sister had waved a dismissive hand and mumbled something about mountains and molehills and Jess getting the wrong end of the stick. And when Jess had persisted, Abby had got cross with her too.

Frightened by Gav and feeling betrayed by her sister, Jess gave up. But she wasn't going to forget what Gavin had said and done. Or about the wedge he'd driven between her and Abby. Not ever. She didn't trust him, she didn't like him and even though Abby had eventually married him, she wasn't about to change her mind. And she still wasn't, even though years had passed since then.

Of course Jess wondered what had made Gav so irresistible to Abby. For a while she'd thought it was just the supply of illegal substances that had made him seem so edgy and glamorous, but it had to be more than that. She allowed herself, despite her antipathy, to concede that he was quite good-looking. So was it, she supposed, that Abby was so flattered he took an interest in her and was so doped to the eyeballs some of the time that she didn't see his faults? Jess wondered if she did now, especially as she didn't think her sister had smoked cannabis for years. Or maybe familiarity had replaced the pot for creating a haze of oblivion as far as Gav's shortcomings were concerned.

However, Abby was promising to make it up to her now – which had to be a good thing. Jess wondered just how that promise would be manifested; an extra helping of nut roast, a celebratory trip to the recycling centre, a chance to help turn the compost heap? *Oooh wow, hold me back!* Then she reprimanded herself – she was being unfair. Maybe Abby wanted to build bridges. Maybe . . . but Jess was pretty sure Gav wasn't going to. Abby might think he radiated so much sunlight his backside could power a solar panel, but Jess wasn't deluded. As far as she was concerned, he was mean and nasty and possibly even violent. Jess wasn't going to trust him further than she could throw a Toyota Prius, but she *was* going to make an effort with her sister.

14

'So what shall we do this afternoon?' said Abby brightly as she and Jess did the washing-up together after lunch.

Outside the window, Gav was studying the veg patch that took up half of the long, thin garden at the back of the little terraced house. Jess reflected that, in the several years that Gav and Abby had lived here and in all of her half-dozen visits to the house, she'd never seen him actually work on it despite the way he paid lipservice to the importance of lowering food miles and the empowering effect of growing one's own food. Abby was out in it at every spare moment, digging, weeding, composting – but Gav? Get his hands dirty? Nope. In fact, once he'd married Abby, his enthusiasm for everything Green had seemed to lessen hugely, although Jess admitted to herself that maybe she was doing him a disservice just because she disliked him so much. Even so, he still seemed rather bogus.

But considering Gav's shortcomings wasn't answering Abby's question. Just what *did* Jess want to do to pass the afternoon? The wicked side of her longed to suggest something like going on a seal-cull, just to see Abby's reaction but, as she knew that she'd pushed her luck with the taxi, instead she said she could quite fancy a walk, which was the truth.

'The parks in London are okay, but they're not proper countryside. It would be lovely to go for a ramble. Won't the bluebells be out about now?'

'Probably a bit early still.' Abby put the pan-scourer down and turned to her sister. 'We ought to go up to the Common. It'd be just like old times.'

'Although I can't see us playing hide-and-seek or tree-climbing,' Jess grinned.

'I dunno. I reckon I could still make it to the top of that old oak in Gran's garden before you could.'

'Bet you couldn't.'

'Bet I could,' Abby challenged her.

'How much?'

'A fiver.'

'Done!' Jess fished in her handbag and extracted a note. 'Come on, put your money where your mouth is.'

'There's no point. We can't get there to prove it one way or the other.'

'Why not? Gav's got a car. He could take us.'

Abby shrugged. 'I don't think that's likely. Besides, it wouldn't be ethical to use his car for a jaunt like that.'

Jess rolled her eyes. 'It's only a few miles. I'd suggest we could walk to the Common, only by the time we got there it'd be dark. Besides, at some stage this weekend I really think you and I need to talk about the future of the place. We've been renting it out for months and months now, and if we're not going to get it done up to sell it I've got a proposal.'

'What sort of proposal?' asked Abby, a note of wariness in her voice.

'I'd rather talk about it later. Maybe over a drink. I've brought a bottle of wine with me; I thought we could have a couple of glasses with our supper tonight and go over everything.' Jess changed the subject. 'So when did you last see Gran's house?'

'Months and months ago. You?'

Jess just shrugged in a vague way to indicate it had been so long ago as to be beyond her recall. For some reason she didn't think Abby would respond well to the idea that her sister had been in the area without telling her, and had been checking up on their inheritance – without Abby. 'We ought to see it together, then we both know exactly what state it's in.'

'We won't be able to go in. The tenants wouldn't like it.'

'I suppose not. But aren't you curious to see how it is these days?'

Abby nodded. 'I suppose I *could* ask Gav.' She stared out of the window at her husband, oblivious that he was the subject of the girls' conversation.

'Or, if he won't take us today, how about tomorrow? If we set out early he could even run us past the place on the way to the station. That way, it wouldn't be an unncessary journey.'

Abby sighed. 'He might go for that.'

'Well, ask him.'

As Jess continued with the drying up, Abby went out of the back door and walked down the garden. Jess couldn't hear their conversation but she could tell by the body language that Gav didn't seem to be opposed to the idea. In fact, from the smile on Abby's face, he seemed to have agreed pretty readily.

Jess was flabbergasted. Never, since she had known Gav, had he greeted anything that involved her with less than barely concealed animosity. Okay, it was a sentiment that she returned in equal measure so there was probably fault on both sides but he'd started it, she thought. If he hadn't gone for her, on that first visit to Gran's house, she would have regarded him a whole lot differently, but the way he'd lashed out at her, completely unprovoked, meant that she would never trust him.

Abby came back in the house and told Jess with a grin that it was 'all sorted' and then muttered something about nipping to the loo, leaving Jess to tidy up the kitchen and finish the last of the drying up.

'So you want to see your gran's house,' said Gav, lounging against the back door.

'It seems like a good idea,' she replied. 'We ought to think about what we're going to do with it. But Abby and I,' she emphasised the *I* very deliberately – this was *not* Gav's business, this was not his inheritance and she wasn't going to let him forget it – 'are going to discuss it later.'

Gav stared at her. 'Good idea.'

Jess hid her surprise at Gavin's reaction. This man was just so out of character at the moment. What had happened to him? A bang on the head? A lobotomy?

'Great.'

'So how's life in London?'

'Busy – you know, new job and everything.'

'So you got that job at Shoq that I told you about.'

Jess threw a nervous glance at the kitchen door but Abby was still busy upstairs. 'I wasn't going to go for it,' she said quietly, 'but, well, I met the owner – a total coincidence really – and somehow I ended up having an audition. But it's not the career I'd planned on. Abby doesn't know about it,' she added.

'And you'd like it to stay that way.'

Was there a hint of a threat in the way Gav said that, or was she just being paranoid? 'It might be easier all round, don't you think?' She tried to sound casual, as if she didn't really care, but she had a horrid suspicion that Gav knew she was bluffing.

'So what does your boyfriend think of what you do?'

'He's . . .' Jess stopped. Bum, she'd been worrying

about Abby finding out about her job so she'd let her guard down about other aspects of her private life. Gav had set a trap and she'd walked into it. And why did he care? Why was he interested? He'd never done anything except ignore her in the past – ignore her or be horrid to her. His change of tack was worrying.

'He's . . . what?' prompted Gavin. 'Ecstatic? Horrified?'

'He's okay about it. It's just dancing, after all.'

'Yeah, just dancing.'

Jess turned her attention to wiping down the counter in the kitchen.

'Tell me about your man,' said Gav.

'He's a bloke and a friend.' She was suspicious. Actually, she was very suspicious. Gavin had been nice to her, had agreed with her suggestion to go and see the house, and was now taking a completely out-of-character interest in her. What was his game? He had to be up to something. Jess wished she knew what.

'How did you meet him? Is he a regular at Shoq?'

Jess shook her head. It was none of his business where she'd met Matt and she didn't want to talk about it. 'We worked together,' she said, using a tone of voice that she hoped would indicate to Gav that this wasn't a conversation she was enjoying. Whether or not he got the hint she would never find out, as Abby clattered down the stairs before Gav could pry any more.

'Ready?' she said.

Jess, thankfully, sped out of the house in her sister's wake and into the back seat of the car, hoping to God Gav didn't raise the subject of either Matt or her job in front of Abby. She felt she might be able to fob Gavin off with woolly answers and semi-truths, but Abby wouldn't settle for that. No, once her curiosity had been roused, Abby would want every blooming detail, and when she'd found them out – that Matt was a police officer and her sister was a pole-dancer – her reaction would be ballistic. Abby might have signed up to CND but she would go nuclear despite her pacifist tendencies and Jess would suffer from the fall-out.

Thankfully, Gavin refrained from talking about anything scary, like Jess's boyfriend or job, on the way to the Common and Gran's house, and instead made occasional small talk and commented on the passing scenery, as if Jess was some sort of tourist who was unfamiliar with the area. Boring and banal though this was, it was preferable to fielding awkward questions about her personal life.

They drew up at the end of the track that led to the big house that had once been their home.

'It's ages since I've been up here,' said Abby, staring along the rutted drive.

'Hmm, ages,' said Jess, noncommittally. She caught Gav staring at her in the rearview mirror. His face was a study in disbelief. Did he know she'd been up here just a matter of days previously? How could he? Jess shivered. The look on his face *and* her suspicions about his motives made her even more convinced something was going on. Or was it that Gavin always gave her the heebie-jeebies? Creep.

'Come on, let's go and have a look at the old place,' said Jess, desperate to escape from Gavin's proximity. She got out of the car and began walking along the track before either of the other two had a chance to object.

'Wait, Jess!' called Abby, panting along behind her.

'Come on,' responded Jess, not slowing down.

'But we can't trespass,' came a plaintive complaint from behind her.

'Trespass? We own the ruddy place.'

'The tenants won't like it.'

Jess stopped. 'I'm sure if we knock on the door, explain politely who we are and ask nicely, they won't object to us having a look around. We're not inspecting the place, we won't ask to go in. What's to mind?'

'Suppose so,' said Abby doubtfully, finally drawing level with her sister.

Jess turned and walked purposefully on, emerging from the beech-lined track in to the garden at the front of the house. She realised that Gavin wasn't with them and looked back along the drive to where the car was parked at the end. Gav appeared to be leaning against the bonnet, texting. Good, she thought. The further away from her he was, the happier she was. Shame he wasn't round the other side of the planet.

The sound of birds twittering and tweeting, the faint soughing of the breeze in the branches and the mewing of the red kites that wheeled overhead were the only things she could hear. She'd forgotten just how peaceful it was up here on the Common – such a contrast to London, with the never-ending roar of traffic, the blare of two-tones and the drone of aircraft descending into Heathrow that was the constant background to life, day or night.

She could see Gav's thumbs flicking over the keypad on his phone, then he used his index finger to jab a button repeatedly. If his phone was like hers, once the message was finished it asked if you wanted to send it. *Sure? Are you* really *sure? What – now? Certain?* Or at least, that's how it seemed to work, and you kept having to press the 'select' button until the phone finally realised that you were serious about the text going to the intended recipient. Gav finally managed to convince his mobile that he wanted to communicate with someone as he stopped jabbing, flipped his phone shut and shoved it in his pocket.

She turned back and studied the house; were any of the tenants in? It was a weekend, after all, and a couple of the smaller windows in the bedrooms were open, indicating that someone probably was at home. That, or they had a complete disregard for security.

Bing-bong. The faint but unmistakable signal of a text being received came from the house.

'I'd forgotten how lovely it is here,' said Jess, gazing at the wooded scenery.

Abby nodded. They both stood in the dappled shade and savoured the tranquillity for a little while, waiting for Gavin to join them, although he didn't seem to be inclined to. The faintest 'bing-bong' drifted to them from over by the car.

Gav got his phone out again, stared at it and then his thumbs started moving again. Then, jab, jab, jab, jab, the phone flicked shut.

Bing-bong from the house, again.

Jess stared at Gav and then the house. Once was coincidence. Twice was . . . Gav was now walking towards them. Should she ask him if he was texting one of the tenants? Should she let on about her suspicions? And anyway, if he was, was it a crime? Or was it that she was now so wound up about him and his motives that she was going to question anything he did. If he stopped to tie his shoelace she'd probably find she was looking for some sort of ulterior motive in that! Jess meandered away from Abby as she turned her thoughts over and over. So what if he was texting the tenants? Maybe he knew the guys who lived there; after all, he had managed the let from the start. Maybe he was just telling them that their landlords were around.

Abby broke the peaceful silence. 'So are you really going to knock on the door?'

Jess dismissed her thoughts, slapped a smile on her

face and turned towards her sister. 'Yes, why not? The worst they can say to us is "bugger off" and if they do, we will.'

'You never used to be like this,' said Abby.

'Like what?'

'Assertive.'

Yeah, well, eighteen months as a Special had a way of bracing you up, thought Jess. Being told where to go by a couple of tenants would be nothing compared to some of the situations she'd found herself in. 'I expect I've grown up a bit. Living in London does that to people.' To say nothing of working in a pole-dancing joint. But Abby wasn't going to know about that either.

15

Jess strode to the old oak front door and rang the bell.

Bing-bong again – but the door bell this time, not Gavin texting. There was a pause and then footsteps. A pale, slightly scruffy twenty-something bloke opened the door and peered round.

'Yes?'

Jess stepped forward so that if he shut the door he'd probably hit her with it. Not quite a foot in the door but almost, she thought. 'Hi,' she said cheerily. 'I'm Jess and this is my sister Abby. Your landlords,' she added helpfully.

'Oh, hi.' The scruffy bloke sounded surprised. Good acting, thought Jess. Or maybe not. 'What can I do for you? Nothing wrong, I hope.'

'No, nothing at all. It's just we used to live here and we're taking a trip down Memory Lane.'

'Oh.'

Jess caught a look he shot past her to Gav. She was tempted to turn round to see her brother-in-law's response but decided against it. She smiled instead. 'We wondered if it'd be okay to have a look around?'

The scruffy man's Adam's apple bobbed. Nervous – why? What on earth had he to be nervous about, unless he and his mates had done something unspeakable to the place? 'It's a bit of a mess.'

'We don't mind about that. Do we, Abby?'

Jess willed Abby not to say something dumb like *Oh, we don't want to disturb you. We'll just have a look at the garden.*

But Abby, bless her, said, 'Absolutely not. And it would be so lovely to see the old place again. If you don't mind?'

'Come in, then.' Again that nervy look at Gav. Then: 'I'm Dave.' He held out a none-too-clean hand which the girls shook as they introduced themselves.

'Any of the other tenants in?' asked Gavin.

'No, just me,' said Dave.

'Oh.'

'Does it matter?' asked Dave.

'I just wanted to check something with Paul. Never mind.'

Dave held the door wide and they all trooped through into the huge hall with the big staircase that wound round three sides of it, up to the first floor. Jess gazed about her and was transported back through the years to the time when the house smelled of her grandmother's cooking, furniture polish and flowers from the garden. But now the house smelled of cheap air freshener and, she sniffed again, trying to identify the smell . . . mothballs. Mothballs? Unpleasant, thought Jess, and wondered why. They'd never had a problem with moths.

Jess and Abby drifted around the downstairs, noting how different the house looked devoid of Gran's furniture. The kitchen, although messy and grubby, was exactly the same – and horribly dated. Although the old fuse-box on the wall had gone and had been replaced by a neat new one. It had needed doing, of course, the old one was probably a fire-risk and a liability, but Jess couldn't remember the agency contacting her about replacing it. They were supposed to; she and Abby were allowed to have the final say in any alterations or repairs done to the property. Maybe it was something that had to be done before it could be let. Oh well, but she ought to ask Abby for a look at all the paperwork about the place. For a start she wanted to know how much had been put aside for the modernisation.

And boy, did the place need it, if the kitchen was anything to go by! The units were battered and tatty and the quarry tiles on the floor were cracked and chipped. The sink was stained and caked in limescale round the taps. The whole thing needed ripping out and replacing. But despite the unappealing aspect, memories flooded back to Jess: she and Abby sitting there exchanging confidences; Gran teaching them how to make pastry; doing her homework. For a second she could almost visualise her grandmother, standing by the table, mixing bowl and wooden spoon in hand, and the immediacy of it was quite painful. Jess felt tears pricking behind her eyes. Quickly she pretended an interest in the view from the window as she smeared the tears away with the back of her hand.

As her vision cleared she saw that the grounds were in a terrible state; the flowerbeds had disappeared beneath a tangle of brambles and couch grass, the shrubs were in desperate need of pruning and the place was now more like a wasteland than a garden. It was too sad and the tears she'd thought she'd banished welled up again once more. Coming here was a mistake.

Maybe if she went to another room in the house, one with different furniture, the blokes' furniture, the memories wouldn't be so raw. Dave, Abby and Gav had moved off and were now chatting in the sitting room about a few repairs that Dave seemed to think needed doing, so Jess was able to slip past them, unnoticed, and quietly climb the stairs to the first floor. The old linen press still stood on the landing and it brought back instant memories of her gran and the smell of lavender that had always wafted out when the door was opened. She paused beside it and stared at the shut doors of the various bedrooms. For a second she toyed with the idea of having a peek into them, then dismissed the notion. For a start the bedrooms might be occupied and secondly . . . Secondly, even she couldn't bring herself to be quite that nosy.

But the attic, now that was a different matter entirely. There was no reason for the tenants to have anything to do with that fantastic space that had been a kid-heaven. She recalled all the junk that had been piled up there – old toys, old clothes, suitcases, bric-à-brac and knick-knacks. She and Abby had had such fun playing make-believe games with it and building dens. On a couple of occasions they'd even been allowed to sleep up there – almost like camping but without the perils of getting frozen or soaked. Bliss.

Jess went to the end of the landing and drew back the curtain that concealed the narrow stairs that led up to the top of the house, but instead of stairs there was a new door complete with a Yale and a mortise lock.

When had that been put in? And why? She certainly hadn't been consulted about it. She wondered if Abby had. Even though Jess was pretty sure it was useless, she still reached a hand out and tested the door. Locked fast. No one was going to get up to the attic in a hurry. Disappointed, she redrew the curtain and made her way back downstairs. The others were still in the sitting room and when Jess slid in through the door she reckoned they all thought she'd joined them straight from the kitchen. She'd ask Abby later if she knew about the new door. Maybe she'd be able to shed some light on it.

'I had it installed,' said Gav curtly as they tramped through the beechwoods on the walk Jess had demanded they should go on when they'd left the house and Dave.

'But what on earth were you doing upstairs?' He sounded quite angry with Jess. Obviously, keeping up the Mr Nice Guy routine with her was proving too hard.

'Just having a look round *my* house. I didn't go into any of the bedrooms, if that's what you're worried about. But that doesn't answer my question: why the new door?'

'Because when I arranged for the place to be let unfurnished I took the decision to store some of your gran's stuff up in the attic and I didn't think you'd want the tenants having access to it.'

'But we had the house cleared after she died. Neither of us wanted the furniture and Abby and I took the bits and pieces that we felt were special or meant something.'

'Well, there were a few bits left.'

'But there shouldn't have been. We paid to have the house cleared completely. If the contractors didn't do their job properly you should have told us.'

'Well, it's no big deal.'

'So what was left?'

'Furniture.'

'What?'

'What do you mean?'

'What furniture? Beds? Chests? The three-piece suite?'

'I can't remember.'

'What, even though you had to lug it up those narrow stairs into the attic?'

'It was a while back.'

Jess was sure he was lying. There was no way you would forget which items of furniture you'd shifted about. Well, you might if you were a removal man, but Gav worked in IT and presumably the only bit of furniture he moved on a regular basis was his swivel chair as he pushed it back to get out from behind his desk. And anyway, if Gav had been so concerned about her gran's furniture, why hadn't the linen press been moved? What he said just didn't make sense.

'What does it matter, Jess?' asked Abby sharply. 'Gav's only been trying to help us.'

Had he? And judging by the look of triumph he shot her, Gav felt that he'd won the argument, or got away with whatever it was he was trying to hide. And Jess was completely convinced that he *was* hiding something.

She let the subject drop. The last thing she wanted to do was antagonise her sister any more than was absolutely necessary. She intended to tackle the subject of buying out Abby's half of the house this evening, and if Abby was in a real strop with her it was only going to make a potentially tricky conversation even more fraught.

'What do you mean, you'd like to buy the place?' asked Abby angrily, waving her glass around so the wine it contained almost spilled over the rim. 'How?'

'With money. How else do you think?' Jess's reasonableness and cool infuriated Abby even more, but given that they were on a second bottle of wine, it was also, thought Abby, remarkable. But then she hadn't noticed that Jess was only half-filling her own glass when she topped up her sister's to the brim.

'What money?'

'Well, obviously I haven't got enough yet but I'm saving quite hard.'

'So when will you have enough – before the turn of the next century?' Abby couldn't keep the sarcasm out of her voice.

'I should think I'll have more than enough for the deposit in a year or so.'

'Yeah, right. Building societies want about ten per cent these days.'

'I know.'

'So . . . That's a lot of money.'

'I know that too. I've got a job that pays well, I work long hours, I don't go out much, I live fairly frugally—'

'But I thought the idea was that we were going to sell it and split the proceeds.' Abby began to get shrill.

'Is it so very different if I buy it off you? You'll still get your share.'

'But you'll have . . .' Abby stopped.

'I'll have the house. Would that be so bad?'

Abby didn't reply but the look on her face said it all: if she couldn't have the house then neither of them should. And Gavin had always been adamant that he was never going to live in Gran's old place. He was a townie, he liked having neighbours and shops on his doorstep, he liked living near a pub and near a station. Being stuck out in the back of beyond was his idea of complete hell.

'And there's another thing,' said Jess.

Abby wasn't really in a mood to listen but she didn't have much choice unless she stormed out of the room – which she really felt like doing, but if she did it would offer a victory of sorts to her sister.

'What's that?' she snapped.

'I am quite prepared to buy the house unmodernised. We both saw that it's desperately shabby, but if I buy it I'll do it up and then you won't have to share the expense or trouble of sorting it out.'

Abby was on her guard. 'What you mean is that you'll buy it at a knock-down price because it's in such a state and I'll get less.'

'But you'd get a big lump sum faster.'

'And you'd get your hands on it faster.'

'Now you're being unreasonable.'

'No, I'm not.'

'Yes, you are.'

'Girls!' shouted Gav.

They both stopped and stared at him.

'Enough. This argument isn't getting you anywhere and you're both pissed.'

'We're not,' said Abby, putting her glass on the table with studied care so as not to spill the contents.

'It's time you both went to bed. If you must, you can talk about this in the morning.'

Jess glowered at him and Abby opened her mouth to argue but then saw the look on her husband's face and shut it again. Grumpily and with scores to settle, words to say and axes to grind, the two sisters made their way up the stairs. There were no friendly 'goodnights' on the landing, just the sound of doors shutting and the residual gloom left by simmering anger.

16

Jess, waking early, feeling hard done by and fuelled by a sense of righteous indignation that her reasonable offer had been slapped down, decided she might as well ring for a cab and get the train back to London rather than stay with her sister a moment longer.

'Sod it,' she muttered to herself as she searched Abby's living room for a *Yellow Pages* to get a taxi firm number.

'What you looking for?' asked Gav.

Jess jumped and spun round to be confronted by her brother-in-law, lounging against the doorjamb with way too much of his chest revealed by his unbuttoned pyjama top. Jess repressed a shudder as she answered his question. 'Looking for the number of a cab company.'

'Why?'

'Why do you think? I doubt that Abby and I are going kiss and make up any time soon and it would be better all round if I went back to London.'

'You were both pissed.'

'So you said last night.'

'I'm impressed you remember.'

'Actually I wasn't – pissed, that is – which is why I do.'

'My mistake. Which explains why you're so bright and early and looking as lovely as always.'

Jess wasn't inclined to acknowledge his compliment,

which she thought was slimy. Her suspicions about his motives were raised again; he was never nice to her and yet for almost a whole twenty-four hours he'd been verging on civil, apart from that brief lapse the previous afternoon. What was his game, she wondered for the umpteenth time.

'Maybe Abby won't feel quite as strongly about your tiff when she wakes up.'

'You mean she'll change her mind about me wanting to buy Gran's house? I don't think so.'

Gav shrugged. 'She may. Well, not immediately, but I reckon she can be persuaded.'

'Huh. I think I know my sister better than you do and I can see hell freezing over first.' Jess narrowed her eyes. 'Besides, why do you want her *persuaded*?'

'Because it gets us out of the hassle of having to do the place up and it'll be less complicated if the sale is between you and your sister, as we can probably manage it without having to use estate agents – which will save us a packet in commission.'

What Gavin said made sense, but Jess had never been inclined to trust him and wasn't going to start now. There was an ulterior motive going on here but she was buggered if she could work out what the hell it was.

'Right,' she said slowly. 'Well, if you can do it, that'll be good. Otherwise we'll just go ahead as planned and I'll wait till it goes on the market to put in an offer. But it seems like an almighty waste of time and effort, if you ask me.'

'I'll do my best. So . . .' Gavin grinned at her, which made Jess's skin creep. 'Will you change your mind and stay?'

Jess considered the offer for all of a second or possibly two and made her mind up. It was his smarmy grin that really clinched it; Gavin being rude and vile she could cope with, but this new persona? She shuddered. 'I think it's a case of least said soonest mended, don't you? I'll fetch my things and get out of your hair. Leave you in peace and give you the chance to work on Abby. If you could just let me have the number of a taxi company.'

'I'll get the car and give you a lift if you like.'

Actually Jess *didn't* like, but it would have been beyond rude to say so. 'At least if you do that you'll know you're shot of me.'

'Don't be silly. Abby and I love having you.'

Jess raised her eyebrows and said nothing. That was a porky if ever she heard one. If he'd said 'tolerate' she might have gone along with it, but 'love'? Oh no, another lie from Pinocchio.

'I'll get my bag.'

It was only when Jess was standing on the platform at High Wycombe that she remembered that she hadn't asked to see any of the paperwork relating to the house. She still had no idea about expenses and outgoings, nor about the amount saved towards modernisation. Damn. And it probably wasn't a good idea to rile Abby further by asking her to photocopy the stuff and send it to her. She'd just have to wait until the next time – whenever that was likely to be.

'I'm on the train,' she told Matt over her mobile, ignoring the look from the passenger opposite her.

'But you'd gone away for the weekend.'

'Long story. Tell you when I see you. What shift are you on today? Any chance of seeing you?'

'I'm on the late turn. Do you fancy lunch?'

'That'd be nice.'

'I'll come over to your flat at about eleven-thirty, pick you up and we can go and find somewhere nice.'

'Sounds wonderful. See you then.' Jess flicked her

phone closed and turned to watch the passing scenery. The Chilterns were giving way to more and more houses, the outer sprawl of London, but she wasn't really paying attention to the view, such as it was. Her mind was totally occupied by the ridiculous excitement and anticipation of seeing Matt again. Her insides felt all fluttery as she glanced at her watch and worked out just how many minutes it was till he'd be at her front door. That long! Ages – hours almost. She ought to have suggested that he met her at Marylebone station, then she'd only have half an hour. She could have coped with that.

Jess sighed and re-opened her phone. She really ought to ring Abby and apologise both for leaving early and for upsetting her the previous evening. She took a deep breath and pressed the keys to get the number. Unsurprisingly, Abby was more than a little cool.

'I'm not going to discuss the house. I know Gavin will agree that you're bang out of order. I'm going to take advice on this, Jess, so don't go planning on moving into it in my lifetime.'

Jess bit her tongue. She wasn't going to rock the boat by letting Abby know that she'd got it completely wrong about Gav's attitude. Let her bloody sister find out from Gav himself. Although Jess quite fancied being a fly on the wall when she did. The row was going to be a blinder to watch.

'I'm sorry you feel this way,' she said placatingly.

'How the fuck else did you expect me to feel? Just because you're suddenly Miss Moneybags and now you're rubbing my nose in it.' There was a pause as Abby thought about what to say next, but apparently words failed her. 'I can't be doing with this right now. I'm going to talk to Gav. I'll be in touch.' The connection was severed.

Jess leaned against her seat, suddenly feeling quite

drained. Well, she thought, good luck, Gav. And was it worth falling out with her sister over the house? Did she want the house more than she wanted to be on good terms with her sister? After all, Abby was her only close living relative – well, the only one she knew about. God alone knew where their father was. House or sister? Hmm, right now, the house won and unless Abby stopped being such a pain in the arse, it would continue to do so for the foreseeable future.

Jess gave up worrying about her relationship with her sister, since there was nothing she could do about it until Abby calmed down. Instead she turned her thoughts to something infinitely more pleasant and sank into a delicious day dream involving Matt and vague plans for the time they would have together until he had to go to work; this pretty much occupied her until they drew into the terminus.

Jess raced along the platform to the exit from the concourse, ahead of the wave of her fellow passengers. She was determined to get to the taxi rank first; she didn't have long to get to her flat, shower, wash her hair and decide what to wear. Although she was almost beside herself with impatience at seeing him again, she also wanted enough time to make herself look her best for Matt. Even Jess realised she couldn't have it both ways but thought, on balance, she would rather risk him seeing her slightly less than perfect than wait a moment longer than necessary.

With a sigh of relief she saw a line of cabs and no queue as she hared out of the station. She grabbed the first one, flung herself on the back seat, hauling her overnight case in after her, gave the cabbie her address and tried to look cool and calm as he moved off to join the Sunday-morning traffic. However, she couldn't help glancing at her watch every few minutes as the cab sped along the almost-empty streets to check how long she had to gild the lily – how long till she would be with Matt.

At the entrance to her block of flats she thrust a twenty-pound note at the grateful cabbie, telling him to keep the change, pressed the key code to get through the front door and charged into a waiting lift.

'Ta-dah! Surprise!' said Matt as she exited.

Jess nearly jumped out of her skin, giving a little shriek. She'd been intent on finding her key in her handbag and the last thing she'd expected was to find Matt waiting for her.

'Don't *do* that,' she said, laughing, dropping her case and flinging herself into his arms.

Matt hugged her and nuzzled her neck. 'Sorry, honey. I didn't mean to frighten you.'

'Nice fright though,' replied Jess, her voice muffled by his woolly jumper. Being enveloped by his arms just felt so right – bliss. She looked up at him. 'How did you get in?'

'Just waited till someone came out and dodged in before the front door shut. Easy really.'

'Devious. Comes of being a copper, I suppose.'

'Comes of being desperate to see you.'

'I was going to make myself look nice for you.'

'You look perfect to me.'

Bless him, he was so lovely. Still in need of a trip to SpecSavers, but lovely. 'I need a shower.'

'I could scrub your back.'

Jess raised an eyebrow at Matt. Now that was an offer. 'Then I'd better get the door open.'

She slid out of his arms, found her key and let them both in. As Matt pushed the door shut behind them both he grabbed her.

'I've got a better idea,' he said. 'Let's have a shower afterwards.'

Jess didn't need to ask what he planned to do first. Lunch could wait.

'So it was a shit visit,' said Matt after they had ordered their drinks – orange juice for him and white wine spritzer for Jess.

'Not all of it. There were some good bits. I just wish I knew what Gav's up to. He's never been nice to me, but recently . . . He put the idea of working at Shoq into my head, he's supporting me about buying the house, he gave me a lift to the station . . . Honestly, it just doesn't add up.'

'Maybe he's decided that, as you're family, he shouldn't keep upsetting you.'

Jess shrugged. 'I just don't see why now he doesn't mind the idea of me buying the house. But when I suggested, a matter of weeks ago, that I should live there, he was dead against it.' She sighed. 'I suppose I've just got to accept the fact that he's weird.'

'Nowt so queer as folk,' agreed Matt.

'And talking of weird – the house smelled of mothballs. How odd is that?'

'Maybe they'd had an infestation.'

'I just hope it isn't a difficult smell to get shot of. It was really rank.' Their drinks arrived. 'Anyway,' said Jess, taking a long slurp, 'let's not talk about my house or the weekend. What shall we do after lunch?'

'I expect something'll come up.' He wiggled his eyebrows suggestively.

Jess giggled. 'It's a shame you've got to work tonight.'

'I'm off at midnight. And I'm off duty for all of tomorrow.'

Jess licked her lips. 'Are you thinking what I'm thinking? And I don't mind waiting up for you if you'd like to come back to mine.'

Their lunch arrived and Jess realised she was ravenous. One thing about sex, she thought, it didn't half give you an appetite. She'd either have to work extra hard at her dancing or indulge in even more energetic sex to try to keep the pounds off. She glanced up at Matt as she thought about 'even more energetic sex'. She didn't think he'd object.

17

By the end of the week, Matt had almost moved in. His shaving gear was in the bathroom and Jess had found him an empty drawer so he had somewhere to keep a few of his underpants, socks and shirts. He was also getting used to the hours Jess worked, but as he was a shift worker himself the fact that she worked from mid-evening to early morning didn't seem so bizarre as it might have done to someone who had a nine to five job. Besides which, as most of their time together seemed to be spent in bed, it didn't really matter if it was day or night when neither was working.

Life in Jess's flat consisted of wonderful tumbles in bed, followed by snacky meals or takeaways, ordered in so as to leave as much time as possible for more tumbles in bed, or in the shower, or on the hearth rug or anywhere that seemed to take their fancy. And Jess found that when they weren't making love they were chatting and laughing. Perhaps this is what being in love is like, she thought to herself, on her way back to the flat in a cab in the early hours of Friday morning. It was a warming, comforting thought, although she didn't consider that she and Matt were 'in' love, not yet, although she knew he'd become a very important part of her life.

She let herself into the flat as quietly as possible so as not to disturb Matt, but as she crept into the bedroom determined to get ready for bed in the dark, he rolled over and offered to switch the light on.

'Don't,' said Jess. 'It'll wake you up properly if you do that.'

'Maybe I want to wake up properly,' he replied with an unmistakably lecherous tone in his voice.

'And I'm knackered. Dead on my feet.'

There was a disappointed sigh from the bed.

'But there's tomorrow morning,' offered Jess. 'And afternoon, although I mustn't forget today's Friday and I'm due at the police station at eleven,' she said as she pulled off the last of her clothes. Outside the bedroom window the sky was already beginning to lighten as dawn approached.

'I'll just have to contain myself,' murmured Matt sleepily. 'And it's a shame I'm not on the same shift as you. I'll miss you tomorrow night, all alone in this big bed.'

'I'll be back in the morning.'

'And I'm on the early turn. We'll pass like ships in the night.' He yawned deeply. 'We'll just have to make the most of the opportunity as it arises.'

Jess giggled. 'Not heard you refer to the old fella as an opportunity before, 'cos it certainly does quite a lot of arising.'

'Dirty wench.' As Jess got into bed, Matt curled around her to warm her slightly chilly limbs up. Jess thought she'd never felt so content and loved in her life. Matt kissed the back of her neck and, as she snuggled deeper under the duvet, she heard his soft snores resume.

When she awoke hours later, Matt was already out of bed and was sitting reading the paper by the door to the balcony.

'Ah, the Sleeping Beauty,' he said, hearing her footsteps. 'Tea?'

'Please. It's great, having someone to look after me,'

she added appreciatively, realising, not for the first time, just how lonely her life had been until quite recently.

When she'd been temping, there had been numerous occasions when she'd come home, shut the door and not spoken to another living soul till she'd gone back to work the next day. And even at work, because she was the temp, she hadn't been a part of the in-jokes, the office politics, the gossip or the banter. She'd been there to fill a gap and nothing else. Being a pole-dancer might not be a job that got you respect with the general public, but the other girls in the dressing room were fab, the customers tipped her well, and now and again she found herself being chatted up by some footballer or TV star, which was bizarre. Flattering but bizarre. There was no way she could describe her life as humdrum now, it was really quite glamorous, and the icing on the cake was wonderful Matt.

She did so love him being around. In many respects he was a great bloke, someone she could even consider becoming a more permanent feature in her life. She wondered if he'd be frightened off if she suggested he should move in with her properly. Perhaps it was a little early for that, although it did seem a shocking waste of money for them to be paying two lots of rent when his flat in the unfashionable part of Notting Hill now seemed to be surplus to requirements. Perhaps she'd broach it over the weekend. They could have a late lunch on Saturday, she'd cook something delicious for them both for when he came off his shift, and then she could mention it after that.

She and Matt went back to bed, and then they spent the rest of the day doing domestic things like the washing and shopping, enjoying each other's company and behaving, Jess thought, very much like a couple. The more she thought about it the more it seemed right and appropriate for Matt to move in. By the time she'd changed into her uniform trousers and shirt she had completely made up her mind to make the suggestion to him the next day. Then life really would be perfect, she thought.

Jess arrived at the police station a good half-hour early, ready for her shift and wondering who she was going to be rostered with. The duty sergeant beckoned her over to him as she walked past the front desk on her way to the locker room at the back of the building.

'Inspector Baxter wants to see you,' he said.

Jess stopped in her tracks. 'Me? Why on earth?'

'Search me. All he said to me was "Tell Dryden to come straight to my office when she gets in". So I am. And if I were you, I wouldn't hang about.'

Jess felt a nasty knot of foreboding. What on earth could this be about? What had she done? Shoving her bag into her locker, she hurried up to the top floor of the station to the inspector's office. Hoping she didn't look as nervous as she felt, she knocked timidly on the door.

'Enter.'

Taking a deep breath, she made her way in. Inspector Baxter was sitting behind his desk and two rather scruffy men perched on chairs beside the wall.

'Ah, Dryden. Come in.'

She moved forward and stood in front of his desk. Although the presence of the two strangers probably meant this wasn't a disciplinary interview, she still felt extremely uneasy.

'I've reason to believe, Dryden, that you're not being entirely straight with the Met Police.'

'No, sir?' Where on earth was this going?

'When you applied to be a Special, you told us you were employed in clerical duties. I understand that this is not true.'

Fuck. They knew.

Jess swallowed. 'No, sir.'

'So you lied.'

'No, sir. That's what I was then, when I joined. I did a lot of temp work.'

'But you don't now.'

'No, sir.'

'And do you think it's appropriate for an exotic dancer to work for the Met?'

Well, thought Jess, at least he hadn't called her a stripper. And she knew from his tone of voice that he expected the answer 'no'. She didn't agree with him, but she wasn't in a position to argue.

'Probably not,' was the compromise she offered.

'And you didn't think to tell us about this career change?'

'I didn't believe it was important. I don't get paid by the Met, so I didn't think it was their business how I earn my living.'

The inspector stared at her. 'I am fully aware that you work for the police in a voluntary capacity and I suppose that your point of view has a certain logic.'

A logic he obviously didn't agree with. Was he going to ask her to resign from the force? She'd be so pissed off if he did. It would scupper her chances of ever being a real constable – which was still her ambition. Pole-dancing was okay and the earnings were great, but when her youth and suppleness began to go, what then? And she wasn't going back to temping in a hurry. That was a mug's game with crap money. Besides, she'd really set her heart on being a police officer and her time as a Special had reinforced that ambition rather than the reverse.

'However,' said Inspector Baxter, 'I have a proposition for you.'

'Sir?' Jess could only think he wanted her to do a turn

at some sort of social event. Did the local Masonic Lodge fancy getting their rocks off watching her perform? Well, he could stuff that. She wasn't going to dance for a bunch of his lecherous mates. Hell, no.

'I'd like to introduce you to these guys.'

She'd almost forgotten about them. She turned to the two scruffs and Inspector Baxter said, 'McCausland and Dodds.' They nodded. 'They work for the Drugs Squad.' That would explain the get-up, and she now noticed the tattoo on McCausland's neck and Dodds's piercings. Essential if they were going to blend in with the sort of people they kept company with, but not attractive – or at least, not to Jess. There was a tiny bit of her that seemed to recognise the one called Dodds, but it was pretty unlikely. She didn't know anyone with multiple piercings. Well, that wasn't strictly true; she had a number of girlfriends with several studs in each ear and some with their belly-buttons done too. But not blokes.

The scruff called McCausland stood up. 'We've had information that the skunk on the Windmill Estate is being provided by someone with a connection to the club where you work.'

Jess wasn't vastly surprised at the suggestion that Shoq and drugs might be linked. Several of her fellow dancers almost certainly snorted coke, as did quite a number of the punters. It was that sort of environment. But skunk? That wasn't the sort of drug the well-heeled bankers, footballers or flashy celebrities were into. But McCausland had said there was a connection between the dealer and the club. Maybe the skunk just gave the dealer the money to be able to afford the exorbitant cost of the drinks in the place.

'Our informant wasn't able to be specific; he was just passing on a rumour. He said it could be anyone, a customer, one of the staff, a dancer, anyone.'

Had there been a special emphasis on the word *dancer*? Shit, they didn't think she was implicated, did they? She felt her eyes widen at the awfulness of the thought. Terrified of saying anything that might be misconstrued, she remained silent, waiting for an accusation.

'We can lift the pushers on the estate, but someone is supplying them with high-grade, home-grown cannabis and we want the supplier. If there is a connection with Shoq we want to know about it.'

'But I don't know anything,' blurted out Jess. 'Honest.'

'But you're there,' said Dodds, speaking for the first time. 'And you don't look like a copper.'

Not an accusation then, or not yet. She still wasn't sure where this conversation was going. But she got even more worried when Dodds continued, 'And we're assuming they don't know what you do on Friday and Saturday nights. Or do they?'

'No, they don't,' Jess said, feeling suddenly very auxious indeed. There was something faintly sinister and threatening in the way Dodds and McCausland were talking to her. Was their implication that they could make life very difficult for her at Shoq if she didn't do something to help them? And what the hell was that likely to be? She felt cornered. Inspector Baxter had said she was going to be offered a proposition and Jess had a sickening feeling that she wasn't going to like it – or that she wasn't going to have much of an option about accepting it.

She stood stock-still in front of the desk, feeling like a rabbit frozen in the proverbial headlights, aware that her fate was thundering towards her but powerless to avoid it.

'Then I think we would like to keep it that way,' said Dodds. 'Although our grass doesn't know who it might be at Shoq, we have our suspicions,' he went on. 'From what

I've heard nothing gets past the owner – and if there's anything dodgy going on at his club, it's only because he allows it.'

'Who, Miles?'

'Miles Morgan is a nasty piece of work who has put the frighteners on more people than I've had hot dinners. If you piss Miles off enough, you might find someone trying out their Black and Decker on your kneecaps. So if there is anything that connects his club with this drug ring, there is a very strong chance that he's involved.'

'Oh,' squeaked Jess, feeling suddenly quite frightened. Shit, how scary was that. Up till now she'd neither liked Miles nor disliked him; he was her boss, that was all. There were rules about behaviour in the club – his rules – and the girls obeyed them because they were well-paid and wanted to keep their jobs, but Jess had never suspected him of being seriously nasty – not the sort who might resort to a bit of casual violence to settle a score. That put Miles in a whole other light, and the thought that she was working for some sort of underworld hard man was totally terrifying.

Shit, what would Matt say when he found out about Miles and his criminal connections? He was a copper and he'd be completely against her having anything to do with such a character. He'd probably demand that she gave up working at Shoq – which meant that she wouldn't be able to buy the house. All her dreams, all her hopes, everything that had seemed tantalisingly attainable was fading.

Suddenly her life, which until a short time ago had seemed almost idyllic, was plummeting into some unknown abyss filled with horrible people and situations. But still she couldn't see why she needed to be involved. Couldn't they just nick Miles? In fact, it was so obvious she couldn't help voicing her question.

'If it was as easy as that, we would,' said McCausland.

'We need evidence, we need intelligence, we need someone to keep an eye open on the inside. When we've got enough to lift him, we will – and anyone else he's connected with. We think there's quite a ring.'

The last piece of the jigsaw was there. 'Someone to keep an eye open on the inside', McCausland had said. Jess knew it was going to be her. She swallowed. 'And what do you want me to do?'

'You cosy up to Miles. Be nice to him – *very* nice. Listen to what he has to say, hang around him, out of hours if you can manage it. We want you to get as close as you can to him.'

But they'd just told her he was horrible and dangerous.

'We're not expecting miracles,' said Dodds. 'Just do your best. We daren't risk hanging around Shoq ourselves very much, but we'll try and pop in occasionally to give you a bit of moral support.'

Well, that'll make *all* the difference, thought Jess.

'And don't tell anyone what you're doing or that you're working with us. Not a soul. Seriously. You'd be amazed how stories get round. If he gets a sniff of what you're up to, it could be very tricky indeed. So you make sure that no one – and I mean *no one* – at Shoq has the least idea about you working for the Met when you're not getting your tits out for the boys.' Dodds had a lascivious leer on his face as he said that, almost as if he expected Jess to whip her kit off there and then and give them a quick flash.

'And come to that,' added Baxter, 'you want to be very careful about who at the station knows that you work at Shoq. A story about a police officer who moonlights as a pole-dancer is likely to get round the force faster than greased weasel shit, and once it's out there, there's no telling who else will hear about it, Miles Morgan included. The last thing we want is for him to start looking at his strippers to try to decide which one is working for us. Understand?'

Jess did. Very well indeed.

As she left the office she decided that her life was getting compartmentalised even further. The girls at Shoq were never going to know about her work as a Special, and when she was around Matt she had to make sure he never found out about Miles and his dodgy connections, because if he did he'd go mental. And over and above all that, she had to keep Abby and pretty much everyone else she knew from finding out about the pole-dancing.

Just great, she thought as she reeled downstairs feeling quite shaky. How was she going to cope with all the subterfuge? And how was she going to keep Matt in the dark about Miles and Dodds and McCausland? All that lying was going to be hideous, almost as if she were being unfaithful. This morning her life had seemed so simple and now it was just a mess – a mess of lies and conspiracies and secrets.

'You all right, Dryden?' asked the duty sergeant.

But Jess wasn't sure how you explained that your life had just been turned upside-down, so she simply nodded and stayed silent.

It was only later, when Jess was out on the beat, that she wondered how they had found out about her work as a dancer. She was always so careful to keep the different sections of her life separate that it was a worry that one compartment now seemed to be leaking into another. Someone had found out stuff about her, but who?

And the only crossover point between her work as a dancer and her voluntary role as a Special was Matt. She couldn't believe he would have dropped her into this mess, but who else could it be? Of course, it could be that someone other than Matt who'd been at Simon's stag do had spotted her – and told Dodds and McCausland or even Inspector Baxter. So they must already know that things mightn't be completely watertight from the off. Oh what a shambles, and she was right in the middle of it.

18

Shoq was buzzing. Thursday nights were always busy. The music throbbed, the tables were crowded, and bursts of laughter punctuated the loud conversations. The club was very warm, verging on the uncomfortable, which also meant that there was the odd whiff of sweat from some of the male customers, which competed with the girl's expensive perfumes. The beautiful waitresses wove their way between the tables carrying trays laden with bottles of wine and champagne, the glasses clinking gently as the girls sashayed around on their incredibly high heels that made their long, slender, fake-tanned legs look even more fabulous, their hips swaying under their microscopic skirts. On the podiums three dancers entertained men who gathered around, their tongues practically lolling onto their ties, and lust and desire written plainly across their faces.

Jess had turned up to work every evening that week and made a conscious effort to look normal, to act just as she had before she'd been told about Miles and his dodgy connections. Underneath though, she was hideously aware that the minute she walked through the door of the place she became tense and edgy – and why wouldn't she? Miles was a nasty piece of work, probably a criminal with a great deal to lose, and she was a copper. This was hardly an ideal situation.

A couple of the other girls had noticed her changed demeanour and Jess had brushed off their enquiries with vague answers about boyfriend trouble and even vaguer mutterings about being slightly under the weather. These confidences were a slightly risky tactic as Carrie wasn't the least bit sympathetic about any personal problems the girls might be having; the rule was that they were there to entertain, to look their best, to make the customers feel happy. They were not expected to bring their personal life with them to work, and if they felt they couldn't comply with this then they were to stay at home. At least Laura and the others seemed to have understood her entreaties about not telling Carrie that she had some problems because nothing had been said to Jess by her boss. Jess really didn't want Carrie sniffing around her, asking concerned questions. The woman was as sharp as a scalpel and would soon cut through any crap and reach the truth.

Jess was perched on a stool by the bar, waiting for her turn on the podium, trying to look relaxed. She found it hard to believe why, and indeed how, given that the place was run by a known criminal with a violent track-record, the police allowed the club to operate at all. How had Miles got within a mile of a licence? Had he greased palms? Scared people into submission? Made a pact with the authorities? Of course, outwardly Shoq looked like a perfectly ordinary night-club in Central London run by a perfectly legitimate businessman making an honest buck – no hoods in shades and fedoras, no shooters in shoulder-holsters, no shifty characters by the door answering coded knocks by peering through a sliding panel, no 'Bernie sent me' or violin cases with machine guns or raids by the Feds.

Jess smiled to herself at the way her imagination was leaping off. Next thing, Jodie Foster and a gang of singing kids in 1920s costumes would be romping through doors firing splurge guns. This is the real world, Jess, she reminded herself, not the set of *Bugsy Malone*, so get right back into it.

Except in the 'real world' she was an undercover policewoman and she didn't think that Miles, given that he *wasn't* a perfectly legitimate businessman, would be too happy about that.

She tried to put thoughts of her boss and the way he operated to the back of her mind but the trouble was, since her interview the previous weekend, it had pretty much dominated every waking thought. But even having been told what the score was and keeping her eyes as open as possible, she'd seen absolutely nothing that was the least bit supicious. Would McCausland and Dodds believe her? Or would they think that she was in league with Miles and protecting him, feeding him information about the Drugs Squad? How she wished she'd never got involved with this whole business.

It would have helped if she'd had the slightest idea what she was supposed to be looking for, other than people with something to do with Miles, people he knew and drugs.

Not that *that* narrowed it down much; *Miles and people he knew*. So, just most of London, then. He was always out on the main floor, glad-handing his regulars, greeting newcomers, schmoozing the celebs, playing the part of the perfect host, encouraging the girls and generally keeping all his staff on their toes. Any of the people he spoke to could be the recipient of some sort of hidden message or codeword. Or maybe money or drugs changed hands in the gents' loo – not a place Jess could be expected to keep an eye on. And then there were the suppliers – catering, wine, cleaning – who came to Shoq during the day to do business with Miles; maybe they were doing business other than selling him caviar, champagne and bleach.

It was impossible, she thought as she scanned the punters for anyone who might be the dealer McCausland and Dodds were after. 'Needles in haystacks' was a phrase that kept popping into her head, along with 'hopeless' and 'lost cause'.

Just then, a large sweaty man wearing a Rolex watch and a beautifully tailored suit, plonked himself on a stool beside her. Along with the smell of perspiration, there was also the unmistakable aroma of money. Jess might be here to keep her eyes open for McCausland and Dodds but she also had a living to earn; if she could persuade this guy to buy an hour of her time, her bills would be paid till the end of the month – and it wasn't as if she'd have to do anything other than chat and entertain him. However unappealing he was, she could do that with her eyes shut. Which might be the best way.

Jess revved up her most alluring smile and turned towards him.

'Hi, stranger,' she purred. And then her smile froze as she saw, over his shoulder, Dodds enter the club. At least she thought it was him, only this bloke was wearing quite a smart pair of slacks with a shirt and there were no apparent studs shoved through parts of his face. She stared at him but the new arrival completely ignored her. Blanked her completely. But if it was Dodds, of course he would. As far as anyone at Shoq was concerned, they had never met. In fact, as far as *anyone* was concerned, they had never met. Period.

But then some portion of her memory kicked in and she was sure she'd seen this smart version of Dodds in the club before, only she'd never entertained him or chatted to him; he'd sat at the bar and had a small beer and hadn't encouraged any of the hostesses to join him.

So they hadn't. Besides, with a cheap watch, scuffed shoes and only drinking beer he didn't give the appearance of a bloke who was going to splash the cash, and the girls knew better than to waste their time on men unlikely to tip generously, and that included Jess. The girls relied on tips and they weren't going to flock around a cheapskate – even if he did look lonely.

Trying not to look as if she was taking any interest at all in the new arrival, Jess risked another glance at him. She was certain it was Dodds, so was he here to check up on her or Morgan?

Jess turned her attention back to the sweaty bloke but she couldn't help flicking the occasional glance over his shoulder at Dodds, who studiously ignored her, gazing around the room but never at her. She tried not to look at him but it was like knowing there was a wasp in the room – she just had to keep an eye on it.

It was a relief to Jess when she was called to one of the podiums to perform her set, since it was a chance to get away from the sweaty bloke who had limited conversation and even more limited social skills. He was obviously wealthy, having made his pile, so he informed her at some length, from derivatives – whatever they were – and now he just wanted to show off how big his stash of cash was. Had Jess been truly shallow, she might have been impressed, but sadly his loaded bank balance didn't make up for his lack of humour nor his obsession with himself and certainly not his low standards of personal hygiene.

For twenty minutes Jess writhed and slithered round the polished chrome pole, hoping that her performance might result in some decent tips and an invitation to entertain some customers who might be more fun to be with than Mr Sweaty-Rolex. When her set came to an end she whisked off to the dressing room to change, avoiding all eye-contact with him. She wasn't going to blow her chance of escaping from being bored to death.

She was passing Miles's office when he called her name.

Jess froze, her guilty conscience and fear causing her heart to thunder against her ribs.

'Nice routine,' said Miles.

'Th-thanks,' said Jess, hoping he'd think her stammer was caused by breathlessness not terror.

'You're quite a hit.'

'Thanks,' said Jess again.

'You're tired and you want to change and I'm keeping you.'

Jess nodded. Dismissed, good.

'Just one thing.'

'Yes?'

'That bloke you were taking an interest in?'

'Who?' Mr Sweaty-Rolex, only she mustn't call him that.

She was casting about for some other way of describing him, when Miles added, 'Sitting drinking a beer. You kept looking at him like you knew him.'

Fuck! Nothing got past this man. How scary was that!? 'Really? Never seen him before in my life.' Please God don't let her nose shoot forward and impale Miles. 'I was intrigued by him – didn't look like he was happy or comfortable here so I wondered what he was doing. Fish out of water, I thought.' She hoped that sounded plausible.

'That's what I thought too. And it's not the first time I've seen him. I want you to find out what his game is. He's not spending money, he doesn't seem to be interested in my girls, I don't think he's meeting mates, so just why is he here? And because I'm a good boss I'll make up the tips you're going to be missing out on while you talk to him, because he doesn't look the sort who'll make it worth your while to spend time with him.'

Jess had an urge to giggle. While the Met were asking her to cosy up to Miles, Miles was asking her to spy on Dodds. This was getting surreal.

Jess showered, changed and returned to the main bar, rather hoping Dodds had gone, but there he was at the end of the bar, still nursing a half-pint. She slid between the crowds of blokes, wending her way between the bulging paunches and the pudgy, grabbing hands (why was it always the fat, unattractive businessmen who tried it on?) to her quarry.

'Hello,' she said.

Dodds's eyes widened and then he looked bored. He certainly didn't appear the least bit pleased to see her, but then he probably wasn't. Jess wondered where all his studs and piercings had gone; perhaps they were stick-ons.

'You look lonely.' Jess pulled a stool up close beside him and sat down. With the noise of the music and loud conversations around them, the only way he was going to hear what she had to say was if she spoke almost directly into his ear. Which meant the chances of anyone overhearing them were non-existent. Besides, there was no one close who was taking any interest in them. The nearest group of guys were all yelling and boozing and laughing, and the racket they were making would mask any other conversation for yards around.

'I'm fine,' he growled, his face close to hers, something Jess found quite distasteful. She noticed their knees were almost touching. She made sure they didn't.

'We like our customers to have a good time. And you really look as if you're not.'

'Really.'

'Really, Mr Dodds.'

'I thought you had a job to do. Aren't you supposed to be dancing or something?' There was more than a hint of innuendo in the way he said 'or something'.

Jess ignored it. 'I just have. And now Mr Morgan has asked me to look after you, because you're on your own.' Again the faintest flicker in Dodds's eyes.

'Really.'

Blimey, in comparison to this, Mr Sweaty-Rolex's conversation was sparkling. 'Yes, really. And what's more, you don't look like you belong here and he wants to know what your game is. He's asked me to find out who you are and what you are doing here. So what do you want me to tell him?' Jess smiled and forced herself to pout prettily at him, like she was chatting up someone who was enjoying her company. 'And I suggest you smile back,' she said. 'I wouldn't be surprised if Miles is keeping an eye on the two of us so it'd be better if you *did* manage to look as if you're enjoying my company, however much of an effort it is for you.' Because she was certainly finding it an effort.

'Morgan isn't here, is he? I haven't seen him about.'

'Well for your information he is. That wall behind me – and please don't look directly at it – is a two-way mirror. He misses nothing.'

Dodds's face instantly lit up. But as a fake smile it was reasonably convincing. 'Enough of a grin for you? Will Morgan think it's genuine?'

It didn't fool Jess, but then she was sitting right by him. 'I should think so, just keep it there. So what's the story?'

'I don't know. Just some lonely sad-sack looking for a good time?'

'That's not going to wash. Our prices don't encourage people like you. To be honest, you're sticking out like the mutt's nuts. Wrong clothes, wrong shoes, wrong drink.

Don't they teach you anything where you come from?'

'What's wrong with my clothes?'

'Look around you. The sort that come here have money with a capital M. Just spot the number of Patek Philippes and Rolexes at the bar. And handmade shoes? Two a penny here. Guys who wear your sort of clothes don't come here for a pint and a cheap thrill. There are hundreds of bars in London where you can get similar for a great deal less money.'

'Okay, so what's my story then, if you're so bloody clever?'

Jess cocked her head to one side as she considered the problem. 'How about I tell Morgan you're an author, you write crime stories and you're researching a book, your next thriller. Unlike JK Rowling, your advances don't pay for champagne in joints like this. Believable?'

'I would imagine so. But speaking as someone who knows nothing about books – except how to read one – what would I know about how authors do their research. And another thing – if I'm an author, he can check me out. Look me up on Amazon or something.'

'This is your first deal and you're not published yet, although you've got an agent. He won't have heard of you yet and neither will anyone else. Except your agent, of course.'

'Very good, but he'll still want a name. What do I tell him?'

'Well, can't you think of something? I've come up with the rest of the story.'

'Charlie Curzon.'

Jess almost snorted. 'Sounds like a porn-star name.' Which, given the way Dodds came across, seemed to really suit him, she thought. If anyone was the sort to hang out in questionable clubs in Soho in a grubby mac, he was it. Jess wondered fleetingly whether he'd gone into the Drugs Squad because the Vice Squad hadn't wanted him.

Dodds smiled; genuinely this time, but it still wasn't pleasant. Jess suppressed a shiver. 'Yeah, but it's actually the name of my first pet and first address, but it'll do, won't it?'

'I imagine so.'

'So do you think Miles Morgan will buy the story?'

'I think there's a fair chance. And I'm going to tell him I'm quite excited because you've promised to mention me in the Acknowledgements of your bestseller.'

'Why on earth would I want to do that?' He sounded genuinely intrigued.

'Because I'm going to help you with your research, tell you about the dressing room and the girls and stuff like that. Which gives us the perfect excuse for me to talk to you if you come in here again.'

'Nice one, Dryden.'

'Please, in here you must call me Jess.'

'Jess. And on the subject of research, how is yours going?'

'Not good, but as I've got to go and tell Miles all about you in a minute I shall take the opportunity to be very nice to him, just like you asked me to.'

'That's great. Exactly what I want to hear. I'm pleased with you.'

But sadly, thought Jess, if Matt got to hear, he'd be horrified. And it was his opinion and friendship she valued, not Dodds's.

'Just one thing before I go though. You've been here before, haven't you?'

'Might have.'

'And you recognised me.'

'Might have done.'

'And then you told Baxter about me.'

Dodds just shrugged, but Jess knew she was right. Well, at least she knew who the toad was who had got her into this mess. Not Matt and not any of Simon's mates, so that was one thing less to worry about. Although given the huge array of other concerns she had, it was hardly going to make a difference.

Jess knocked on Miles's open door with apparent confidence. Inside she was feeling queasy with nerves. Miles seemed to spot everything, every nuance, every twitch that went on in Shoq and he'd almost certainly been watching her encounter with Dodds. What if he'd spotted that she and Dodds weren't complete strangers, what if he didn't believe Dodds's story, what if . . . She quickly stamped on the thought. It didn't bear thinking about if he really was the nasty piece of work she'd been told.

'Come in, Jess. Take a seat. Champagne?' He brandished a bottle in her direction.

Jess refused politely. She didn't want to fuzz up her brain with fizz. 'Thanks,' she said with her best and brightest smile, 'but no thanks. I like to keep a clear head when I'm working.' And I certainly need one when I'm around you, she added mentally as she slid into the chair in front of Miles's desk and crossed her legs.

'So,' said Miles, pouring a glass for himself. 'Who's the mystery man?'

'Actually, he's not very mysterious at all,' she said casually. 'On the other hand he is quite – because that's how he makes his living.'

Miles's eyebrows shot up at this.

'He's an author. He's doing a spot of research,' Jess said reassuringly, although she took a bit of secret amusement from having tweaked Miles's strings like that.

'Is he now.' Miles looked less than pleased.

'I'm sure it's all perfectly harmless.'

Miles looked doubtful.

'He just wants to get a feel for this sort of gentlemen's club, what the girls are like, that sort of thing.'

'A long as he doesn't want to get a feel of the girls,' said Miles pointedly.

'He won't. The likes of Tom will keep him in check. Besides, he doesn't look like the sort who'd get fresh with the dancers.'

'So this author guy – what's he write?'

'Crime, I told you.'

Miles pulled the computer keyboard towards him. 'Anyone I'd have read?'

Jess bit back the retort that she didn't know Miles could read and parroted the agreed story about this being a début novel. 'He says his name is Charlie Curzon.'

Miles's fingers flickered over the keyboard and then he clicked the mouse a couple of times. 'You sure he's an author? I can't see anything on Amazon.'

Jess reiterated that it was his first book.

'So he's a wannabe.'

She shrugged. 'He says he's got an agent.'

'Anyone can get an agent, can't they.'

'I suppose.' She laughed. 'Actually you must be right because I even had one once, when I wanted to work in showbiz.'

'When you wanted to be a proper dancer.'

'As opposed to an improper one,' she shot back, but she softened her retort with a smile; she was supposed to be making Miles like her, not alienating him.

Miles grinned. 'You're a sharp cookie, Jess. I like you.'

'That means a lot to me, Miles,' she said. Was she being too obvious, she wondered. She certainly sounded corny but then it was exactly the sort of line blokes liked. Flattery, that was always a good way to a man's heart. If Miles had one, which was debatable.

'Does it now?' he said. He contemplated her over the rim of his champagne glass. Jess flashed him a smile and he smiled back at her. 'Tell you what, how about I treat you to dinner one night.' Jess was about to protest that she never ate a big meal before she performed, when he added, 'I know what you girls are like about food but I'm sure you can manage a lettuce leaf or two. Perhaps a glass of Chablis? I'd like it,' he said finally in the sort of tone that made Jess think it wouldn't be a Good Idea to turn him down.

Jess suddenly developed a completely split personality; one half of her brain was turning cartwheels that she'd managed to do the Met's task of cosying up to Miles really well, while the other half of her brain was cringing in disgust that she appealed to him. But she smothered her shudder of revulsion and smiled back. 'I'd love to,' she cooed, 'but you'll have to book early to avoid disappointment. I've a very busy social life.'

'But I'm sure you'll find space for me. Won't you.' It wasn't a question.

Jess almost shivered again but got a grip on herself. Was there a veiled threat there, or was she imagining things because she knew stuff about Miles that she didn't like? He wanted her company and she wasn't expected to decline, but was that because he was keen or because he had some other agenda? She wished she knew.

'Of course.'

'I'll ask Carrie to get some dates to you.'

Matt was getting ready to go on the early turn when Jess got home. He was yawning and stretching as he made a cup of tea and Jess was dead on her feet so neither was paying a great deal of attention to the other as they swapped a perfunctory kiss.

'Good night?' asked Matt.

'Not bad. Nice tips.' Jess extracted a cheque from her bag and waved it under Matt's nose.

'You know there's a law against living off immoral earnings.'

Jess bridled against a hint that she did more than just dance. And from Matt, too. 'My earnings are *very* moral,' she protested sharply. 'Just because you don't like how I earn them, there's no law against it.'

'You're right, I don't like it. In fact, I really *dis*like the idea of you taking your kit off each night for a bunch of baying louts.'

Jess slipped out of her skimpy red dress and hung it up carefully, as she did every night with the other costumes she'd worn, ready to take them to the cleaners at the end of the week.

'But women do as much on the beaches of Saint Tropez.'

Matt couldn't meet her eye. 'I know, honey, but that's different.'

'It's only a bit of nudity. The fact I get my tits out for public consumption doesn't make me a bad person.'

'I know.'

'Are the models who posed for Titian or Michelangelo tarts because millions of people have now seen them naked?'

'No.' Matt sounded defensive.

'So because what I'm doing is entertainment and not art it makes it something to be ashamed of.'

'I didn't say that.'

'But it's what you think.'

'I'd just rather you didn't do it, that's all. I think the way the punters at the club look at you as a sex object cheapens you.'

'But I'm not cheap. You of all people know that and who I really am.'

'I never said you were and I'd never think of you in that way, but I don't like the fact that they do.'

'Despite the very *expensive* way it pays.'

'Despite that. And I don't think that that sort of money,' he pointed at Jess's fat cheque, 'is entirely moral either. But it's bloody good so maybe I should shut up.' He leaned forward and kissed her on the nose.

Jess kissed him back. 'Look, if I'm honest I can't say I think what I do is the ultimate and most enviable career for a girl, but I'm not going to be doing it for ever so let's just both of us get over it, huh?'

'You're right.' He took a swig of his tea and glanced at his watch. 'Got to love you and leave you, babe. See you this afternoon.' He passed his barely touched tea to Jess. 'I haven't got time to drink this. You take it to bed with you.'

Jess smiled at him gratefully as he legged it out the door and then flopped onto a chair with a sigh of relief and toed off her shoes. She thought about the conversation they'd just had. Was what she did a really big problem for Matt? Did he really hate it? She sighed again. Well, he'd have to cope with it for a bit longer because what with her plans for the house and the task she'd been set by Dodds and McCausland, she wasn't going to be able to give up any time soon. And then there was the hideous question of whether or not she ought to own up to Matt about her date with Miles. Which would be better – owning up or praying that Matt didn't find out? Jess yawned. She was too tired to think about it right now. She'd wait till she woke up again. And anyway, she wasn't two-timing Matt; anything she had to do with Miles was strictly business, Met Police business.

She took her tea into the bedroom, set her alarm for

midday, finished undressing and slumped into bed. She was knackered and drifted off instantly.

She was projected out of sleep, however, by the sound of the front door slamming really loudly.

What the fuck!

Matt strode into the bedroom, barely glancing at her as he opened his drawer in the chest and began to haul his few possessions out of it and pile them, any-old-how, into a plastic carrier bag.

'Matt!' cried Jess. 'What is it?'

Matt ignored her, as having emptied his drawer he moved to the bathroom.

Jess leaped out of bed and followed him.

'What's the matter? What's going on?'

'What's going on?' he mimicked. 'That's rich. Perhaps you'd like to tell me.'

'Tell you what? I haven't a clue what you're talking about.'

'I know what your job is, and try as I might, I can't bring myself to like what you do. But I cope with you taking your clothes off for a bunch of leering bastards. What I can't cope with is you lying to me about the extras you offer and two-timing me behind my back.'

'But I'm not two-timing you with Miles,' said Jess, completely bemused and still groggy with sleep. 'In fact, I'd rather not go out to dinner with him but he's not . . .'

'Miles?' shouted Matt, sounding aghast. 'What, Miles from the club? So he's getting some action as well? This gets worse and worse.'

'What do you mean?' Jess was aware her voice was shrill but she didn't care. She was completely at sea here, she didn't have a clue what Matt was on about, she was being accused of something when she was sure she'd done nothing, and it was all horrible. 'What do you mean, "getting some action *as well*"? Who else is getting some action?'

'Don't give me that. Don't play the innocent with me,' shouted Matt. 'Or are there so many men you've lost track?'

Jess was close to tears. She didn't understand why Matt was being so vile. Until a few hours ago, everything was perfect. What on earth had happened to change it while she'd been in bed asleep? 'You know there isn't anyone but you,' she said, gulping back a sob.

'No, I don't. In fact, I haven't a clue about what you get up to when you're at the club.'

'Nothing. I dance. And I take my clothes off. It may be tacky but that's all I do. You know that. You've seen me do it, for God's sake.' She saw the sneer of disbelief on Matt's face. 'Well, come along and watch me again, then you'll see there's nothing else involved.'

'Forget it. You wouldn't try to pull anyone else while I'm around so what's the point. And that's exactly what I heard you'd done when I was down at the station – and frankly I'd rather believe my own ears than the crap that you spout.' Matt swung the carrier over his shoulder and stormed out, slamming the door behind him.

Jess reeled back into the bedroom and sank on to the bed. Fuddled with sleep, Matt's words just rolled round and round her brain making no sense. What had he heard about her? Lies, obviously, but from whom – and why?

She rolled on her side feeling sick with misery as a sob welled up into her throat. She swallowed it back down. Feeling sorry for herself wasn't going to solve anything, she told herself bravely. It wasn't going to get Matt back. But as the image of him slamming out of her flat surfaced, she lost control and a howl of utter dejection clawed its way out of her. Burying her face in her duvet, Jess wept until exhaustion took pity on her and she fell once move into a sleep of sorts.

As Matt returned to his flat at the end of his shift he reflected that, one way and another, it had been a truly shit day. It had started off well enough but had gone downhill from the moment he got into work, until it had finally hit rock bottom shortly before his meal-break. And now to cap it all, he'd come home to discover that when he'd abandoned his own pad for Jess's a week ago, he'd forgotten to empty the bin in the kitchen. He had no idea how much or what he'd left behind to rot, and he wasn't inclined to investigate, but the place now stank like a sewer and he didn't think, even when he'd emptied the bin, the stench would lift. It seemed to have got into the very fabric of the place.

Gingerly he lifted out the dripping bag from the pedal-bin and, holding it at arm's length, scurried outside to the big communal dustbin. Just as he got there and was about to flip open the lid, the bottom of the bag gave way and dumped a foul dollop of slimy rubbish at his feet.

'Just fucking perfect,' he snarled as he disposed of the remains of the bag and returned to his flat for a dustpan and brush. With his breath held and his anger only just in check he cleared up the noisome mess, rinsed the pan under an outside tap but then saw the state of the brush and chucked them both into the bin and slammed the lid. Sod it.

He returned to his still smelly flat, grabbed a beer from the fridge. At least the presence of a cold beer meant that something was right that day, although it was a precious small compensation for the rest of the crap that had happened. He slumped in a chair and mulled over the day's events.

It had seemed such a good start when he'd met Jess coming home just as he was about to go to work. Her pay cheque had been impressive too, although he had been pleased for her sake; her earnings were nothing to do with him and he'd told her long and often that he'd pay his way, that he didn't want to freeload and she was to save her money for herself. And then he'd got to work. That was when it had all gone pear-shaped.

First of all, there'd been a problem in the canteen and he hadn't been able to have the cooked breakfast he'd promised himself. It had been a bit of a bummer but, hey, worse things happened at sea as the cliché went. So a bit hungry and not in the best mood, he'd gone out on patrol. It had all been fine to start with; the London streets in the early morning had been quite pleasant. It was light, dry and the air temperature had been higher than average so, what with those conditions and the fact that he and his accompanying PCSO had paced along the pavements for a while before the rush-hour crowds began to jostle them, the morning had begun to look up.

But then, a while later, they got a call to go to a store in a shopping mall near High Street Kensington to assist with a shoplifting incident – and that was when it had all begun to go wrong. They'd got to the shop to find an ashen-faced, youngish woman in the manager's office. Instantly there was something about the shock on the girl's face and her abject remorse that made Matt think there had been a terrible mistake. He'd been to numerous shoplifting incidents, and the reactions of the accused usually varied from sullen resignation, through vehement denial to aggression – but this woman's reaction was a first. There was something about her which really convinced him she was innocent – or at least, she had never intended to shoplift. Either that, or if she bothered to apply to RADA she'd be a shoo-in.

He asked the PCSO to keep an eye on the accused woman while he went into an adjoining office to have a word with the store manager and the security guard who had caught her.

'There she was, as bold as brass, outside the store, with the shoes and lipstick in a wire basket and not a single intention of paying for the goods,' said the security guard.

'And I want her made an example of,' insisted the store manager. 'Do you know how much stock a week I lose because of scrotes like her? Two grand. Two grand! I ask you.'

Matt couldn't recall expressing an interest but he did know it was a problem for all the big stores so he made some placatory comment and asked the security chap to show him where the girl had been apprehended.

They walked through the shop to the entrance, only, as Matt pointed out, the entrance wasn't exactly obvious.

'What do you mean, "not obvious"?'

'Well, there isn't a door, is there? This whole wall is one huge entrance.'

'Precisely. How do you miss a door *this* size?'

'But if you're not paying attention, if you're distracted, it would be easy to walk out of the shop without noticing.'

The security man didn't agree.

Matt returned to the office and began to question the woman. He took down her name – Shelley Wilson – and her age – twenty-one – and her address.

'Tell me in your own words what happened,' he prompted.

'I didn't do it,' she began. 'I was going to pay, honest.

My dad's going to kill me. I've never been in trouble, not even a detention at school.'

'Just tell me what happened,' Matt insisted gently.

'I'd chosen the shoes and then I saw the lippy. I'd just decided it would be perfect with a red dress I bought at the weekend when my mobile went. It was my dad, and what with Mum being ill in hospital . . .' Shelley's voice faded and her eyes shone suspiciously brightly but then she swallowed, regained her composure and continued. 'Anyway, I couldn't really hear what Dad was saying, what with other people in the shop and the piped music, so I tried to find somewhere a bit quieter. I suppose I must have walked out of the shop, because the next minute I felt this hand on my shoulder.' She stopped and this time the threatened tears did fall.

'I see,' said Matt.

'And you believe her,' said the manager sneeringly.

Matt didn't say a word but left the office and beckoned the manager and the PCSO to follow him.

'Tim,' he said to his colleague, 'get on to the station and see if Shelley Wilson's got any previous.' Tim whipped out his radio and got busy while Matt turned to the manager.

'Frankly, I believe her.' The manager looked incensed. 'As I said to your security guy, it'd be easy enough to walk out of the store; there's no physical barrier, no line between the shopfront and the shopping mall. Why don't you give her a break and not press charges.'

'Because she walked out of here with fifty quid's worth of shoes and an expensive lipstick.'

'Come off it, they were still in the wire basket. She was hardly concealing the items.'

'Just makes her brazen, that's all.'

'For heaven's sake.'

'No.' The manager stared at him belligerently. 'I want

this one made an example of. She took the goods out of my shop, she didn't pay and that's an end to it. I want her nicked and I want it done now.'

So Matt had had to call for a van and watch as the poor woman, tears streaming and white with humiliation and shock, had been stuffed in the back of it, and then he'd had to climb in beside her, feeling like an absolute heel. They'd driven back to the police station where she was interviewed, a statement taken and the whole rigmarole of the justice system began to grind. He'd been livid with the shop manager, livid with the system and livid that there was nothing he could do about it.

At about midday he'd escaped from the inter-views, the statements, the forms and the mountain of paperwork that followed an arrest, and went off to the loo. He spent a second or two staring at his reflection in the mirror, wondering if job satisfaction was the be-all and end-all and deciding that it would be nice to feel happy in his work in the future as he certainly wasn't feeling happy right now, and then he entered a cubicle. He was just unzipping his trousers and lower-ing them round his ankles when the door banged open again, followed by the sound of feet on the tiles and a conversation in mid-flow.

'So Jess came through.'

'I should say so. She was amazing. Much better than I expected.'

Matt froze. Jess?

'It's the training.'

'Nah, she's a natural. She understood exactly what I wanted and how to produce it. Christ, when I saw her in Shoq last night I really wasn't expecting anything, but she's prepared to pull out the stops. Made my evening, I can tell you.'

'Blew you away, did she.'

There was a guffaw of filthy laughter followed by another comment Matt didn't catch.

Matt felt his blood sink to his ankles and pool there, along with his trousers. Jess . . . Shoq . . . My God, it was *his* Jess this pair were talking about. And what the fuck had she been getting up to? And who with? He didn't recognise the voices but if they were in the locker-room gents they weren't members of the public. Someone at the station knew all about Jess and in a really horrible way. Matt felt quite ill.

'She's got quite a devious mind – almost as bendy as her body. I tell you, she was much better than I ever dreamed, especially considering what we pay her.'

There was a raucous laugh followed by the sound of the urinals flushing automatically and then the door banged again.

Matt sat, shocked, on the toilet, his reason for being there completely forgotten. The two men had been talking about Jess and one of them had paid her for sex. Matt put his head in his hands and groaned. He felt as though he'd just been kicked in the crotch. That joke he'd made about Jess's immoral earnings wasn't a joke any more. She'd lied to him, she'd betrayed him and now she disgusted him.

The trouble was, as he now sat in his chair in his gloomy, smelly flat, sipping his beer, he couldn't quite believe that she could have duped him so easily. All those times she'd told him she was just a stripper. Hah! And he'd believed that the huge sums she earned each night were just for taking her clothes off. Fool.

Obviously her air of innocence was an act, unlike the girl in the shop. And the knowledge that Jess's dancing was just a cover for something infinitely more sleazy was almost more than he could stand. As far as he was concerned, when she wasn't getting stuffed by her clients, she could go stuff herself.

Miles Morgan sat in the big swivel chair by the window of his penthouse flat and looked at the view of the sun setting behind the Houses of Parliament. The rays of the sun had turned a portion of the Thames into a river of copper rather than its usual muddy-grey hue. Miles wasn't the kind of man to appreciate the aesthetic side of life – the only sort of beauty he liked was when it came packaged in expensive lingerie, Fuck-Me shoes and a dab of Chanel No 5 – but even he could see that this view was what had hiked up the price of his flat.

However, nice though it was, the view wasn't earning him any cash. He spun his chair round to face the big desk and picked up the phone. Jabbing at a series of numbers with his index finger, he then tapped the same finger impatiently on his desk as he waited for the phone at the other end of the line to be picked up.

'Gav,' he said, as soon as his call was answered.

'Hello, Miles.' Gav's voice sounded weary.

'How's things?' Not that Miles was really that interested, but some vestige of the good manners his mother had once taught him remained.

'Abby's giving me grief.'

Well, there's a thing, thought Miles, but if you will marry a prize cow, what do you expect? But he said, 'What's the problem?'

'She's dead against Jess buying the house.'

'That's a shame. It'll take years for Jess to save the deposit, even with the money she earns with me. Quite enough time for us to finish our business and move on. What does Abby want to do instead?'

'She wants it put on the market right now, as it stands, unmodernised.'

'You've told her how bad the market is right now, I take it?'

'What do you think? And I also pointed out that if we sold it to Jess we could save on an estate agent's commission which could amount to thousands.'

'And?'

'And she's adamant.'

'Then you've got to persuade her otherwise.'

'I've tried, believe me.'

'Then try harder. All we need is another three years to clean up and be sorted for life financially. We've invested a great deal of time and effort into this project and I don't want it wrecked by your fool wife when we're in sight of our goal. Do I make myself understood?'

'Of course.' Gav sounded nervous, which was exactly the result Miles wanted. If Gav was scared then he was more likely to sort out his hippy-dippy wife. The only reason he'd encouraged Gav to get involved with her in the first place was the house – and now she was like a bloody albatross; a dead weight, hanging about, no sodding use and causing all sorts of problems. Just as soon as they'd wrapped their business up at the house he knew Gav would be in the front door of the divorce courts like a rat up the proverbial, but until then they had to keep the silly bitch sweet.

'But you know what Abby's like.'

'Your problem, Gav. And I don't want problems, I want solutions.'

'I took the girls up to the house. I wanted to get Paul to confirm it had been Jess snooping around.'

'And?'

'And he was out.'

'Ah, well, can't be helped. In the meantime I suggest you concentrate on sorting Abby out. Savvy?'

'Yeah, I understand. I'll do my best.'

'Your best had better be good enough then, hadn't it?' Miles pressed the button to end the call.

Abby and Jess. Miles raised his eyebrows. Christ, if it wasn't one sister being a pain it was the other. Although to look at them it was hard to believe that Jess and Abby shared a gene pool – Jess, lithe, gorgeous and sexy and Abby, prickly, plain and to judge by the photo that Gav had once shown him, with as much sex appeal as a billiard table. Similar legs though.

Miles sighed at the thought that his solutions to the problems the girls presented weren't turning out to be as simple as he wanted. When Gavin had phoned him to say that Jess wanted to move into the house rent-free because she was stony broke, he thought he was being smart by making sure she earned enough money to stay in London. It hadn't crossed his mind that once she was earning bucketloads of the stuff she'd want to blow it on that rundown pile of crap in the middle of nowhere. Most girls he knew would have wanted a glitzy apartment in a fashionable area, with shops and gyms on the doorstep, not some sort of *Good Life* fantasy with half of Buckinghamshire for a back garden.

And now, because Jess wanted the house, Abby was going to play dog-in-the-manger and demand that it went on the market straight away. Which would wreck everything for Miles and Gav. He was having dinner with Jess in a couple of days; he had to persuade her to try to stop Abby selling the place because he couldn't trust Gavin to do the job properly. All he needed was a couple of years – three, tops – and then the girls could burn the house down for all he cared.

He'd just have to hope he could make Jess see sense and then get her sister to do the same. He didn't want to get heavy, but if that's what it took . . . it was always an option.

21

Jess thought about calling in sick to the station when she awoke a second time from a fraught and restless sleep. She still felt exhausted and her throat ached from crying, but as she lay amongst her twisted sheets and her damp pillow she realised that she was living so many lies at the moment she couldn't face another one. She'd forget who she'd told what, or who knew what about her. It was a given she'd get caught out if she made life any more complicated. Besides, as Matt had been on the early turn it was unlikely she would run into him that night. Which was something to be grateful for in her otherwise very bleak world. How had things changed so quickly? When Matt had gone off to work he had seemed to be in love with her, and then when he'd stormed in on his meal-break he hated her. In the interim, someone or something had poisoned his mind about her – but who, or what? And *why*? Someone at the station had told lies about her. Was there someone there who hated her so much that they would do something as malicious as that?

But her world was especially bleak because Matt no longer seemed to be a part of it. He'd crashed out of her life with harsh words, and although she desperately wanted to see him to tell him the truth, put her side of the story, she didn't think she could bear seeing that look of disgust upon his face again; disgust at her and something he thought she'd done. Would it be worse to see him again or not? Which would cause her more pain? It was like having a knife stuck in her; would it be worse leaving it where it was, or trying to pull it out?

Jess hauled herself out of bed, her head and her heart as heavy as each other, and spent the last bit of the day before she went on shift sitting morosely in a chair, nursing successive mugs of tea and bursting into tears intermittently because everywhere she looked, everything she thought about, took her back to her recent happy time with Matt when life seemed wonderful and she felt truly loved for the first time in an age.

She mulled things over and over until she could bear it no more and her thoughts became jumbled and incoherent. As dusk fell outside she dragged on her police uniform and got ready to go out, but that, like everything else in her life and her flat reminded her of him; washing, eating, going to the fridge, making the bed, tidying up, even breathing involved something that caused a bolt of sorrow to pierce her that Matt had gone. The flat smelled of his aftershave, there was a lump of his favourite cheese left in the fridge, his shower gel was in her bathroom . . . And she wasn't going to get rid of the reminders; not yet, at any rate. She held a tiny spark of hope that he might change his mind and come back. Or maybe he'd realise that he'd left some bits and pieces behind and come back to collect them, giving her a chance to talk to him, to find out exactly what had been said and by whom. The possibility that might happen was all she'd got to cling on to and she wasn't going to let go easily. She felt if she did, it really would be over between them. And she couldn't face up to that.

Not now. Maybe when she felt stronger, maybe when she stopped crying every couple of hours, maybe when she didn't feel sick each time she remembered the way he'd cleared out, had shouted at her, had made those awful accusations, maybe then she'd be able to come to terms with it. But now, now she'd rather live with the pain as a reminder of what she'd had, what *they'd* had, than expunge it.

Moving like an automaton, she got ready and left the flat to go to the station. It would be better to spend the night working, she decided. At work she'd be busy and her mind would be occupied elsewhere. Besides, when she came off shift she'd be so exhausted that oblivion was bound to come. Keeping going might stop her from falling apart completely.

When she got to the station she found that once again there was a message for her to attend a meeting. The desk sergeant looked at her curiously, but Jess didn't know whether it was because she looked like death warmed over or because of the cryptic message. Either way, she didn't care. On the way to the office she'd been directed to she checked her face in her reflection in a window on the stairs, the dark night outside turning the glass into a mirror. She didn't think her eyes looked too red, or her face unduly blotchy, so it wasn't obvious she'd been crying her eyes out, but she certainly didn't look her best. If she'd been going to work at Shoq she'd have slapped on layers of make-up – Carrie, Miles and the punters expected nothing less than perfection. But here? They could get what they were given. Besides, if she looked like shit maybe the bastards who had been spreading lies about her would realise the damage they'd done. She hoped they did and wound up feeling guilty. It was nothing more than they deserved, although deep down she suspected that the rumour-mongers wouldn't give a toss about any harm they'd caused.

She climbed to the top floor of the stark, uncarpeted stairs and headed down the corridor to the correct office.

Inside, McCausland and Dodds were waiting for her, both of them sprawled untidily on orange, moulded plastic chairs by a scarred and battered wooden table. Jess grabbed another chair, hauled it over towards them and sat down heavily. She stared from one to the other, waiting for them to say something. 'Good evening,' or 'Hello,' would be a start.

'How's it going?' said McCausland eventually.

'Nice to see you too,' she snapped back.

The two men exchanged a glance.

'Get out of bed the wrong side, did we?' said Dodds.

She really wasn't in a mood for this sort of game. Jess glowered at the two coppers. 'I suppose you want to know how I'm getting on with Miles? For your information, he's taking me out to dinner on Tuesday.'

'Well done.' But it wasn't said with any sort of emotion; no enthusiasm or gratitude were present.

Jess's irritation and annoyance began to rise and with it the temperature in the room plummeted. The relative bonhomie she and Dodds had shared at Shoq the night before was forgotten.

'So I've got cosy with him –' she didn't add that her life was a mess as a result, on the principle that it was none of their business and they wouldn't care anyway; that sort didn't. 'Now what?'

'Stay cosy with him and keep your eyes open. Pay attention if he makes or receives any phone calls in your presence. If you go back to his place . . .' there was a definite hint of nudge-nudge-wink-wink as Dodds said that '. . . have a bit of a nose about.'

'Go back to his place? Just what do you think I am?'

Dodds looked at her coolly. 'Seeing you work in a stripjoint I think we all know exactly what you are.'

Jess found herself starting to shake as an uncontrollable rage began to race through her, fuelled by adrenalin. Not them as well. This was the last fucking straw. 'How dare you! I dance. That's all I do – and don't you dare imply I do anything other than that.' She could feel tears pricking her eyes and she blinked, willing herself not to let herself down by crying. She knew if she did, she would be unlikely to stop.

Dodds raised an eyebrow and a look of cynical disbelief crossed his face. That did it. The tears were swept away by a tsunami of rage that barrelled through her. She launched herself forward and landed a slap on his cheek that made her palm smart. She hoped it hurt him just as much.

There was a silence following the crack of her blow. A silence that continued as both men stared at her; Dodds shocked and white-faced, except for the red handprint on his cheek, and McCausland amused. But no one spoke and Dodds glared, his fury obvious as the temperature in the room fell still further. Awkwardly Jess resumed her seat but still no one said anything.

Eventually, she apologised. 'Sorry,' she mumbled. Although she didn't feel it, not at all. The bastard deserved it.

'I should think so. I could have you for assault,' said Dodds coldly.

'And I'd have you for defamation of character,' shot back Jess.

'Enough,' said McCausland. 'We're not here for you two to have a cat-fight.' He stared hard at Jess and Dodds to emphasise his point. 'Right, it's good news that Jess is on Morgan's radar. That's exactly what we want. And it *would* be a good thing if you managed to get yourself invited back to his place, regardless of what you might think.' Jess remained silent but her face made it clear she disagreed. 'Yes, I can see he's not your idea of a dream date,' said McCausland, 'but just think of England, or whatever girls do. The important thing is that you get the chance to snoop around; look and see if his address book is lying about, see if you can get your hands on his mobile and look at his texts, anything.'

'I don't know,' said Jess. This sounded quite extra-ordinarily risky. 'Don't you have proper people on the case, people who know about surveillance?'

'Of course we do, but Miles is no fool and although we've got various procedures in place he's clever and cagey and doesn't give anything away. We've not picked up anything useful yet, certainly nothing incriminating. Maybe he'll be less cautious with you.' McCausland looked her up and down. 'Frankly Dryden, you're the last person he's going to suspect. You don't exactly look like the fuzz, do you?'

Jess considered his last comment and wondered if there was some veiled insult or double entendre hiding within. Probably not. Dodds wasn't smirking, although as he was still looking pained from the slap maybe he wasn't in the mood to find anything funny.

'No, I don't suppose I do,' she answered cautiously.

'Look, we're not expecting miracles but we're convinced Morgan is involved in this drugs ring and we've got no proof, not even a whiff of a lead. Anything you can help us with can only be a bonus. Seriously.'

'But you want me to get close to him. You told me yourself he's a nasty piece of work. Supposing he finds out I'm not just a dancer?'

'If you take my advice, you'll make sure he doesn't,' said Dodds. 'But I wouldn't go around upsetting people, if I were you. Because if you do you'd be surprised who might get so pissed off that they grass you up: let slip to one of his mates about the sort of company you keep, how you spend your spare time.'

Jess felt a frisson goose-bump her skin. Dodds had

just given her a stark reminder of the seriously dodgy position she was in, and how, if he wanted to, he could make life a whole lot worse for her. The thought was quite disturbing and she had no doubt that either Miles himself or his associates would turn very ugly indeed if they knew about her. She felt quite rattled, but she wasn't going to let Dodds see it, no way. He might have been impressed with her cool performance the previous night, he might have praised her, but she still didn't like him and she certainly wasn't going to forgive him for his previous implication. As far as she was concerned, he was a sexist creep. And now she thought he was a nasty sexist creep.

'I'm very careful who I tell about my personal life.'

'Then I suggest you keep it like that and maybe other people will too.' Dodds suddenly smiled at her, which was even more unsettling. 'Anyway, to make it easier for you, after tonight you're off the beat and out of uniform.'

Jess was baffled again. She didn't understand. Was she being dismissed as a Special?

'We know you don't work weekends at Shoq,' said McCausland, 'so you can work here, but we'd rather you didn't. Instead of reporting here, you'll be working in plainclothes at the club instead.'

'Oh.'

'As far as we're concerned, what you do there is more important than you pounding the beat, and there's less chance of anyone spotting you in uniform. So after tonight, you can hang up your handcuffs—'

'Unless you've got any other uses for them,' interrupted Dodds, with a leer. Jess was sorely tempted to slap him again.

'Shut it, Dodds. You can hang up your handcuffs,' reiterated McCausland calmly, 'until we've nicked Morgan. So you can tell Morgan that you can work for him as often as he wants you to. Okay?'

Jess supposed it was. Besides, the money at weekends was much better than what she could expect during the week, and it really would be easier for her if she gave up being a Special. She nodded.

'Right then, good luck with your date,' said McCausland. 'And remember, keep your eyes open for any opportunity to find out more about Mr Miles Morgan. Any information might be of use – anything odd, out of character, anything at all. But be careful.'

Jess was dismissed.

'By the way, if you need one of us, that's our number.' Dodds handed Jess a piece of card. She glanced at it and saw that it looked like contact details for a recruiting agency. 'Don't lose it. And if you can't be careful, be good.' He smirked again at her.

Jess's palm itched as she tucked the card into her trouser pocket.

She made her way back down the stairs to the locker room to finish getting ready to go on shift. It was only when she was out on the beat with a colleague that she wondered if it was something Dodds might have said that Matt had heard. After all, as far as she was aware, it was only Matt, Inspector Baxter and those two goons who knew about her dancing. She didn't think Baxter would drop her in it but Dodds . . . Nothing he did would surprise her; she didn't trust him any further than she could throw him. Someone had said something out of turn about her and had ruined her relationship, and right now, the only person in the frame for the blame was Dodds. That was good enough for Jess to have him in her sights for the firing squad.

22

'Choose anything you like,' said Miles, looking at Jess over the top of the enormous menu.

Jess hid behind hers, feeling awkward and out of place in the huge, ornate grill room. She knew Miles was loaded – he had to be, to own a club like Shoq – but even so she'd expected to be taken out to some little bistro or discreet restaurant, not to be paraded into this swanky West End hotel full of flunkies, rich tourists and over-paid, over-loud industrialists and bankers and their trophy wives. Jess was floundering, and the vast assortment of choices on the menu didn't help matters. Half the things on it she'd never heard of. She wasn't some uneducated country bumpkin, but Gran had been a 'good plain cook', and since she'd left home, eating out tended to be pub or pizza. What the hell was a *carpaccio* – and did she really want something that came with a *coulis*?

A waiter hovered by her arm. 'Would sir and madam like a drink to start with?' he asked.

Jess was sure that 'madam' did. But not alcohol, she wanted to keep her wits about her.

'Jess?' prompted Miles.

'Please may I have some sparkling water?'

'Whatever you like,' said Miles expansively, as if she'd just asked for the finest champagne, not the cheapest thing on offer. 'And a large whisky and soda for me.' The waiter slid away. 'I can recommend the oysters,' Miles told her, 'and their Châteaubriand steak is to die for.'

Jess clocked the price of the steak and nearly choked. *How much?!* The cost of the one course would keep her in food for a week. At that price the steak would have to offer more than the simple deathbed scene that Miles suggested it did. She'd expect it to come with a copper-bottomed guarantee of a fast track through the Pearly Gates, a private audience with God and a requiem mass composed especially for her.

She smiled at him to acknowledge that she'd considered his recommendation, then shook her head.

'Don't you like steak?'

'Not really,' she answered truthfully.

'You're not some sort of vegetarian, are you?'

'No, not at all. I'll eat anything, me. And before you gave me a job at Shoq I'd eat anything that was on special at the supermarket, and I mean anything. Although I draw the line at tripe. Not that supermarkets sell it.'

'Tripe? I should think so too. Can't abide sweetbreads either.'

Jess couldn't comment on those but she didn't think it was something she'd want to try just in order to be able to hold an opinion. And as they didn't seem to be on the menu she would be perfectly happy to go with the sea bass or veal and a green salad. She dithered, then finally plumped for the veal.

'You sure?' Miles asked. 'Doesn't seem like enough to keep body and soul together, if you ask me. Mind you, you don't seem to have much of a body to keep together with your soul. Hardly anything at all. In fact,' he said, 'I've seen fatter cigarette papers.'

Jess forced a smile. She assumed he was offering her a compliment, but if that was his idea of a compliment she'd love to hear an insult.

The waiter reappeared with their drinks; the bottle of fizzy water was in its own cooler and the tumbler adorned with slices of lime and lemon and filled with ice cubes, while Miles's whisky was accompanied by a bowl of ice and an old-fashioned soda siphon so he could serve himself with the amount he liked. Once that was all dealt with, another waiter appeared to take their food order.

'You are going to have a proper drink with your meal, aren't you?'

'Maybe a glass of wine, please.'

'Glad to hear it. I'm perfectly happy to drink alone, but I'd rather not.' Miles ordered their food plus a bottle of red and a bottle of white wine. Jess was astounded – two bottles! She had a nasty feeling he was showing off; rubbing it in just how wealthy he was, and it wasn't attractive. However, she was aware that she wasn't there to enjoy herself so she kept her mouth shut.

While they waited for their order to appear they were fussed about by various attendants who solicitously arranged their napkins on their laps, offered bread rolls and butter, topped up Jess's drink every time she took a sip and enquired if everything was all right. Jess wanted to tell them things would be a whole lot better if they just pissed off and left them alone, but didn't think that was the done thing in such a place. Much as she liked the comfort of the chairs, the view over the Thames, the thick carpet and the soft music played by a real-live pianist at a real-live grand piano, there was a lot to be said for the sort of restaurant where you weren't fussed over quite so much. However, she noticed after a while that it was Miles they swarmed around in particular rather than herself. And no surprise there. Miles was the one who would be paying – and tipping.

The girls were like that with some of the clients who

came to the club; the ones who were the biggest tippers always got the most attention. Jess suppressed a smile. Human nature was the same whether in a class joint like this or a club like Shoq.

'Enjoying yourself?' asked Miles.

'What's not to enjoy,' answered Jess obliquely. *Your company for a start, Miles.* But she smiled sweetly and tore off a piece of roll to nibble.

'I'm surprised at you having veal. Your sister wouldn't approve.'

The saliva drained from her mouth and the morsel of bread became as unpalatable as cottonwool. She stared at him, horrified at the implications of that innocent little remark. She'd told him about having a sister but she had never, ever mentioned that Abby was a vegetarian or someone who had protested against the export of veal calves. So how had he found out? Who had he been talking to? And why? She swallowed the bit of roll painfully and just managed to stop herself from choking on it. Her face must have given away her thoughts.

'Someone at the club told me your sister had strong feelings about food,' said Miles smoothly.

'Really, who?' She tried to cover up the shake in her voice.

'Laura? Carrie? Can't really remember, to be honest. Does it matter?'

Yes, it fucking did! She was sure, absolutely certain she'd never spoken to any of the girls at the club about her private life. In fact, she knew for a racing certainty she hadn't. A wave of panic swept through her. Shit, if he knew about Abby, what else did he know? That she was a Special? Oh my God – supposing he knew that. The panic increased. The blood pounded in her ears and she felt physically sick. But she forced herself to breathe normally and reasoned that if he thought she was some sort of threat to his criminal activities she'd be more likely to be swimming with the fishes than dining with him. As calmly as she could she replied, 'No, not at all. Just wondered.'

'Anyway, is your sister funny about food?'

'A bit.' Jess wished to kill this conversation stone dead. She didn't want to give Miles any more information about herself, her sister or anything to do with her private life.

'But you're not.'

'I'm not what?'

'Funny about food.'

Jess shook her head. Her mind was still thumbing through the implications that Miles's knowledge about her sister had thrown up. She was utterly convinced she hadn't had a conversation with anyone at Shoq about Abby, but might she have let something slip? It seemed unlikely, but she trawled through past conversations she'd had with Laura and the others. Some of them were a bit fuzzy but only because they were now relatively distant; she'd never got pissed at the club, although Miles didn't seem to care how much the girls drank, as long as they didn't get lewd, abusive or fall over. But Jess had always made a point of just sipping drinks bought for her before 'losing' them and drinking water at all other times.

She realised that Miles was looking at her curiously. 'Well?'

Well what? Had he asked her a question? She didn't have a clue, since she'd been lost in her thoughts. 'Sorry?' she said guiltily. 'I was thinking about how nice it is here,' she blustered.

'I was just asking how you are enjoying your work.'

'Loving it,' she gushed. She flashed Miles a full-on smile.

'Good. As I said the other evening, you're very popular. The punters like you.'

Jess smiled and shrugged. 'That's very flattering.'

'You're a class act, Jess. A cut above my regular girls. You talk nice – you're articulate.'

'Thank you.'

'The fact that you were a professional dancer really shows.'

'Hardly. I mean, I trained a lot but I never really earned a living dancing. Not till now, anyway.'

The wine waiter appeared with the two bottles Miles had ordered. There was a pause in the conversation while the bottles were opened, tasted and poured. Jess thought the white wine he'd ordered for her was like nectar, but she restricted herself to saying that it was 'nice'. She didn't feel inclined to pander to his ego by praising his choice more than absolutely necessary.

'So I've got a proposition for you,' resumed Miles.

Jess looked at him over the rim of her glass. A proposition? She didn't like the sound of that. 'Yes?' she answered, trying not to sound too wary.

'I want you to dance for some friends of mine.'

Jess put her glass down on the table. 'Dance?'

'Yeah. Just dance. Only somewhere,' he paused, 'somewhere a little more private. Not the club.'

Jess took a large gulp of wine. Sod sobriety, she needed Dutch courage to cope with this situation. 'Where?'

'A mate of mine's got a gaff in the country. It's his fiftieth birthday and he's asked me to arrange the entertainment. He'll pay well.'

'Just dancing?'

Miles nodded.

Did she believe him? 'How much?'

'A couple of grand for a couple of hours.'

'Can I think about it?' Two grand for a couple of hours. For dancing? On the face of it, it was a great offer, but if these mates of Miles expected more bangs for their bucks . . . Oh God, 'bangs for bucks' was not the turn of phrase to use. And anyway, these mates – who were they? Jess had visions of some sort of gangster get-together. Like something out of *The Godfather*. Get a grip, she told herself. This is real life, not a crime thriller. But then she remembered the Kray twins who had been real-life characters not works of fiction – and look what happened to some of their associates! She gulped nervously.

It was Miles's turn to shrug. 'Don't take too long. I expect some of the other girls would jump at the chance.'

Their food appeared and Jess found that Miles's offer of a trip to the country to meet his mates had effectively removed her appetite, but Miles seemed to think that her disinterest in her food had more to do with worries about her weight than anything else. Jess didn't put him right. She picked at her food while he tucked in with gusto.

'So,' he said, as he pushed his empty plate away, 'how's your plan going to buy a place in the country?'

'Well, nothing's really happening,' Jess told him. 'Apart from anything else, I need to save enough for the deposit.'

'You do know, don't you,' said Miles, looking very serious, 'that this is absolutely the worst time to be trying to deal with property. Mortgages are like hen's teeth. You'd be much better off leaving it for a couple of years. You're not in a hurry, are you?'

Jess shook her head. 'No.'

'Or is your sister wanting her half of the money?'

'No, or rather yes, but not from me.'

'Oh dear. That doesn't sound good.'

'It's complicated.'

'Well, if you've got any sense the pair of you will do nothing about your house for a year or two. Frankly, I doubt if you'll get a mortgage with the way things are with the banks, and if you sell it to strangers you'll probably get a crap price. You're far better off renting it till the market sorts itself out, and you'll have time to get a good big deposit together which'll give you the best shot at getting a mortgage. Trust me.'

'Yeah, well, Abby's made her mind up.'

'Try and persuade her to change it.'

Jess stared at Miles, trying to make out whether he just liked interfering in other people's lives or whether he really was trying to help her.

'I doubt if anything I say will make any difference to Abby,' she sighed. 'She's never paid any attention to anything I want.'

'Maybe I could help,' offered Miles. 'I'm told I can be very persuasive.'

Given what Jess knew about him and some of his alleged associates, she didn't doubt it. 'That won't be necessary.'

'Let me know if I can help, although I seriously suggest you don't rush into things.'

Jess wondered why he cared but nodded in agreement anyway. It was harmless enough advice and presumably impartial. After all, the house was nothing to do with him.

It was a relief when at nine o'clock he suggested that they ought to make a move to get to the club.

'Carrie will be wondering where we are.' He glanced at his watch again. 'In fact, I'll text her. Tell her we'll be another half-hour by the time I've paid the bill and got us across Town.'

Mile sïgnalled to the waiter for the bill as his thumbs flicked across the keys of his mobile. He'd just about finished when the maître d' arrived with a discreet folder and a cardreader. Miles dropped his mobile on to the table as he read the bill.

'I think there's a mistake here,' he said bluntly, his finger jabbing at an item listed.

The maître d' looked at it, then signalled to the waiter who had served them. Jess looked about the room as the three men discussed exactly which vintage of claret Miles had ordered and which vintage he was being charged for.

'Maybe sir would like a word with the sommelier,' offered the head waiter.

'*Sir* would like that very much,' said Miles.

'I'll ask him to come to your table.'

'Don't bother,' said Miles. 'I've no doubt I'll only have to wait an age for him to come to me and I'm in a hurry. Why don't you take me to him?'

'If you wish, sir.'

Miles stood up, throwing his napkin on the table where it landed on his mobile. He stomped off behind the waiter leaving Jess, feeling acutely embarrassed, behind.

Under the napkin Miles's mobile chirped. Presumably Carrie replying to his earlier text.

Keeping one eye on the direction in which Miles and the waiter had gone, Jess reached out a none-to-steady hand and retrieved his phone. She flipped it open and saw that the incoming text was indeed from Carrie. But under that information was the word *Contacts* in a corner of the screen above a button. She pressed it and a list of names filled the screen. She recognised a couple as girls that worked at Shoq but most of the names meant nothing. She scrolled down the list but there were dozens of names flowing past, too many to note really, and anyway some of the names seemed to be more gobbledy-gook than proper names – a string of letters and then a couple of numbers. Still looking out for Miles's return, she kept her thumb pressed on the scrolldown button. A movement from the doorway through which he'd left made her heart race, and her thumb shot off the button just as the name *Gavin H* came into view. She barely registered it but already she had flipped the phone shut and slipped it back under the napkin, her hand shaking like an aspen leaf in a gale.

She looked up to see if Miles had spotted her, only to see it was just a waiter, alone, re-entering the dining room.

Gavin H? Her brain finally caught up with what her eyes had seen. Or had they? Had she really seen Gavin H or had she imagined it? Part of her wanted to reach out for the phone again but the other part of her was still so shit-scared at the prospect of getting caught that it glued her hands to her lap and refused to let them move.

So was it just coincidence that there was the name Gavin H on Miles's phone when her brother-in-law was called Gavin Harris, or was it her imagination, or – and this was the most likely solution – was it an entirely different Gavin? It was hardly an unusual name, when all was said and done. Although Gavin must have known someone at the club because he'd suggested that she worked there in the first place.

Gavin and Miles . . . And Miles knew about Abby – had he learned about her from Gavin?

Jess thought her head was about to explode with all the implications, and alarm bells were jangling horribly.

23

The way Matt glowered at all and sundry in the station when he was next on shift didn't encourage his work colleagues to approach him. And when Simon plucked up the courage to ask Matt what the matter was, he almost got his head snapped off.

'Jeez. Who rattled your cage?' he responded.

'Shut up, Simon.' His split with Jess was only a couple of days previously, and the wound it had left was red-raw. He knew he ought to tell Simon what the matter was, but he couldn't bring himself to do so. It was too painful.

'Well, I hope you're going to be better company next weekend at my wedding. It's supposed to be a happy occasion and if you're in a mood like this it'll spoil the day for everyone.'

Matt had forgotten it was Simon's wedding so soon. Shit. And he and Jess had both been invited. His heart sank. The last thing he wanted to do was to go anywhere socially where he might run into her. Maybe he'd try to find out if she still intended to go, although he certainly wasn't going to talk to her directly to find out.

Although the thought of running into her at work was appalling, the prospect of meeting her socially was worse. At work he could keep things on a professional footing – at least he hoped he could – but socially he might be expected to make small talk, and he knew he wouldn't be able to bring himself to do that. His emotions were too sore still.

Stronger than the hurt of their failed relationship was the feeling of outrage that she'd managed to dupe him. That he'd been so gullible as to believe every word she'd said, when all along she'd been lying. He'd believed her when she said she just danced, he'd believed her when she said those big pay-cheques were tips for just chatting to the punters – but that overheard conversation had shown him it was anything but the truth. How could he have been such a blind fool as not to wise up sooner? Matt – the guy who wanted to join CID – couldn't even detect that his girlfriend was lying and was working as a prostitute.

And the knowledge that she was on the game put him in an enormous quandary. Prostitution was against the law, and as a lawbreaker she had no place in the Met, but although he felt hurt and betrayed by her, and although he wanted to hurt her back, to blow the whistle on her was quite another thing.

Matt felt that to do that would be an act of vindictiveness – and could he really stoop to that? Besides, she was good as a Special Constable; even feeling the way he did right now, he had to admit that much. And she'd once told him that her idea of a dream job was to be a proper police officer, so could he wreck that dream? Or was that just another lie, another tale she'd spun? Could he believe anything she'd ever told him? Matt sighed.

'So, my wedding is boring the pants off you,' said Simon with a sad shake of his head.

Shit, he'd been miles away. 'No, Si. No, absolutely not. Really. It's just . . . Oh, never mind. I've just got a lot on my plate at the moment.'

'And I haven't? Blimey, Matt, you have no idea how much effort goes into getting married. I just thought I popped the question, bought the ring and that was that. But the reality is . . .' and Simon launched into an account about hiring suits and choosing music and guest-lists and a whole plethora of details about the minutiae of a wedding which left Matt free to think about his dilemma with Jess.

By the time Simon had got onto the subject of his and Sal's dealings with the caterers, Matt had made his mind up and had come to a decision about what course of action he was morally obliged to take.

'Fascinating, I never knew there was so much to it,' he said to Simon as he drained the last of his tea and stood up. 'I'll come to you for advice if ever I tie the knot.' Not that that's likely to happen any time soon, he thought, given his recent track record.

'World's living expert, me,' agreed his friend. 'Although all this knowledge is probably going to be wasted as I'm only going to do this the once.'

Matt nodded, hoping he looked supportive and caring, then he hurried off. He sped up the stairs to Inspector Baxter's office and rapped his knuckles against the closed door. He had to do this before he changed his mind.

'Come.'

Matt opened it and peered round. 'Sir, I need to talk to you.'

Baxter looked up from some papers he was perusing. 'Green, isn't it?'

'Yes, sir.'

'What can I do for you, Green? Take a seat,' he added as an afterthought.

'It's not about me exactly.'

'Okay. So what is it? Someone harassing you? Someone promoted ahead of you? Stress?'

'Nothing like that. I'm fine.'

'Good, good.' Baxter was doing the 'concerned

superior' bit very diligently, which made Matt wonder if he'd been on some sort of man-management course recently.

'It's about one of the Special Constables.'

Baxter's eyebrows rose. 'Is there a problem?'

'There certainly is.' Matt took a deep breath. He felt like he was about to take a bungee jump. Once he launched himself into this, he wouldn't be able to claw his way back to a place of safety. 'Sir, I have reason to believe Jess Dryden, a Special Constable, is unsuitable to continue working for the Met.'

Silence. Baxter stared at him, then at his hands, clasped together on his desk, then back at Matt. More silence. Matt swallowed.

'Constable Dryden,' said Baxter eventually.

Matt nodded.

'In what way?'

'She works as a dancer at Shoq and I believe as a prostitute.'

Baxter stared at him, not a flicker of emotion on his face. 'I see.'

Was that it? Was that all he could say? Here was Matt, making a really serious accusation involving a fellow member of the Metropolitan Police, and all Baxter could say was, 'I see.' Matt added, for good measure, 'I don't think she'll deny her work at Shoq.'

The inspector waited.

'But the fact that I am certain Dryden is also a sex worker is another matter entirely. She may deny that, but I'm pretty sure of it,' insisted Matt.

'Hmmm.' Baxter stared at his hands again.

Matt shifted uncomfortably in his seat. And . . . silence. Then, after an interminable pause, Baxter spoke again.

'I appreciate your concern, Green. The fact is, Dryden has already been removed from the beat.'

Matt felt as though the wind had been knocked out of him and then he felt relief, a huge surge of it. So he hadn't blown the whistle; Baxter already knew and that meant that he wasn't responsible for shopping Jess, so he wasn't being a vindictive shit. And there was no chance of him running into her again at work. Thank God for that too.

'However,' continued Baxter calmly, 'I'd rather you didn't say anything to anyone else about this, about your suspicions, or about what Dryden does out of uniform. Just keep it to yourself.'

'Yes, I quite understand.' Although Matt wasn't quite sure he did. Baxter seemed remarkably sanguine, almost too sanguine, about the whole business. And if Jess had already been suspended then Baxter must have been confronted with more than just Matt's suspicions. The inspector would only suspend her if he knew something fairly concrete, so wouldn't he want evidence from Matt to corroborate it, to build a case? Still, it wasn't up to Matt to question his superior, and if Baxter wanted him to stay schtum then he would.

'Right, sir.' Matt waited. He'd given Baxter the cue to dismiss him and yet he felt the man was going to say something else to him. He saw his boss open his mouth, shut it, then open it again. *Come on, man, spit it out.*

'Can I just ask how you know about Dryden? About her other job?'

So he did want Matt's evidence after all. 'We had a short relationship.'

'I see.'

'I ended it when I found out about . . . her other life. Not her work as an exotic dancer, but the other stuff.'

'I see. She told you she worked as a prostitute, did she?'

'Not exactly. I found out by accident; I overheard a

conversation between two men who had paid . . . paid for her services.'

'I see. So you're sure of your facts.'

'Yes, sir.'

'And you could recognise these two men again, could you?'

'Er, no,' Matt admitted. 'I was in a toilet cubicle in the locker room here and they were taking a pee in the urinal.'

'So you didn't see who it was.'

'No.'

'So your evidence is an overheard conversation between two unknown males.'

Put like that, Matt suddenly felt doubtful. He thought about what he'd heard, how certain he'd been at the time. But they hadn't actually *said* Jess had had sex.

'Yes, sir,' he admitted. 'But I know what I heard, and whoever it was talking they were pretty explicit.'

'Are you sure about that?'

Matt thought back to the snippet of conversation again, and although he did have some doubts he also remembered how, at the time, he'd been so certain he knew exactly who and what the men had been talking about. 'They made some comments about her abilities and about how much they paid her.'

'Tell me exactly what you heard.'

Matt repeated what he'd heard, about Jess being a natural, about how she'd pulled out all the stops and how she'd blown her client away and was better than the man speaking had ever dreamed. 'So you see, sir, there isn't any doubt, is there?'

Baxter didn't look convinced one way or the other. 'Thank you, Green,' was all he said. 'I'd like you to leave the matter in my hands now. Like I said before, just forget all about it.'

'Yes,' said Matt. Although he didn't think it would be that easy. Not when he considered everything that had happened in the weeks before, and how intense his relationship with Jess had been. But it would be easier if he didn't discuss anything to do with Jess with his colleagues. Yet he knew he was going to think about her. He wasn't going to be able to stop himself doing that.

Baxter tapped his fingers impatiently as he waited for Dodds and McCausland to make an appearance before him. On his desk was a briefing from the Home Office on policing policy and targets but he couldn't bring himself to read it, even to pass the time, waiting for the two officers to turn up. Finally there was a rap on his door.

'Come,' he barked.

The pair strode in looking as scruffy as always. Baxter didn't offer them a chair or coffee. This wasn't a social occasion, far from it.

'What do the pair of you think you're playing at?' Baxter rapped out.

'Sorry, sir, you've lost us there,' replied Dodds, looking completely bemused.

Baxter glowered at them. 'Talking about Jess in a public place, rocking the boat.'

Dodds shrugged. 'Still not with you.'

'You were overheard in the toilets here, talking about Jess and her . . .' he hesitated, 'her skills.'

McCausland and Dodds exchanged a look.

'And her ex-boyfriend isn't happy.'

'She's got a boyfriend? In the force?' asked Dodds.

'Had a boyfriend,' said Baxter, before he filled them in on Jess's private life – or as much as he could tell them – and about his recent conversation with Matt Green. 'Luckily, when Green recounted exactly what he'd heard I understood why he'd got the wrong end of the stick.

And I'm not surprised, frankly, the way you were talking about Dryden.' He glared at them. 'And don't deny it wasn't you two,' he finished. 'Your careless talk may be compromising this whole operation.'

'Can't see how,' grunted McCausland.

'Because if Jess is miserable, she may say, "stuff this" and walk away from it. She may decide that it's not worth her sanity and happiness being associated with a couple of twats like you two.' Baxter's rage threatened to boil over. He took a deep breath to calm down. 'So I'm asking you to be careful what you say about her and to whom. I told Green, after he informed me of his suspicions about Dryden, that I'd taken her off beat duties. Of course he thinks I've suspended her.' The inspector sighed. 'Which is handy. And I've asked him not to talk to others in the force about the matter. He thinks that's because it's under investigation.'

'Equally handy,' offered McCausland.

Baxter's eyes narrowed. Were these two jokers taking the piss? He decided they probably weren't. 'But for all that I want you to treat Dryden with more respect – on duty and off. No more smutty innuendos, understand?'

'Yes, sir,' the pair chorused.

'That's all.'

Baxter watched the two Drugs Squad officers leave his office. Why did he always feel like he needed to wash his hands after he'd talked to them?

24

Jess was leaning by the bar waiting for the punters to start arriving. It was relatively early; there were a few diners in the restaurant which was off the main show room, but Jess hadn't been asked to perform a private dance for any of the tables, nor had she been invited to join them for a drink and a spot of conversation – or what passed for conversation in this place; the blokes bragging about how wonderful/successful/rich they were and Jess making suitably flattering comments right back. Just along from her were a group of other dancers chatting about fashion and shopping, but she was lost in thoughts about Matt and where it had all gone wrong.

'How's things?' said Tom, joining her.

Jess smiled at him and wondered if she should tell him the truth. 'Fine,' she lied. Inside she felt as if someone was clawing her heart to pieces, and every time she thought about the way Matt had stormed out of her life – which was every few minutes – she felt as though she was at the bottom of a deep well filled to the brim with loneliness and loss

'You looked a bit sad, I thought.'

Jess forced a bigger grin. 'No,' she said gaily. 'No, I was just thinking and you know, for a girl like me, that's a pretty big deal.'

'Don't be silly, Jess, you don't fool me. I bet you've got

exams and everything. Your life must be pretty good.'

But she'd fooled Tom away from thinking she was sad, which was something. 'Maybe, but for all that I still work here as a dancer.'

'Don't you like it?'

'The money's cool. I can't say I don't like that but, well . . .' She shrugged. 'It's not exactly what I planned to do when I left school.'

'I didn't expect to wind up a bouncer, neither.'

'What did you want to do, Tom?'

'Dunno. Work in a shop maybe. You know, ordinary hours, so I get some chance to see me mates, take a girl on a date.' Tom looked glum. He obviously knew as well as Jess did that working in the club, the only girls he was likely to meet were the dancers – who only had eyes for the celebs and the rich. Tom didn't stand a chance with any of them. 'I expect it's not much fun for you either, sleeping when everyone else is up and about. No life is it, really?'

Jess agreed with him.

'Still, it can't be all bad. Not if Mr Morgan and you—'

Jess interrupted Tom. 'What do you mean, Mr Morgan and me?'

Tom stuttered, 'B-but I thought Mr Morgan was . . . I mean . . .' His face flushed brick-red. 'Well, I saw you arrive with him the other night, in his car.'

'He took me out to dinner. I don't think that means we're dating.' Jess suppressed a grimace at the thought of being linked with Miles.

'Well, I've worked here for quite a bit and I can't remember the last time he took a dancer out. Honest.'

Goodness, thought Jess. She'd imagined she'd been just one in a long line of girls he'd wined and dined. That was a turn-up. And instinctively, she knew she ought to make the most of Miles's interest in her if she was going to worm her way into his confidence. The trouble was, it was like the prospect of eating an eyeball: she knew it could be done, other people had done it before her and furthermore it wouldn't kill her, but the very idea made her want to hurl.

'Well, I expect he was just lonely that evening and I was available.'

Tom didn't look as if he agreed but he didn't contradict her either.

Jess made up her mind; she'd been told to encourage Miles and now was the perfect opportunity to do it. Pushing her drink away, she told Tom she was nipping to the dressing room to check her make-up. She slid past him and headed for the corridor behind the mirrored wall where, as she had hoped, she found Miles in his office, his feet on his desk looking at some glossy glamour shots submitted by a hopeful.

Jess paused in the door. 'Hi, Miles,' she said softly.

Miles glanced up and swung his feet off his desk. 'Jess. Come in. Take a look at these.' He chucked the pictures onto the desk so they slid across the expanse of polished beech. Jess picked them up and turned them the right way up. The girl was curvy and very sexy, with great legs although Jess reckoned she probably wasn't any older than about seventeen.

'Very pretty,' she said casually. 'I'd have thought she's a bit young though.'

'Her letter says she's twenty-two.'

'I'd want to see proof of that.'

'My thoughts exactly.'

Jess put the pictures back on the desk and sat on the chair opposite Miles. 'I've been thinking about that private engagement, dancing for your mate.'

'Oh, yes?'

'I'll do it.'

Miles's face lit up in a genuine smile. 'That's a cause for celebration. Angus will be dead chuffed.' He went over to the bank of cabinets and cupboards behind his desk and pulled open a door. Reaching in, he produced a bottle of Bollinger and a couple of champagne flutes.

'I know you don't like to drink when you're working but just one glass won't hurt,' he said.

'You're the boss,' said Jess lightly.

He pulled off the foil and the metal cage and then popped the cork. At the moment the cork left the bottle Carrie appeared. Jess wondered if she had homed in on the noise or whether it was just coincidence. Given Carrie's predilection for the more expensive things in life Jess assumed the former, an opinion that was confirmed by the fact that Miles instantly produced a third glass and waved it at her enticingly.

'I won't say no,' said Carrie, 'although I just came to bring you this.' She held up a black briefcase. 'A customer left it in the cloakroom last night.'

'Thanks,' said Miles, putting his glass down, taking it and putting it straight into a cupboard.

Miles? Lost property monitor? Surely not. Nadine, the coat-check girl, did that. So this was odd. And she'd been told to look out for anything, however trivial, that was odd. Her curiosity was aroused and she suddenly wanted to know why this briefcase was getting special treatment. She decided to prod the situation. 'Aren't you going to open it and see if you can identify whose it is?' she asked, trying to sound ultra-casual.

But Miles ignored her and closed the door.

'Don't you want to see if it's got a business card or anything in it?' she persisted.

'I've no doubt the owner will come forward soon enough,' he said, dismissing Jess's suggestion.

'But the owner might think he's left it in a taxi or anything.'

'Leave it,' said Miles. His tone was pretty terse so Jess did. She'd gone too far. She took a sip of her champagne instead. She still thought it odd that Miles was looking after lost property and his reaction to her enquiry seemed to confirm her suspicions.

'People are always leaving things behind here, aren't they, Miles?' said Carrie. 'I think the girls distract them – and I swear some of them have almost forgotten where they live when they leave here. But they always seem to get reunited with their property, even if it takes a week or so.'

Jess forced a laugh but thought that Carrie's comment was clunky in the extreme; it only reinforced her feelings of suspicion. However, Miles's tone of voice had left her in no doubt that he didn't appreciate her cross-questioning him about the briefcase. Time to move away from it.

'So why the fizz?' asked Carrie, possibly mentally agreeing with Jess. 'Or is this a private celebration?'

'Jess is doing me a favour.' Carrie's face registered surprise. 'She's agreed to dance at a private party.'

'Has she now.' The other woman sounded less than pleased.

'Miles made me an offer I couldn't refuse,' said Jess lightly.

'Really? Well, if you take a tip from me, sweetie, I wouldn't tell the other girls. Dressing-room jealousy can be a bad thing. The others might not like it that the new girl is getting special treatment.' Carrie raised her perfectly plucked eyebrows significantly.

Jess hadn't considered that there might be any repercussions to being Miles's personal choice for this gig; she herself didn't think it was altogether desirable to have been picked to perform exclusively for his buddies, especially if they were all like Miles himself. God, the thought of a room full of Miles-alikes . . . Yeuch! Her assumption that the other dancers would feel the same way was obviously deeply mistaken.

But of course, most of the girls were in this game for the short-term; to make a pile of dosh, perhaps become a trophy wife – and then their only connection with laps would be sitting in ones of luxury rather than dancing. Understandable, she supposed. Shallow, but understandable. And given the size of Miles's bank balance, he would obviously fulfil a lot of the criteria the girls had for a catch. Providing, of course, your eyesight was crap and you had no discernible sense of taste.

Carrie finished her champagne and swept out to 'see the girls', leaving Miles and Jess alone once again. Jess always found Miles's office seriously weird for, when the door was shut, she knew it was a private space but with the mirrored walls that looked out across the corridor and into the main bar she couldn't help but feel that she was in some sort of goldfish bowl and that she was just as visible to everyone in the club as they were to her. It was bizarre, and she could never quite believe that she couldn't be seen as clearly as she could see.

'So Jess, how is life treating you?'

Goodness, someone else interested in her private life. Did she have a label on her forehead saying she welcomed enquiries?

'Just peachy.'

'Only Carrie tells me you've decided to work weekends, after all.'

Jess nodded. 'Well, why not?'

'Is it because of the money?'

'I can't say it won't come in handy. Tips on a Saturday night are worth having – or so the others tell me.'

'Which means you'll be able to afford to get that dream house of yours all the quicker.'

'Yeah, well. It's a long-term plan.' But Jess was surprised Miles was still showing an interest in her plans for the house in the Chilterns. 'Even saving hard it'll take a few years yet, I should think. And you're right about taking it steady.'

'Which I find good news. You're an asset to the club, Jess. I don't want to lose you any time soon.'

There was a knock at the door. 'Yeah?' he called.

Carrie poked her head round. 'Can you come to the bar, Miles? We've got a problem with one of our customers. He doesn't appear to have any means of paying.'

Miles sighed. 'A regular?'

'Not really, but he has been here before.'

Jess got up to go.

'No, stay here and finish your champagne,' said Miles. 'Besides, I need to give you details about this party you're going to be starring at. Won't be long.'

The two disappeared out of the room, Miles shutting the door behind him. Jess watched as they went down the corridor and out onto the main floor. She sipped her champagne and swung her stiletto off her toe. She wondered how long Miles would be, and as she did so, realised this was the perfect opportunity to check out the briefcase. While she was at it, she could see what else Miles had stashed away. There was no way anyone could creep up on her; all she had to do was keep an eye on the mirror wall which would give her plenty of warning if someone approached.

Slipping her shoe back on, Jess put her glass on the desk and went around to Miles's chair. Swiftly she opened each of the desk drawers in turn; stationery, a few porn mags, a stapler, a hole punch. She glanced at the mirror wall. Miles and Carrie were still in discussions at the bar and the corridor was empty.

She moved to the cupboards and began opening them; revealing a fridge with wine, a cupboard filled with glasses, another concealing a TV; one was a wardrobe with a couple of suits and some clean shirts hung up, and another contained a washbasin and mirror. It was all so frustratingly innocent and normal, although did she really expect to find a hidden armoury or a skeleton? She pulled open the final cupboard where Miles had put the case – and there it was. And beside it was an identical one. She gave them a closer look: yes, same make, same model. How weird was that? When you considered how many different briefcase manufacturers there had to be in the world, to have two of the same design left behind in one club . . . So maybe they hadn't been left behind accident-ally. Maybe, if Miles was into distributing drugs, this was a way of concealing a drop and a pick-up. Maybe *that* was why he'd been so tetchy when she'd asked about it.

Or maybe, thought Jess, her imagination was in over-drive. There was only one way to find out. Taking a deep breath to steady her nerves, she glanced out at the bar area and, seeing that the coast was still clear, she pulled one of the cases towards her. It was locked. She tried the other one. The catches flipped open but inside was com-pletely empty. She pushed it back into place. As she did so she realised that the locked case was full – it weighed quite a bit more. She tried the catch again but it wouldn't budge. Frustrated, she shoved it back in the cupboard and shut the door. Miles and Carrie were heading back towards the office so she hurried round to her chair and was sitting, outwardly calm, sipping her drink and swinging her shoe off her toe when they re-entered. Just as well they couldn't see her pulse-rate – it was through the roof.

202

I'm really not suited to skulduggery, thought Jess, trying desperately not to hyperventilate and praying to God she looked innocent. She hoped they didn't notice how much her hand, holding the champagne flute, was shaking.

Jess's pulse was still thundering through her body when she escaped from Miles's office and her cosy chat with him and into the corridor. In fact, her heart-rate was so high it was making her feel quite dizzy, and the throbbing beat of the dance music wasn't helping any either. Fresh air was what she needed. Moving gracefully through the bar, now packed with clients, avoiding the pudgy hands that reached out towards her, smiling at some of the familiar faces, exchanging a few greetings and pleasantries, she reached the door at the foot of the stairs. The draught that fed down instantly cooled and refreshed her, and she climbed the flight eagerly. The lobby at the top was empty except for Nadine, the cloakroom attendant, who was sitting behind the counter filing her nails.

'Hi, Jess. What are you doing away from the action?'

'Just got a bit hot and felt the need for fresh air.'

'All those blokes getting sweaty?'

'Something like that.' Jess leaned against the jamb of the main entrance. 'Don't you get bored, up here on your own?'

'Bored to sobs, but it's a job and it pays the rent. I don't get the kind of tips you lot get, but I don't have to be nice to the buggers neither.'

'That's probably a bonus. Some of the prats we have to talk to – I ask you.'

She shut up as a customer approached the door. He paid his entrance fee then leered at Jess in her skimpy spangly frock. Jess smiled sweetly back.

'I'll buy you a drink later if you play your cards right,' he said with a lascivious wink.

'I shall look forward to it,' Jess replied. As soon as his back was turned she wiped off her smile and stuck her fingers down her throat. 'Still, forewarned is forearmed,' she whispered to Nadine, then hitched herself onto the counter and dangled her endless legs.

'Shouldn't you be getting back?' the girl asked.

'Don't you want my company?'

'It's not that, but don't you have to earn your keep?'

'I suppose.'

Another guest arrived, paid, handed over his coat to Nadine and slipped his cloakroom tag into his shirt-pocket.

After he'd gone down the black staircase Jess said, 'Carrie says loads of guys manage to forget their kit.'

'You'd be amazed. I get all sorts left behind here. Mostly coats and scarves, but also presents for their wives, lunchboxes, cases – and then there's the stuff the guys leave on the tables, like their wallets and keys. Honestly, I swear some of the men that come here really shouldn't be out without a minder.'

'So what happens to all the junk?'

'Got a cupboard here where I store it for a couple of months or until they claim it.'

'So it doesn't get locked up anywhere?'

'Yes, it does – here. I just told you. Anyway, why are you interested? You got a fetish about lost property or something?'

Jess laughed – casually, she hoped. 'No, just curious.' So, Miles wasn't the lost-property monitor, just as she'd thought. Or maybe it was different for some things – like the more valuable items. She longed to ask about left briefcases and if they were treated differently but she reckoned that she'd pushed things a bit too far as it was. The last thing she wanted was for Carrie or Miles to know she'd been snooping, and it would be just her luck that Nadine would say something and drop her in it. But it seemed from what Nadine said that *she* was the guardian of all lost property, which made the identical briefcases in Miles's office seem even more curious. As she'd been asked to keep her eyes open for anything odd, Jess knew she'd have to ring Dodds and McCausland – a prospect which filled her with almost as much distaste as her enforced association with Miles.

Pounding the beat just didn't have the same appeal for Matt now there wasn't the chance of sharing the task with Jess. And to make matters worse he'd been teamed up with Sally – Simon's fiancée and fellow wedding obsessive.

'So, do you know what Jess is wearing on my big day?' she asked as they crossed Kensington High Street and headed towards Church Street, being the visible presence of law and order which paid lip-service to the Government's promise to bring down crime figures rather than actually producing any results.

'Sorry, can't help you there, Sal.'

'It's a big secret, is it?'

'Actually, I really don't know.'

Something in his tone must have alerted Sally. 'You two had a tiff?'

'Drop it,' pleaded Matt. He didn't want to discuss his private life with her. Apart from the fact it was so painful that even to think about their break-up was like dripping vinegar onto a carpet burn, he knew that anything he told

Sal would be round the entire Met Police before his next meal-break.

Sal took the hint and shut up, but only for a few seconds. 'So is Jess coming to the wedding?'

'You'd better ask her yourself.'

'But I haven't seen her around the station lately. Has she gone away?'

'Look Sal, I'm not seeing her any more. We're no longer an item, we're an ex-couple, our relationship is as dead as Monty Python's fucking parrot. Get it?'

'Oh.' There was a pause. 'So anyway, how will I find out if she's coming to my wedding?'

Matt seriously considered throttling her but decided against it, not because Sal didn't deserve it but because it would wreck his promotion chances. And Si mightn't be too pleased, either. Ignoring the question, Matt turned his thoughts to Jess. She might have made a fool out of him but he still missed her desperately. He didn't think men did 'lovesick' but he now knew he was mistaken. It wasn't just soppy teenaged girls who thought they would rather be dead after being dumped, hulking great blokes could feel that way too. And *he'd* done the dumping. Only now a great big chunk of him wished he hadn't. Or rather, he wished he hadn't found out about her. No, that wasn't right either. Bugger, he didn't know what he wished – apart from wishing the hurt would go away.

They plodded along High Street Ken in silence until Sal suddenly let out a piecing shriek. 'Cooee!' she yelled. 'We were just talking about you!'

Matt snapped out of his introspection and turned to see who the hell Sal was accosting. For a second he could see no one, then he realised that Sal was heading into the open doorway of Shoq. And there was Jess. Looking stunning in a silver lamé dress that just skimmed her crotch and showed off her flawless legs. He had always liked her in that dress, she looked amazing in it. Then he noticed an expression of horror mingled with panic on her face. Was it because he was there, or possibly because she was about to be cornered by Sal, or because if Sal knew she worked at Shoq the whole of the Met Police would soon know too.

'Love your frock. You look quite different out of uniform. Hardly recognisable. So why you all poshed up like this? Party?'

Jess opened her mouth and then shut it again.

'So what's this place?' Sal checked the neon sign. 'Shoq? Isn't that some sort of night-club?'

'Sort of,' said Jess.

Sally stopped gassing for a second and took in the pictures on the billboard outside the door, the name of the place and signs blaring the words 'topless' and 'girls'.

'Funny place to hang out if you're a girl,' said Sally, perplexed. Then it was almost possible to hear the cogs turning and grinding. 'I know what this place is. It's a strip joint.'

Shit, thought Matt, Sherlock Holmes had better watch out.

Jess just stared at her. 'It's a nude dancing club,' she said coldly.

'Like I said – a strip-joint.'

Matt's eye was caught by a movement behind Jess. A beautifully groomed woman of about thirty-five, wearing a long dress, appeared at the top of the stairs.

'Good evening, officers,' she said. 'Can I help you?'

'Nah,' said Sal. 'We're just being sociable. Chatting to a friend of ours.'

Carrie's eyebrows shot up her forehead. 'You know Jess?' She turned and scrutinised Jess. 'You didn't tell me you have such interesting friends.'

Matt watched Jess's face which was draining of colour.

'You never asked me,' she said lightly, but her eyes didn't match her tone. She looked terrified, really scared. 'Besides, we're not really friends.'

'No,' said Matt quickly before Sally could say a word. 'We've just run into each other a couple of times.'

'Not professionally, I hope,' joked Carrie, her eyes dead and cold.

'Hell, no,' said Matt. 'Purely social. Actually I met Jess here at a stag do. Sal's fiancé's. Didn't I, Sal?'

Sal shrugged. 'Oh yeah, Si said you'd ended up here.'

'Really.' The older woman looked supremely bored. 'I hate to break up your reunion but some of our clients get a bit twitchy if they think the police are taking an interest in this club. Not,' she added hastily, 'that anything happens here that we wouldn't be entirely happy for you to examine. And we're always pleased to welcome the boys in blue – out of uniform.'

'Of course,' agreed Matt.

'And anyway, we have a gentleman downstairs who has asked for a private dance from Jess.'

There was a splort from Sally. 'You dance! You mean you're a stripper?' Her mouth hung open slackly as she assimilated the information.

'Exotic dancer,' said Jess and Carrie in unison.

'Does Inspector Baxter know about this?'

Jess glared at Sally, her face ashen, while Carrie looked thoughtfully at the pair of them.

'We need to get going,' said Matt firmly. Whatever he felt about Jess and her job – the way she'd lied to him – he could see that the fact she was also a Special Constable was not something she was keen for Shoq to know about. Part of him hated her, hated what she'd done, but when he saw her looking scared and vulnerable he couldn't harden himself to deliver a metaphorical kicking or to put her in a position where Carrie might deliver one.

'Night then,' said Sal, as they moved away.

As they did Matt heard the older woman say, 'And who the fuck is Inspector Baxter?'

'I'm sorry, Jess,' said Tom as he escorted her to Miles's car. 'You know I like you, but orders is orders. And I can't afford to upset the boss.'

Jess made some sort of strangled noise that she knew Tom wouldn't be able to interpret, but then people with a wad of tissues in their mouth generally found it tough to make themselves understood. However, he would be able to tell by the look on her face that what she'd tried to say hadn't been 'never mind' or some other platitude. And what she'd actually tried to say – 'Go stuff yourself' – had come out as 'Hnnn hnnn hnn-hnn'. And had her hands not been tied behind her back she'd have accompanied it with some rude gestures just to make sure he really got the message. And she had thought he was her friend. Pah!

'If you struggle, I'll just carry you so it'll be easier all round if you walk properly.'

Again Jess made a sound between a squawk and a cough but complied. What else could she do? Going along the bare, concrete service corridor to the back entrance of the club she knew she wasn't going to meet anyone, and even if she had been able to make a sound, the racket going on in the bar on the floor above would cover up World War Three breaking out, let alone the sort of scream she could raise with a face full of Kleenex.

Tom kicked open a door and led Jess to the black limo

parked in the corner of the underground garage. As he approached it he pulled the keys from his pocket and plipped it open. Jess half-expected to get shoved in the boot so was almost pleased when he opened the rear door and laid her down on the back seat.

'Mr Morgan'll be along in a minute.' Tom sat himself in the front seat and swivelled round. 'He's not pleased, you know.'

Really? She'd never have guessed, but despite her brave thoughts another frisson of fear ran though her, clutching at her innards and giving them a sickening squeeze.

She'd first felt really worried when Carrie had said, 'And who the fuck is Inspector Baxter?'

Jess had blustered that he was also just a mate. 'Honest, he was at the stag party too.'

'Really,' said Carrie, as they both descended into the main bar. 'Anyway, that's as maybe. There's a gentleman who wants you to do a private dance for him so you'd better get yourself over to him before he changes his mind.'

Jess breathed freely again as she shimmied across the floor towards the client who wanted her to perform exclusively for him. She'd got away with it, her secret was safe. But only by the skin of her teeth.

She decided there and then that she just couldn't cope with this sort of pressure; she wasn't cut out for it and she didn't have any training for this sort of work. It was all very well them saying, 'just keep your eyes and ears open and cosy up to Miles' but even doing that seemed to be fraught with perils and pitfalls. No, next time she saw Dodds and McCausland she'd tell them about the briefcases and then break it to them that she wanted out. She'd quit the Met, dance till she'd got enough cash saved for her house and then reapply to become a copper.

As she twirled and danced, pouted and pirouetted and entertained her rich admirer, Jess was planning exactly what she would say. And if they didn't let her go immediately she'd take some leave; she was sure she was owed some. Or she'd go sick. She smiled at her client again to make him think she was enjoying performing for him and then reimmersed herself in her thoughts of getting out of her association with the police.

The music finished, she blew her one-man audience a kiss and made a break for the dressing room to shower and change.

'Don't go,' said the bloke. 'I'd like to buy you a drink.'

Jess suggested it would be nicer for him if she showered first and promised to hurry back. Not. He was okay as punters went but he looked about as interesting as a ball of dough and it didn't help that he resembled one as well. Flaccid and puffy and pale. She took her time showering and changing, re-doing her make-up with care, and it was quite a while before she moseyed down the corridor again.

As she passed Miles's open door he called out to her. 'The details of that private party have changed. Go and chat up that punter who's taken a shine to you and then come back here so I can fill you in.'

An hour later and not suspecting a thing, Jess walked into his office. 'I'm all yours now, Miles,' she said.

'You certainly are.'

And that was when she heard the door slamming shut behind her as a hand was clamped over her mouth, the moment when she discovered it was possible to almost faint with terror as she saw Miles come round his desk with a plastic tie in his grip. He grasped her hands roughly and pulled them behind her back. She heard the rasp of the tie as its little plastic teeth were pulled through the opening until the strap bit into the skin of her wrist. She yelled out in pain but all that came out was a muffled squeak. She could feel her eyes pricking with tears as she wondered if she was going to be sick; her skin went clammy with sweat and her ears rang, and she realised that she had never known such gut-wrenching fear in her entire life. Those earlier moments, when she'd thought she'd been experiencing fear as she'd rifled through Miles's cupboards and checked his phone, was like comparing a bucket of water to an ocean.

'You're hurting me,' she protested.

Miles's face was so close to hers she could see every pore on his nose and feel his breath on her cheek. 'Tough,' he said without a trace of emotion as he stared into her pain-filled eyes.

Jess's legs felt so wobbly she thought they were going to give way, so she leaned against whoever was behind her for support. The hand over her mouth shifted, making her wonder just for a second if whoever it was, was taking pity on her but then, as she went to open her mouth to say something, to ask what was going on, to attempt to lie her way out of this appalling situation, she felt tissues being shoved in it. It was horrible, making her want to gag. She half-retched and wondered whether, if she actually was sick if she would choke – but then she managed to quell the reflex, although the tissues seemed to fill her mouth with fluff and dryness, and little bits of them stuck to her tongue and teeth.

'Now I don't know exactly what your game is,' said Miles, his face still uncomfortably close to her own, 'but you've been nosing around, asking questions, and it now seems you have a lot of mates in the police. So Carrie got your key out of your locker and I sent our Tom round to your flat.' Fear surged through Jess again. Fear and anger. 'Guess what he found?'

If Jess had had any saliva in her mouth she would have

swallowed because she could guess. All she could do was stare in horror as Miles moved away from her, opened a cupboard and pulled out her police uniform.

'I think this explains a lot, don't you?' said Miles. He threw her jacket at her. The buttons hit her face, causing the tears to roll faster down her cheeks. And then he waved her warrant card at her. 'How could I have been such a mug? Not that you look like the filth, I'll give you that, but I'll be a laughing stock if word ever gets out that I employed a constable as a dancer. You've caused me a lot of problems which I'm going to have to sort out pronto, and when I've done that I'm going to start asking you some questions. In the meantime I need you out of the way and I've got just the place lined up.'

Jess was trembling so violently now her legs did actually give way. As she fell, a pair of hands caught her under her armpits and supported her. She twisted round a little to see who it was behind her. Tom. And she had thought he liked her. Bastard.

'Tom,' said Miles, 'put her in my car. Use the back stairs – we don't want the punters getting curious, now do we? And wait with her till I get there, then you can go back on duty.'

He appeared a few minutes later, dismissed Tom and started the car. He didn't say a word to Jess who was beside herself with fear, with no way of contacting anyone who might be in a position to help, uncomfortable, miserable and desperately trying not to think about what was going to happen next. Except it was the one thing, the only thing, that occupied her mind.

By the time Miles's car drew to a halt Jess was stiff and sore. Her shoulder sockets were on fire from being wrenched back in an awkward position, her fingers had gone numb, and although the back seat of Miles's Merc was designed with comfort in mind, the seats were also designed to be sat on, not lain on. Besides, as she wasn't wearing a seat belt, Jess had to brace herself when the car cornered to prevent herself from sliding off it and onto the floor. She was exhausted, she ached and she was still scared witless. And she didn't have a clue where they had ended up except that it was somewhere right outside London; she reckoned they had been travelling for over an hour but wasn't sure. The sky was pitch black so they were deep in the country – which told her nothing.

At the start of the journey she'd been aware of street-lights flashing past; intermittently the car had stopped and started, presumably at traffic-lights and junctions, and then they must have joined one of the big thoroughfares that led out of London, maybe Western Avenue or the Edgware Road, as they'd picked up speed and had moved steadily without interruption. She kept hoping that drivers of the lorries they passed would look down and notice her on the back seat, and pick up some sort of signal from her that she was in jeopardy, but none turned their heads her way. She'd tried twisting round to see the gantries and road signs to give herself a clue as to which direction they were headed in, but it just wasn't possible. All it had done was give her an appalling crick in her neck and improve her view of Miles's headrest.

Her fears had receded while Miles had been driving. As long as they were moving he couldn't do anything to her. Jess felt sick again as the courtesy light came on. Miles was getting out. What was going to happen next?

27

'Sir,' said Dodds, as he and McCausland entered Baxter's office. 'What do you know about Dryden?'

Baxter leaned back in his chair and dropped his pen onto the stack of papers he was working on. 'What do you mean? Apart from the fact she's a stripper?'

'Correct.'

'And she and Green had an affair?'

McCausland nodded. 'But do you know anything about her family?'

Baxter shook his head. 'Should I?'

'What if I told you that her sister is married to an associate of Morgan's.'

Baxter's eyes widened. 'I beg your pardon?'

'That's right. We've been keeping tabs on Morgan's personal calls, and although he's very careful about what he says, he can't disguise who he's calling. We've been looking at everyone he's been in touch with, and one of his mates is none other than Gavin Harris, husband of Abigail Harris, née Abigail Dryden.'

'Bloody hell.' Baxter almost choked. 'And we thought . . . But she's . . . Fuck.'

'Our sentiments exactly. So the whole operation is probably blown.'

'Well, she's got to go. We can't have her working for us. I'll suspend her immediately. Why didn't you check her out before?' Baxter sighed. 'I suppose you haven't got enough evidence to lift Morgan.'

'Nah. And it's not surprising if he knows what we are doing, our every move, courtesy of Dryden. And to think we told her to get close to him.' Dodds smacked his forehead. 'And we were so impressed when she did. But of course she found it easy – they already knew each other.'

'Get her in here, immediately. And get Green in too. I want to find out what she told Morgan and what Green knew about it all. Because if he knew, if he had the least idea . . . Sheesh.' Baxter could see his chance of progressing further up the promotion ladder disappearing down the pan. He looked apoplectic and neither Dodds nor McCausland fancied being in Jess's shoes. The dressing-down that was coming her way was going to be awesome; it was a crying shame they wouldn't be able to witness it.

Baxter stared out of his office window into the yard below where the area cars and the police vans were parked, but although his eyes were pointing in the direction of the vehicles he didn't see them. The scene was busy as police officers were coming and going for their mid-morning meal-break but he was oblivious, immersed in his own thoughts. Where was Dryden? What was so difficult about finding her? Surely all someone had to do was haul her out of bed and bring her in. And how much had she jeopardised the operation to find the main supplier of drugs on his patch? He drummed his fingers on the windowsill. Surely someone knew where she was.

The frustration he was feeling suddenly surged up and he picked up the phone on his desk, dialled an extension and demanded to know why he still hadn't had a chance to interview Dryden.

'We can't get hold of her,' said the duty sergeant.

'She works odd hours,' he yelled. 'She should be at home sleeping. So if she won't answer her mobile, send an area car round to her address and pick her up.'

'Sir,' said the sergeant. He sighed. This was going to be a long shift if Baxter was in one of his irritable moods.

It was with trepidation that he reported to Baxter's office some thirty minutes later that when the area car had called at Jess's address they'd been unable to get an answer from her entryphone.

'So where is she?' he snarled.

'We don't know, sir. The caretaker said he hadn't seen her for a few days but that's not unusual. He says she doesn't often go out when he's around because he's there from nine to five and that's when she's sleeping. But he said he'd keep an eye open specially and let us know if she turns up.'

Baxter rolled his eyes. 'And you've tried her mobile again?'

'Straight to voicemail each time we ring.'

'You've left a message, I assume.'

'Several, asking her to call in or come to the station as soon as possible.'

Baxter wiped a hand over his face. It'd have to do. If Jess couldn't be found then there wasn't much he could do about it. He didn't have the manpower or the resources to comb London for her.

'In the meantime wheel Green into my office,' he said. 'He knows her. Maybe he'll be able to tell us where to find her.'

It took nearly an hour to get Green into Baxter's office and there was still no sign of Jess.

'So where is she likely to be?' Baxter demanded.

'She was working last night so she would have gone straight home to get some sleep before going back to the club tonight. If she's not at home I've no idea. She's got a sister, Abigail, but they don't get on particularly.' Matt fidgeted irritably. 'Look, can I ask what this is about?'

'No, you can't,' snapped Baxter.

'Is she in trouble? What's the matter?'

'*I'm* asking the questions. Do you know where her sister lives?'

'I haven't a clue but she and Jess co-own a house. In the Chilterns near High Wycombe.'

'I expect we can find the address easily enough.' There was a pause then Baxter said, 'What do you know about the sister?'

Green shrugged. 'Nothing, I've never met her. They lead very different lives. Jess told me that her sister wouldn't approve of her having anything to do with the police so she'd never told her she was a Special.'

'That's what she says,' said Baxter with feeling. 'Although I'm not sure quite what we can believe if it's come from Dryden.'

Matt looked bewildered. 'And I don't think she knew Jess danced either.'

'That's what Jess told you,' Baxter scoffed. 'But for all you know, she and this Abigail are as thick as thieves.'

Green shook his head. 'That really isn't the impression I got.' But then she'd lied to him about other things, hadn't she? 'Look, is she in trouble?'

'We just want a chat with her and she doesn't seem to be around.'

'She was definitely working last night. I saw her at the club.'

'You *what*? But you were on duty!' The colour of Baxter's face reflected his anger.

'Sir, I was on the beat and we passed the night-club. Jess was standing by the door getting some air. We had a brief chat.'

'Who's "we"?'

'Myself and Sally Clifton. I think it came as a bit of a shock to Sally to find out what Jess's day job is.'

'What time was this?'

'About two or three in the morning. Probably nearer three because shortly after that we came in for a meal-break. I don't think Jess was that pleased to see us, especially considering that she and I . . . Well, it was awkward. And there was someone else there who didn't seem too happy that Jess was talking to us.'

'Miles Morgan?'

'No, not a man, a woman.'

'Another dancer?'

'I don't think so, sir. She looked a bit old to dance, to be honest. And Jess said there was someone who manages the girls, looks after them, gets them taxis home, that sort of thing, so it was probably her. All the girls Jess works with are about her age – early twenties.'

'Would they know where she might be?'

'You'd have to ask them. But Jess'll be working at the club again tonight, so couldn't someone get hold of her then?'

'Has Jess ever spoken to you about Morgan?'

'Not really. He took her out to dinner the other day.'

Baxter frowned. 'You don't sound happy about it.'

'Would you, sir, if it was your girlfriend?'

Baxter raised his eyebrows. Did he look like the sort of man who would date a stripper? 'So what's their relationship then?'

'We didn't really talk about it. We had a bit of an argument.'

Baxter was silent for a moment or two. 'About that date? Or the other matter you told me about?'

'Both.'

'What if I told you she went out with Morgan because

we asked her to? She's been helping a couple of guys from the Drugs Squad since we think Morgan's got something to do with the drugs on the Windmill. Of course we didn't know at the time that her brother-in-law seems to know Morgan too.'

Matt's jaw sagged. He found it hard to articulate a sentence. 'Her brother-in-law? Morgan?' he got out eventually.

'Exactly!' Baxter snapped. 'And what else hasn't she told us? Our Miss Dryden seems to lead quite a complicated life, which is why we're rather keen to have a word with her.' Matt couldn't answer. 'So, as far as you are aware, she should be working again tonight.'

Matt nodded again.

Baxter leaned back in his chair. He didn't want to wait till tonight to get hold of Jess, he wanted to talk to her now. But he supposed he didn't have any choice. He'd just have to be patient. Although it was going to be tough because he really wanted to know what the connection was between her, Miles and her brother-in-law. Frankly he was finding it hard to believe it was just coincidence.

Jess was cold. The silver lamé dress she had on was warm enough in the club but currently she was in some sort of unfinished property development with no carpet or heating. She could see from the locked window that she was pretty high up – so even if she managed to get the window open or break it there was no way she could escape out of it. Miles had assured her that no one would hear her if she shouted, and having checked out the door to the room she was locked in, Jess had no reason to doubt him.

'You're lucky,' Miles had said as he'd shoved her brutally through it. 'I've decided to give you one of the studio flats that's almost sorted. You've got a sink in the corner and a toilet behind that sliding door. All your needs catered for. If I wasn't feeling so generous I'd have put you in one of the really unfinished flats.'

Jess tried to feel grateful and lucky but was just aware of being numb and dazed. And nauseous. She supposed that was brought on by fear and shock. But at least Miles had untied her hands. The trouble with her hands being free was that she could now see the face of her watch so she knew how long she'd been there; it was five o'clock so coming up to twelve hours since she'd been bundled out of the club.

She wondered when she'd be missed. How long did it take for a grown-up to be reported as 'missing'? The only person who might worry about her at the club was Laura, but if Miles said that she'd handed in her notice or that she was poorly, would Laura query it as an answer? Probably not. Especially as Carrie would corroborate anything Miles said.

For the first time in her life Jess wished that she didn't keep her life quite so private. If she had more friends, if she worked regular hours, if Matt was waiting at home for her . . . Feeling lost, alone, and very, very frightened, she hauled herself over to the mirror and removed her contact lenses. She couldn't possibly keep them in any longer, but now everything was going to be a blur. Maybe under the circumstances things wouldn't look quite so bleak if it was all out of focus.

Gav was being shifty. He was up to something, or was hiding something from her; Abby could always tell. And it wasn't the first time in recent months that she'd felt Gav was being less than level with her. He didn't seem to be able to come up with any figures about how much the house had earned them, then there'd been that sudden interest he'd taken in Jess and her welfare, and now . . .

Now what? Something was bugging him. Since he'd come home from work he'd been acting oddly – jumping to get the phone when it rang, staring into space, deep in thought, and then there was the way he seemed to be about to tell her something and then he'd change his mind.

What on earth was worrying him? His job, finances, something going on with his colleagues?

'Gav, is something the matter?'

The expression on his face as he looked up from the paper he was reading seemed to confirm that all was not well; it was one of guilt and fear.

'No, should there be?'

'Come off it, Gavin, I'm your wife. I've been married to you for four years now and I can tell when you're lying. And you're lying to me now.'

'No, I'm not.'

Abby put her hands on her hips. 'You're worried about something. Surely you can tell me what it is. Is it your job?'

'The job's fine, I'm fine, everything's fine. Just leave me alone.'

'Is it money? If so, we can sell the house. OK, we'll make a bit less—'

'It's not money, it's not anything – just shut up!'

'No. You're acting odd. You've been odd since you invited Jess here but now you're really weird. There's something going on and I mean to find out what it is.'

'Get off my back.'

'Is there something going on between you and Jess? Are you planning to do something with the house that you both know I wouldn't like? Is that it?'

'Just shut the fuck up!' yelled Gavin, finally completely losing his temper.

Silence fell and Abby just stared at him.

She took a deep breath. 'Fine,' she said. 'If you're going to be like that I'm going to phone my sister, ask her.'

Gav shrugged as if he didn't care, but Abby detected a look in his eye which gave a lie to his actions. 'Go on,' he said, 'but won't she be working?'

Abby looked at her watch. 'I shouldn't think so. I know she works funny hours but she's always around at this time.' She got out her phone and brought up Jess's number. She listened to the automated message for a second before she flipped the phone shut. 'Voicemail,' she muttered. 'I'll try again later.' But she still got put through to voicemail when she phoned later and the next morning, and as Jess was the sort of person who was welded to her mobile, Abby began to worry.

28

'Gavin, I'm really worried about Jess,' Abby said as he came through the door from work, twenty-four hours after their row. She'd forgotten about that now; she was more concerned with what was going on with her sister.

Gavin didn't look her in the eye. 'She'll be fine,' he mumbled.

'How can you say that? You don't know for certain. Suppose she's been in an accident, or mugged, or anything.'

'She'd find a way to get hold of you.'

Abby bit her lip. 'I can feel it in my bones that there's something wrong.'

'Now you're being ridiculous.'

'Am I? The feeling won't go away.'

'Because you haven't been able to get hold of her for a few hours? You're being stupid,' Gavin said nastily.

'No, I'm not. She always answers her phone. And it's not a "few hours" it's a whole day.'

'So she's switched it off to stop people like you from interrupting her all the time.'

'But that's what I'm saying – she never does.'

'So she's changed her mind.'

Abby stared at him. How could he be so dismissive of her worries? She made her mind up. 'I'm going up to London.'

'What?'

'I'm going up to her flat, to see if she's okay.'

'You're mad, she'll be fine. She's just had her phone nicked or she's lost the charger. It's going to be something simple – and rational.'

'Look, if I could ring her at work I would, but I haven't a clue where that is. I don't know the names of any of her friends either, and the only way I have of reassuring myself that my sister isn't on a slab in a mortuary is to go and find her.'

'Now you're completely over-reacting.'

'I'm not!' yelled Abby, perilously close to tears.

'And working yourself up into a state.'

'I'm not,' she sniffed, more quietly, getting a grip.

'You will be wasting your time and money.'

'So?'

'Don't go,' said Gavin.

'If you had a sister you were worried about, wouldn't you go and see her?'

'Not necessarily.'

Abby gave Gavin a cold stare and walked out into her garden. She couldn't be bothered to argue with him. She'd wait till tomorrow when he went off to work, Google a map of London and work out how to find her sister's flat – then she'd go there.

Jess stared at the casement, numbed by boredom interspersed by moments of total terror. Any noise, any creak the old house made set her heart thundering in her chest. And apart from anything else she was now famished. She'd had a meal before going to work the night Miles had abducted her, but that had been two whole days ago. All she'd had to live on had been water from the tap. Miles had promised to return with food 'later' but now, apart from hunger gnawing at her stomach, Jess had a hideous horror that something might have happened to him. Supposing he'd had a car crash? No one knew where she was, no one would have a clue where to begin searching for her. How long was it possible to survive on just water? Jess knew it was longer than you might expect, but that was cold comfort.

Wearily she got up from the mattress and went over to the window. She noticed that her legs were shaky – lack of food, she supposed. Or maybe it was lack of exercise. Either way, if Miles didn't come soon she thought she might be in a bad way. To take her mind off her problems she looked at the view – what she could see of it.

She had no idea where this property was except that it was somewhere deep in the country and on the edge of a hill. Like that narrowed it down. And even if she developed telepathic powers and could work out where she was, Jess realised that no one else would be any the wiser. She blinked at the blurry sweep of countryside in front of her. On any other occasion she'd be admiring the view and thanking her lucky stars to be in such a rural setting, but now it just increased her feeling of loneliness. On the horizon the sun was glowing red as it began to set. The sky above was darkening and the treetops that covered the side of the hill that spilled down to the fuzzy patchwork of arable fields below had gone from green to black.

Jess leaned her elbows on the windowsill, put her chin in her hands and stared morosely at the scene. If there were houses nearby she couldn't see them. In the distance was the glow from a town, miles away, but closer to hand there wasn't a sign of any human life. Surely there couldn't be anywhere in south-east England that was this isolated, but sadly for Jess, it seemed as though she was stuck in the one place that was.

Going to the sink in the corner, she cupped her hands under the cold tap and drank a few mouthfuls of water. Her stomach grumbled noisily that it wasn't being fed anything more sustaining. In order to try to keep warm and to conserve as much energy as possible, she padded across the bare floor to the mattress and curled up there.

The nights, she had discovered, were worse than the days and she dreaded the approach of another one. She had almost welcomed her first one as a captive, thinking that sleep would pass the interminable hours. However, the darkness and the cold made sleep difficult, and the long hours of extreme boredom and silence meant her imagination could run riot. All her fears and phobias, any dreadful images from slasher movies that she had watched in the past, scrolled through her mind's eye, getting bigger, grosser, more terrifying.

Jess knew she did sleep from time to time during the night but at best it was fitful and much of the time she lay wide-eyed staring into the dark, and at the paler rectangle that was the window because it was preferable to confronting what lay behind her closed eyelids.

Darkness fell as Jess lay on the mattress and she must have dozed off for a brief moment because she was awoken by a torch shining in her eyes. Confused and disorientated, she couldn't work out where she was for a few seconds. Blearily she rubbed her eyes and then, as she realised she was still in her silver lamé dress, reality asserted itself and sick fear clutched at her again. She wished she could see who was behind the light but the glare of the bulb just hurt her eyes.

Something landed on the mattress beside her. Dazzled, Jess glanced away from the mesmerising light and down at the glossy plastic packages. Someone had just delivered some packs of sandwiches, and even if they were only supermarket ones Jess didn't think she'd seen such a delicious feast before in her life.

'I didn't know what sort of sandwiches you'd like. I brought you a selection.' It was Miles's voice. Jess felt a whoosh of conflicting emotions: hatred for her warder and abductor but gratitude that he hadn't forgotten her. And she didn't care what Miles had brought her – rat paté or semolina, she didn't give a shit. She just needed food.

'Thanks,' she said, grabbing the first pack that came to hand and ripping the film off the front. 'And where the hell have you been?' she added angrily. 'I thought you'd left me here to . . .' She almost choked at the enormity of what he might have done to her and she couldn't voice her fear.

'Just got held up.'

Jess took a big bite out of the bread.

'Don't guzzle them all at once. I may not be able to get back for a while.'

Jess swallowed her mouthful so fast it hurt her throat. 'How long is *a while*?' she asked nervously.

'Twenty-four hours at least. You've caused me a lot of grief and I've got a great deal to sort out, thanks to you.'

'Sorry,' Jess said automatically, before she wondered why she had apologised. He was the criminal, he was the one who had kidnapped her. But she was scarily aware that as she was completely dependent on him, she couldn't afford to antagonise him. Was this what psychologists called Stockholm Syndrome?

The knowledge that the sandwiches had to last her for several meals meant that they represented much less of a feast. The next mouthful she took was considerable smaller than the first.

'So I'll get to you when I can. Or if I can't I may send someone else to check up on you. Meantime I suggest you do as you're told; be good, don't damage this room and don't try to contact anyone, because if I find out you've done anything that might annoy me, I won't be very happy. Savvy? And you ought to thank your lucky stars that none of your flat-foot friends have come sniffing around any of my,' Miles paused as he searched for the words he wanted, 'any of my business concerns, otherwise I'd have to start getting heavy with you and find out what you've told them.'

'Nothing. I haven't told anyone anything,' said Jess, suddenly feeling weak with fear. 'I don't know anything *to* tell,' she added.

Miles stared at her. 'You'd better not be lying to me. But maybe we'll find out for sure in a day or two. When I've finished sorting everything out, you and I are going to have a little chat.'

Jess gulped. She didn't dare ask how he planned on finding out or what form the 'little chat' was going to take. She thought it might be better not to know for sure.

Miles left without another word and Jess heard the double click of the mortise lock; the most hateful sound in the entire world, she decided, because of what it represented.

She ate two of the packs of sandwiches slowly, savouring the flavours. She then washed her meal down with several more handfuls of cold water before returning to her mattress. Although her hunger hadn't been sated, at least she didn't feel completely hollow and shaky any more, although she had a nasty residue of fear left after her last conversation with Miles. And when he'd found out everything that she did – or didn't – know, what would he do then?

Clasping a brand-new A-Z, Abby made her way across London towards her sister's flat. It had been a long time since she'd been in the city and she found the hustle and bustle daunting. The whole place seemed to smell of diesel, soot and unwashed people. Or was it just the Tube? Morosely she stared at the Tube map above the heads of her fellow passengers and worked out how many stops till she got to where she had to change lines – again. The train rattled on and Abby was jolted and bounced about while she wondered what on earth possessed people to live in London where they had to travel like this on a daily basis.

She was feeling faintly weary and grubby by the time she re-emerged into daylight at Shepherd's Bush. At the entrance to the shiny new station – so different to some of the ones she'd encountered already that day – she opened her map and studied, yet again, the page she'd marked. Beside her, cars roared along the busy Uxbridge Road as she tried to decide which way she needed to go to get to Jess's flat. Finally she managed to orientate herself and set off, carefully checking the street names at each intersection until she arrived in Jess's road.

At first, she thought nothing of the three police cars parked halfway along it. Since she'd arrived in London she'd been amazed at the number of two-tones she'd heard, hurtling around, and had quickly realised that she was the only person to be so uncool as to turn to watch them as they sped by; it marked her out as a real out-of-towner. But as she walked down the road, checking the numbers of the blocks of flats beside her, it dawned on her that the cars were outside the very block towards which she was heading. A knot of dread began to tangle in her stomach. She quickened her pace.

Shit. It *was* her sister's block that the police were focused on. But at least there was none of that tape you saw on all the crime dramas cordoning the place off. Nothing to say she couldn't enter the lobby, nothing to suggest there was a crime scene to be found. Tentatively she approached the entryphone and pressed the number to her sister's apartment.

A male voice answered, 'Yes?' Abby felt sick.

'I'm after Jess Dryden,' she said. 'It's her sister.'

There was a pause then the door buzzed. Abby pushed at it and entered. She made her way over to a bank of lifts. A sign told her that Jess's flat was on the sixth floor; she took the lift that was open and waiting on the ground floor and hit the right button. Her heart thudded and she offered up a silent prayer that the voice had belonged to some random male friend of Jess's and not someone in uniform.

About thirty seconds later the steel doors slid apart to reveal her sister's front door standing wide open and a number of policemen who seemed to fill the place.

Abby thought she might faint.

'**B**oss,' called out a male voice. It might have been the one that had spoken to Abby just seconds earlier. 'Dryden's sister is here.'

'Bring her through.'

The uniformed policeman beckoned to Abby. 'Follow me please, Miss Dryden.'

'I'm not Miss Dryden. I'm Abby Harris.' Frantic worry made her snappy.

'Sorry, miss. Anyway, the inspector would like a word.'

'But my sister – what's happened? Where is she?'

'The inspector will put you in the picture.'

Abby felt sick as she followed the constable through the main room to the kitchenette. When she was offered a seat she almost collapsed into it, her legs were so shaky.

A policewoman offered her tea before a burly man sat down opposite her. He appraised her in silence for a few seconds.

'My sister,' blurted out Abby, unable to stand the silence. 'Where is she?'

'I was hoping you'd know something.'

Abby felt her entire interior plummet in the way it did on a fairground ride. She rubbed her face, unable to articulate her fears.

'I'm Inspector Baxter and I need to ask you some questions about your sister.'

'But what's happened?' insisted Abby.

'She seems to have disappeared, which is a pity as we'd really like to ask her for some information she might have.'

Abby felt as though she was entering some sort of vortex. The words were swirling about her and she tried to pluck them out of the air and make sense of them, but it was all madness. Why would the police want to question Jess? Why wasn't she around? 'You've lost me,' she said, shaking her head. 'I don't understand at all.'

'How much do you know about your sister?'

'Pretty much everything, of course,' said Abby, accepting tea from the policewoman. 'She's just about my only living relative. When I finished uni we lived together till she left home. We still keep in touch.' She curled her fingers round the mug, partly for comfort and partly to stop her hands from shaking.

'So where does she work?'

'Um . . . Well, she worked for someone who had some-thing to do with night-clubs, or cabaret acts or something.' Abby felt herself colouring up. Shit, she didn't really have a clue. So much for knowing 'pretty much every-thing'.

'So you don't really know.'

'No,' she admitted reluctantly. It was embarrassing to be caught out.

'But you know she also works for the Met as a Special Constable?'

Abby slopped her tea. 'Don't be daft,' she scoffed.

'She works at my station.'

Abby put her tea down and slumped back in her chair. She felt completely at sea now. What else didn't she know about Jess? 'This *is* Jess Dryden you're talking about?'

'Yes.'

'So, if she works for you, *you* must know where she is.'

'Well, we don't. And she hasn't been to her other job for a couple of days either.'

'Her other job with the cabaret . . .'

'Her other job is working as a pole-dancer in a night-club.'

Abby was glad she was nowhere near her tea. It would have gone everywhere. A pole-dancer? Her sister! Shit a brick! No wonder she looked so groomed and glossy when they'd last seen each other.

'You didn't know about that either, did you?' said Inspector Baxter.

Dumbly Abby shook her head. Her sister seemed to be a complete stranger. How could they have grown so distant? Why didn't Jess tell her anything? What had she done to Jess that had driven such a rift between them? So what *did* she know about Jess?

'Do you come up to London to see your sister regularly?'

'No,' Abby said quietly. She didn't want to admit she'd never visited her sister in London before, always preferring Jess to make the effort to come to her.

'So, may I ask why you chose to visit her right now?'

'I . . . I'm worried about her.'

'Why?'

'Because she's not answering her mobile.'

'And that's unusual?'

Abby nodded. 'She's glued to it. I haven't been able to get hold of her for a couple of days and it's so unlike her. And . . . and I just have a feeling.'

'A feeling?'

'Yes.' A bad feeling and one that was being horribly justified.

'What does your husband do, Mrs Harris?'

Abby was taken aback by the sudden change of tack. 'He works in IT for a company near Reading.'

'You're sure about that?'

What? Not someone else she thought she knew who was suddenly a complete mystery. 'As far as I know,' she responded. Although she didn't seem to know anything any more. She gave the name of the company.

Inspector Baxter called someone over and asked them to check out the truth of Abby's statement.

'Does your husband know a man called Miles Morgan?'

'Not that I'm aware of. Why?'

'Your husband and Mr Morgan phone each other regularly.'

'Maybe he's a colleague.'

'Miles Morgan owns the night-club your sister works at.'

Abby felt any remaining colour drain from her face. 'You mean my husband knows she's a . . .' She couldn't bring herself to say the words. 'He knows what she does?'

'Probably.'

How did Gav know when she didn't? Abby now added a sense of betrayal to the range of unpleasant emotions she was suffering. 'How?'

'We don't know when your husband and Mr Morgan met, but they've been associates for some time. We think your husband might have been instrumental in Jess getting the job.'

'No! He knew and didn't tell me?' Abby felt a big ball of anger forming in her chest.

Baxter nodded.

'Look, Mr Baxter—'

'Inspector.'

'Look, *Inspector* Baxter, I haven't a clue about anything that's going on but my sister appears to be missing, I'm scared for her and you're just sitting here in her kitchen asking me a load of questions which aren't getting anyone anywhere.'

'Mrs Harris, we need to interview your sister about an investigation we are conducting, an investigation that initially she was working on. We have no reason to believe she is in any danger, but we are concerned that she's suddenly decided to go away without telling anyone, especially as we now discover that someone in her family has a direct connection to Mr Morgan, when Mr Morgan is the subject of a police enquiry.'

Baxter stared at Abby. She could see what he was thinking; she was guilty by association. What the hell had Jess and Gavin got involved with?

'Might your sister have gone abroad?'

'Jess? Unlikely, since she doesn't have a passport.' Abby stopped. Given how little she knew about her sister, this was something else she might have got wrong. 'Well, she never used to have one.'

'We'll get it checked out.'

'So just what are you alleging my family is mixed up in?'

'I'm not at liberty to tell you.'

Abby had this frightening suspicion that it was serious. 'Has this got anything to do with why she's not here?'

Baxter looked at her and steepled his fingers. 'Mrs Harris, we very much think it has. Before I tell you anything further I'd like you to answer some questions about your husband.'

How much worse could things get? And what the hell were Gavin and Jess up to? Abby felt frantic with worry. Everything seemed to be like some sort of nightmare. And what did Gavin know about it all? No wonder he'd seemed cagey and worried, if he knew about all of this mess.

*

Jess stared at the two packs of sandwiches that she had left. Should she save them or eat them? She was famished again but she had no idea when Miles might reappear. Did she dare risk running out of food? She glanced at her watch although she knew it was well after midday as the sun was now shining through the casement again. Three o'clock. So she'd lived on two rounds of sandwiches since Miles had carted her off here. She wasn't going to have to worry about putting on weight on a diet like that.

Matt had always said she shouldn't get any thinner. He'd said she was perfect as she was. Oh Matt, what had gone wrong? It had been so perfect until that point when he'd stormed out without warning. She wished she understood what it was she'd done. If only she knew, she could try to make it better. Apologise, explain, whatever it took. For that brief week while he'd virtually lived with her, it had seemed so right, so comfortable. They'd fitted into each other's lives like pegs into holes – a bit like those coloured shapes kids had to post into a box under-neath. Until the moment when someone had kicked the box and pegs over and it had all been ruined. She shouldn't think about Matt, she decided. It would just make her even more miserable.

Morosely she lay propped against the corner of the wall, her feet stretched out on the mattress, and watched as the shadow of the window slowly crawled across the floor. About six inches from the edge of the shadow was one of the discarded plastic packs from her snack. She made a bet with herself as to how long it would take for the sun to reach it. Twenty minutes, she guessed. She logged the time and shut her eyes for a moment or two.

When she opened them the sun was nearer to its target but only five minutes had passed. The boredom was numbing. She shut her eyes again and tried to remember poems but could barely get past the first line of most – and to think that once she had them by heart. She tried hymns from school assemblies. She was better on those and got through several verses of half a dozen before her memory gave up. She recited her tables all the way to twelve twelves. She opened her eyes again. The sun was almost at the plastic triangle. Bugger – twenty-five minutes. She'd lost.

She wondered if Miles would agree to let her have a book, or a newspaper. She resolved to ask him next time he appeared. The worst he could say was no. But she so needed something to occupy herself.

The sun reached the triangle. A ray bounced off an irregularity in the stiff celluloid and shone into her eyes. Jess screwed them up and shifted her head out of the way. She watched the bright silver shape creep along the wall beside her and then, like a flash of pure sunshine, she had an idea.

A couple of seconds later, she had the plastic container in her hand and was standing by the window trying to angle it so as to reflect the light back out. She'd seen movies where messages had been sent by resourceful heroines using their handbag mirrors. Well, maybe not messages but they'd attracted attention from rugged-jawed heroes. For the only time in her life, Jess wished she knew Morse code.

Alice Diamond was washing up at the kitchen sink when a flash of light in the middle distance caught her eye. And then another one followed. And another. Woman and girl she'd been washing up and this had never happened before. Kids mucking about in the woods, was her initial thought. She leaned heavily on the sink and craned her head towards the beam, to try and get a better handle on exactly where it was coming from. But she wasn't as young as she used to be and her neck didn't flex like it had when she was a nipper. But that was a sight more decades previously than she cared to think about.

With an uncomfortably cricked neck she stared at the wooded hillside that rose to the east of her cottage. There was that light again but it seemed to come out of the top of the sea of green that billowed up the steep slope. Something was catching the evening sun – but what? Then she remembered that the old house up on Pitt Hill was being done up by some city slicker, although Jed in the village said that no one had worked on the site for a few weeks now, the credit crunch and lousy property prices having done for the project for the time being. There had been a distinct undercurrent of *schadenfreude* when the locals had discussed the reason for this over a Sunday pint a while back. It wasn't that they didn't want the old house done up, but they were all wary of the future inhabitants. Incomers didn't understand country ways, and as none of the villagers would be able to afford the sort of prices that the apartments were probably going to be sold for, it was bound to be commuters who bought them. It was a constant source of grumbling that all their kids were either still living at home or having to move miles away where house prices weren't so ridiculous. So maybe, she wondered, as she glimpsed another flash, work had started again. The intermittent light continued, irritatingly, so she pulled the kitchen blind down to block it out.

When Alice had finished the washing-up she dried her hands on the towel and picked the dog's lead off the hook on the back door. Although she did it without making a sound, a second later she heard the clicking of the dog's claws as it padded across the stone flags of her hallway. The kitchen door was shouldered open by an elderly Labrador which then sat down in front of her and eyed her expectantly.

'Walkies,' said Alice and Jumbo's tail thumped on the floor. 'I think we'll go up the hill today,' she told him. 'I want to see what's going on at Marston House.'

Jumbo cocked his head on one side and waited patiently as Alice clipped his lead to his collar, then accompanied her on her slow way out of the cottage and onto the lane.

M att had not had his eye on the ball for most of the day, distracted with worry about Jess. And why did he care about her? He'd made a decision that it was all over between them – she'd betrayed him, she'd not told him the truth – and yet he couldn't get her out of his mind.

And to add to the trouble of having her haunt him, he now had a horrible and growing feeling that he'd misjudged her. Her date with Miles had not been voluntary; Baxter had told him as much – she'd been acting on orders. That still left the conversation he'd overheard in the toilets, but had he got that wrong too? He recalled a lie he'd told when he'd been in Year Ten at school. A wonderful girl called Anna-Lucia Ferenti, dark, Italian and exotic, had arrived at his comp. All the boys had lusted after her and Matt had been no exception. After a brief fumble in the alley by the science block, which resulted in no more than Matt getting his face slapped, he'd told his peers he'd gone all the way with her. His lie improved his reputation no end. It effectively wrecked hers, but Matt had got his street cred – he was the boy who'd shagged Anna-Lucia. So he'd ignored the fact that the other girls in Year Ten had shunned Anna-Lucia for months afterwards for being 'easy' and 'a cheap Italian tart'. He'd felt hideously guilty about it, but he couldn't redress the balance and tell the truth which was far too big a step for an insecure adolescent. To do that required far more courage than he could muster, so he'd felt nothing but relief when Anna-Lucia had been moved by her parents to the local convent where her reputation could start afresh. The guilt still pricked.

Had the guy in the toilets indulged in a similar exaggeration? After all, it was something blokes did. And if that was the case, it was a distinct possibility that she hadn't lied to him about going with other blokes either.

He could see Jess's face, bemused and disbelieving when he'd made the accusation. The more he thought about it, the more he was convinced it had been the real deal. She'd been genuinely stunned by his accusation. It had been the same reaction as the one the girl in the shoplifting incident had had. He'd believed in her innocence, but not Jess's. So had he made the most terrible mistake? That was a distinct possibility. And could he ever atone? Probably not.

During his shift at the station, he'd asked other police officers on the case for information but had drawn a blank. He didn't know whether they were in as much ignorance as himself or whether they were closing ranks and shutting him out. The pack mentality of shunning the weakest link, getting rid of the danger to the herd. Matt had a nasty feeling that he was definitely lion bait right now, but was he being paranoid? Baxter's questions had left him feeling deeply uneasy, and the silence he met from his colleagues wasn't helping.

The few officers who had been at Jess's flat in Shepherd's Bush knew that she was missing and that she was involved in some sort of operation being run by the Drugs Squad, but beyond that, nothing. But it seemed to Matt that the Met Police's interest in Jess was not concentrated on the fact she was missing but on the fact that her absence was buggering up an investigation. They certainly didn't appear to think she was in any danger.

All Matt could deduce was that Jess had suddenly lit out, leaving her fellow investigators in the lurch – and there was a suspicion that she had more than just a family connection with the drug dealers. Which was pissing off her superiors no end and, since he was associated with her, Baxter had transferred his anger to Matt. In fact, Baxter had told Matt that he was 'fucking lucky not to be suspended from duty'.

As soon as Matt came off the early turn he drove across London to Jess's flat where the caretaker confirmed to Matt that the police had already crawled all over it.

'Wouldn't tell me nothing,' the caretaker told him, 'but someone said she's gone missing.'

'Missing?' Well, he knew *that* but he didn't want to steal the old man's thunder by admitting it. To do so might piss the caretaker off and then he could whistle for any more confidences.

The man shrugged. 'It's what I heard. They had her sister up here and all. She looked right worried.'

'Is she still around?'

'Doubt it, they all buggered off again. Footprints all over the stairs for me to mop up. No thanks from the residents, of course,' he grumbled.

Matt left the block of flats and took himself off to the pub across the road. Morosely he ordered himself a pint of orange and lemonade and mulled over the snippets of information in his possession, which frankly amounted to diddly-squat.

He'd known about the skunk on the Windmill Estate, but Baxter's revelation about Morgan's involvement had been a bit of a bombshell – almost as big a bombshell as Jess's brother-in-law being a known associate of Morgan.

But he couldn't work out if Jess was involved with Morgan and Gavin or whether it was all just a dreadful coincidence. Maybe she wasn't a liar. Maybe she'd been straight with him all along and he'd completely misjudged her. In which case, if she wasn't a friend of Morgan's and the latter had got wind of the fact that she also worked for the Met, she might be in serious trouble.

So why couldn't Baxter see that this was a possibility and not that she'd disappeared because she was worried about getting arrested?

Matt stared out of the window as he tried to work out the conundrum that was Jess. Over the street he saw the caretaker leave Jess's block of flats. Matt watched the man walk along the road till he got to a bus stop where he looked at his watch and then expectantly along the road. When the double-decker pulled up and the caretaker climbed on, Matt swigged the remainder of his drink and almost ran across the road, pulling a bunch of keys from his pocket as he went. He'd meant to return Jess's spare set to her but he just hadn't got round to it. Which was going to come in handy now.

The flat was remarkably tidy given that it had been turned over by the Met's finest in their search for clues. There were still traces of fingerprint powder and a couple of filthy footprints on the laminate floor in the entrance hall, but other than that it looked pretty much as Matt remembered it.

He wasn't sure what he was looking for, but maybe he'd spot something out of the ordinary. Carefully and methodically he began opening cupboards and drawers. It all seemed perfectly normal – except that the dress he'd last seen her wearing wasn't hung up with the others ready to go to the cleaners. He was sure she'd been wearing silver lamé, it was one of her nicest dresses and one he'd always thought she looked fabulous in. The one thing he knew about Jess was that she was a creature of habit. Every night, when she got in, she'd hang up her dress. She could be dead on her feet but she'd sort her kit out first. There were other dresses hanging up, several, but not the silver one. He was sure that was significant; if the dress wasn't there it must mean she'd never come back from the club.

So maybe she *was* with Miles. Maybe, now she and Matt had split up she'd shacked up with him. But it seemed so unlikely. She called him 'slimy Miles', for heaven's sakes. Unless it was all an act. Maybe she was up to her neck with him. Maybe she and he were like Bonnie and Clyde. But if that was the case, why on earth would she be a Special? And given the fact she'd been a Special *before* she started to work for Miles, it didn't make sense.

Which brought him back to the grim idea that Miles had found out about her policework and didn't like it. He and Sally stopping for a friendly chat the other evening might have been all the evidence Miles Morgan had needed to want Jess out of the way. And given what he now knew about Miles, how 'out of the way' would he want her? A chill feeling of awfulness began to seep into him.

Alice Diamond stood in front of the old manor and looked up at it. The place hadn't been touched for weeks, that was obvious to anyone. Weeds had intertwined themselves though the big double security gates and had started to sprout over the piles of rubble and building supplies. The padlock was rusty, and the whole place had an air of dereliction and neglect.

Jumbo snuffled around the long grass that grew at the side of the footpath that ran along the edge of the wood at the back of the building, cocking his leg from time to time as Alice stared at the building. Now that she had satisfied her curiosity that the work hadn't started again, she wasn't that bothered about what had been flashing. She'd vaguely wondered if it might have been a window that had popped open and was banging about in the light wind, but the place looked secure enough. Whatever it was, it wasn't her problem.

Alice ambled further along the edge of the site to the brow of the hill and stood to admire the view. She could see all the way to Sussex from here, miles and miles away. And although the village wasn't far from this point it was hidden by a fold in the land. She couldn't even see her own house, tucked away in the trees and camouflaged by its ancient and mossy thatched roof. To all intents there wasn't a soul to be seen. She looked back at the house. Would she want to live in a big place like this without a sniff of another human being? The view was all very well but you wouldn't have to mind the sense of isolation. But, she supposed, it might be welcome to people who spent their days crammed into Tubes and buses up in London. Maybe isolation was exactly what they wanted.

Something made Alice shiver, despite the warm evening sun that blazed across the fields below almost directly into her face. She glanced back at the building. If Victorian Gothic was your bag then this was ideal, but she'd never had much time for the place. Spooky, she thought. Not so bad on a nice sunny day like this, but in the winter it was always downright sinister.

'Come on, Jumbo,' she called, then turned and set off back the way she came.

She didn't see the figure banging frantically on an up-stairs window, trying to attract her attention. The sound of the hammering fists was mostly blocked by the super-efficient triple glazing, and Alice's hearing wasn't sharp enough to pick up the faint sounds that did penetrate.

Alice was back on the lane that led down the hill

towards the village and civilisation when a large
Mercedes swept towards her. Alice watched it pass as she
and Jumbo pressed themselves into the hedgerow. Not
many cars came up this lane, since it didn't lead anywhere
much beyond the house. She saw the indicator light start
to flash as it neared the crest of the rise. She supposed it
was the developer, coming to check up that his place was
still safe and free from squatters. Serve him right, she
thought, if someone was living in the place. Maybe that
was what had attracted her attention, she thought. Maybe
someone was up there, living there in secret.

31

Jess sagged back against the wall, tears streaming down her face. Why hadn't that dog-walker looked up at her? What more could she have done to attract her attention? And if she couldn't be heard, despite all her efforts, how on earth was she ever going to get rescued? Despair overwhelmed Jess. Despite the sun outside she was cold, afraid and hungry. Miles hadn't visited her since the previous evening and now she was facing a third night as a captive; she hadn't had anything to eat except a couple of packets of sandwiches all day, and the very real fear that he might never come back again was gathering momentum.

What if he didn't? How long could she last? When might someone realise that she'd disappeared off the face of the planet and come looking for her? The answerless questions whirled around in her brain, feeding off her anxieties, supping on her desperation. And the little glimmer of hope she'd just experienced, that little glimmer that had been dashed away, made everything suddenly bleaker.

She looked at the sandwich packet that she still held in her hand. Even if her head told her there was no chance of attracting attention her heart said she mustn't give up. She had to keep trying. Not to would be the equivalent of turning her face to the wall and waiting for death. She stuffed the packet under the corner of the mattress. She didn't want to risk Miles removing all the packets as rubbish and losing it.

The sound of the door being unlocked made her jump out of her skin with guilt. Shit, if he'd arrived a couple of minutes earlier he'd have caught her trying to signal. Then a mix of other emotions raced through her: fear at what his presence might mean – that Miles and she were about to have the 'little chat' he'd threatened during his last visit – and relief that she hadn't been abandoned. She dashed away her tears. She didn't want him to see she'd been crying, didn't want to give the bastard the satisfaction.

'So what have you been up to?' Miles said as he strode in. No preamble, no greeting.

Jess's guilty conscience went berserk. 'W-What do you mean?' she stammered.

Miles's eyes narrowed. 'What I said – what have you been doing?'

'Sitting here. Why? Did you think I might have been watching TV, listening to the radio – or socialising and having a ball?' she added rudely, defiantly.

Miles ignored her sarcastic comment. 'I've brought you some more sandwiches.' He threw the plastic bag he was carrying onto the bed. 'I also brought you some other things I thought you might need.'

Jess grabbed the bag and rummaged in it. A toothbrush, Tampax, loo roll. Then her heart sank. If he was thinking about her needs then he wasn't planning on releasing her any time soon.

'Aren't you going to say thank you?' sneered Miles.

'For what? Kidnapping me?' She glared at him.

'If you're going to be like that . . .' He made a move towards the bag. Jess swept it up and clasped it to her.

'How long are you going to keep me here?' she asked, her voice trembling.

'Like I said before, you've caused me a lot of aggro. I've got stuff to sort out. Maybe when I've done it, then I'll let you go. *Maybe.*'

Jess didn't dare ask what the alternative was, although she thought she could guess. She swallowed.

Miles went over to the window and checked the fastening. He looked out. 'Nice view,' he commented.

'If you like that sort of thing,' she said sulkily.

'It's the countryside. What's not to like?'

'It's just trees and grass.'

'No people, no houses, you mean?'

Jess nodded.

'Precisely. No one to come snooping about.'

That's what you think, Jess thought, privately rejoicing in the fact that Miles was wrong.

'I'll come back again tomorrow sometime to check up on you. And it seems you might have told the truth. The filth have left me well alone; given me the space to tidy up my affairs. It seems no one's noticed you're not around either.' Miles shrugged carelessly. 'Which can't make you feel good – talk about being Little Miss Norma No-Mates – but it suits me just fine.'

Jess stared at him, willing herself not to cry at what he'd just said. She would not show him how much that last sentence of his had hurt her. Instead she said, as coolly as she could, 'Next time you visit, could you bring me some fruit as well as the sarnies?'

'Missing out on your five-a-day?' scoffed Miles. 'Your health is the least of your worries, I'd have thought. Okay, I'll see what I can do,' he conceded as he made for the door. He picked up the empty sandwich packets, looked at them for a moment, while Jess's heart hammered so hard in her ribcage she thought the beats would be visible from the moon, let alone the other side of a smallish room. Then when he suddenly marched back across the room towards her, Jess thought she might faint with fear. However, he didn't even look at her as he picked up the plastic carrier bag, tipped the contents out onto her bed and stuffed the rubbish into it.

'I'll see you tomorrow,' was his parting shot as he opened the door and left. The lock clicked loudly as Jess sagged weakly to her knees, the sense of relief making her want to laugh and cry simultaneously.

Abby got home and let herself in. She was surprised Gav's car wasn't parked outside but then he sometimes got held up at work or by the traffic on the M4. However, she was spoiling for a fight after Inspector Baxter's revelations about his connection with Jess's employer, and it irritated her even more that she wasn't able to have it out with him then and there.

She went into the kitchen to make herself some tea and then pottered around working out what she was going to make them for their supper. Not that Gav deserved any. He'd known that Jess was a stripper and hadn't told her. How could he, the rat? Which begged the question, just exactly what was going on between Gav and Jess? Why on earth did he kick around with a night-club owner? What the fuck had *that* got to do with his job? Unless he was a member of this club . . . But as Abby thought about this she knew she was barking up the wrong tree. Gav rarely, if ever, went out in the evening, and when he did, he wasn't out long enough for a trip to London and back plus a visit to that . . . that . . . Gah! The whole thing was mad, Abby thought as she sipped her tea and rummaged through the bottom of the fridge to see what vegetables she had. Not enough, was the short answer.

Abby finished her tea and went out into her garden to lift some potatoes, pick a couple of courgettes and gather tomatoes. They, together with some lentils and butter beans, could form the basis of a nice vegetable curry. Although she hoped Gav might choke on it as she slammed her fork into the ground and levered out the spuds.

Ten minutes later, she was back in her kitchen, chopping, slicing and dicing, a pan of oil shimmering on the gas ring, ready for the prepared veggies. She looked at her watch. It was nearly half-six. Gav was never as late as this coming home from work. She switched off the gas and went to look for her mobile. A minute later she tried another number since Gavin wasn't answering his mobile. The phone on his desk rang at the other end of the line until the office answering machine kicked in. So he'd left work; he must be stuck in traffic somewhere.

Abby switched on the local radio to listen to the drive-time road reports. It was about ten minutes before the update was broadcast and she was informed that all roads were flowing smoothly with no reported incidents. Maybe he'd had to go to the pub after work with some colleagues. Maybe his car had broken down. Maybe he would walk through the door any minute.

At nine o'clock, the forgotten chopped vegetables were becoming dry and brown on the counter in the kitchen and Abby was frantic. First her sister and now her husband had vanished. What the bloody hell was going on! She found her handbag and took out the small piece of pasteboard that Inspector Baxter had given her and then with a less than steady hand she dialled the number on it.

Matt locked up Jess's flat and returned to his car. He drummed his fingers on the steering-wheel as he wondered what to do next. Jess had to be somewhere.

She couldn't just disappear into thin air. She wasn't at her flat, she obviously wasn't with her sister, so where else might she be hiding out? With a friend from Shoq? It was certainly a possibility. But that was a dead end as far as Matt was concerned because, apart from a few Christian names, he knew nothing about Jess's co-dancers. Laura was one of the names he was aware of. Maybe, if he went to the club he might be able to talk to her. But he was loath to show his face there again. He had a dreadful feeling that it might have been his appearance a few nights previously that had triggered events. Would a reappearance make things worse? On the other side of the coin he was in plainclothes now and there was a possibility no one would recognise him. It was worth a risk.

He turned the key in the ignition and headed east towards Kensington High Street. The journey – stop-start traffic – was frustrating and it took him longer than he expected to get to his destination and even longer to find a parking space. It was gone nine when he finally walked up to the neon-lit doorway of the club. Another customer was paying his entrance fee so Matt hung back until the lobby was empty.

Casually he approached the pretty girl behind the counter. He recognised her as the one who had been working there when he and Sally had run into Jess. A badge on her chest said her name was Nadine.

'Laura working tonight?'

Nadine grinned at him. 'If you pay your entrance fee you can find out, can't you, handsome?'

Matt felt a sense of relief that she hadn't appeared to recognise him.

'What about Jess?' he tried.

A frown creased the girl's forehead but she quickly recovered her composure. 'Same answer, cheeky.'

'Come on, sweetheart,' Matt pressed. 'Jess is my favourite.' He pulled a tenner from his pocket and waved it at her. Nadine shot a glance at a CCTV camera then her hand flashed across the counter and in a second the note had disappeared.

'I haven't seen her for days,' she said quietly. 'She might have called in sick but I don't think so, because Carrie, the woman in charge of the dancers, usually tells us if someone's poorly.'

'Does Laura know anything about Jess?'

Nadine shook her head. 'She's worried about her too. She and Jess were mates, but she can't get hold of her. Jess isn't answering her mobile or anything.'

It was really worrying if she'd cut herself off from her girlfriends too.

Despondently Matt left the club and went to find the car. Jess had to be somewhere. Not at her home, not at her sister's . . . Of course. Duh! He should try the house in the woods, the one the girls had inherited. He banged the car into gear and shot off towards the motorway and the Chilterns.

An hour later he was crawling down a tiny lane, his headlights illuminating the high banks on either side, the trees overarching to form a ghostly green tunnel. Was this the right way? he asked himself. The place looked different in the dark. He knew he'd come off the M40 at the right junction and he'd remembered which way he'd turned off the slip road at the T junction, but now . . . ? The little villages all looked remarkably similar with their chocolate-box brick and flint cottages, village greens and inviting pubs, with locals standing outside in the warm night air, downing their last pints before time was called.

Matt drove on, hoping he'd spot something that would jog his memory – some landmark or other. The trouble was, he didn't even know the name of the wretched house. He came to another fork in the way and stared at the signpost: neither of the options rang a bell. Sod it, he didn't have a clue. He turned left.

And then he saw a blasted oak tree, the branches all bent and misshapen and not a leaf to be seen on the dead wood. A little bell rang. He drove on. If he remembered correctly, there should be a five-bar gate. Eureka. And then a sharp left. Yesss! And then the turning to the old house should be on the left. Ta-dah!

Matt stopped the car at the end of the drive and switched the lights off. The house, which he'd expected to be in near darkness, was ablaze with light; it streamed from every room. Outside were three large white vans. Someone seemed to be moving.

Matt watched for several minutes while a handful of unknown men shifted boxes from the house to the vans. He'd never seen a moonlight flit before but recognised this as one instantly. He wondered why the tenants were buggering off so suddenly. Usually people indulged in this sort of activity to avoid an impending visit from the bailiffs, but when Jess had told him about the house she'd never mentioned that the tenants were late payers or anything. Not that she necessarily would have done, but surely, if they had been, it was the sort of thing she would have dropped into the conversation. So why the need to skedaddle in the middle of the night? It wasn't normal behaviour for tenants.

Matt sat in the darkness and looked at the scene. The activity round the vans had come to a temporary lull. Perhaps the tenants had gone back inside to fill more boxes with their kit. As quietly as possible, Matt got out of his car and closed the door. Keeping well away from the big rectangles of light that lay on the land in front of the house, he approached the building. As long as he kept in the shadows he'd be invisible to the occupants.

Besides, with all that light inside the house, their night vision would be shot. He got close to the first of the vans and made a mental note of the registration. The logo on the number plate proclaimed that it was on hire from *First Fleet Rentals*.

A noise near the front door made Matt dodge back into the bushes. A couple of scruffy-looking youths, long hair, grubby clothes, came out carrying a heavy box between them which they shoved into the back of the van nearest the door.

'That the lot?' panted one.

'Pretty much. Just our personal stuff to go.' The other looked at his watch. 'We should be away in an hour. Miles said he'd meet us at the services north of Dunfermline.'

'Which is a fuck of a long way north.'

The rear door to the van was slammed shut and the two disappeared into the house, closing the front door behind them.

Matt crept out of the laurel bushes and tried the rear door to the van nearest him. It opened. For a second he couldn't get his head round what was inside. Plants? Pot plants? And then he realised that was *exactly* what they were.

And why Jess had been able to smell mothballs. How stupid could he be, not to have cottoned on! Naphtha was what drug growers used to cover up the smell of cannabis plants.

B axter was sound asleep when the phone by his bed rang. Groggily he fumbled for the receiver, forcing himself to wake up.

'Yeah,' he mumbled, sitting upright and turning on the bedside lamp. His wife twitched grumpily and pulled the covers over her head to block out the sudden light. He listened to the voice at the other end of the phone. With each sentence he became more alert.

'Send a car,' he barked as the caller finished his report. 'Pick me up as soon as possible and tell Thames Valley Police what the score is. Then ring the relevant police force in Scotland and get those vans picked up at the service station – but they're to wait for Miles Morgan to arrive. I want him too. Oh, and get Thames Valley to pick up Abby Harris. I want her in for questioning. And if her husband has shown up, nick him too.' He replaced the phone and climbed out of bed.

Glenys Baxter rolled over and opened a bleary eye. 'Trouble?'

'Not really. Go back to sleep.' Alastair Baxter began pulling on his uniform as Glenys snuggled back down. All right for some, thought Baxter a trifle enviously. Still, he was buoyed up by the thought that if what young Matthew Green alleged he'd seen was correct, he was about to get a lot of loose ends all tied up in one go.

Although it was no thanks to bloody Dryden! He couldn't believe he'd fallen for her act of playing the innocent and pretending not to know Morgan, while all the time her house was being used as a nursery for hundreds of cannabis plants. Baxter felt a complete fool – not a sensation he enjoyed. The only positive aspect that was going to come out of this was the result with the Windmill Estate drugs gang.

Twenty minutes later he was in a police car heading for the address phoned in by Green. The car headlights scythed through the inky black of the country roads as his driver took him from the outskirts of London to the Chilterns. Every now and again Baxter glanced at his watch. He was eager to get to Dryden and Harris's house and see what evidence was left so he could nick the lying pair as soon as possible. The Harris woman had to know something about what was going on at her house – the vans loaded with cannabis plants had been rented by her old man, for a start, the plants had been grown in the attic of her house, by people who seemed to be in the employ of Morgan, a known associate of Gavin Harris and a man who employed her sister. He couldn't believe she didn't know anything about this. And as for Dryden . . . Words almost failed him.

As the car sped westward he mulled over exactly what he could charge Dryden and her sister with. In fact, it was more a case of what he couldn't charge them with. It gave him a great deal of satisfaction to think that the scheming, underhand minx and her manipulative sister were about to get their come-uppance.

He had to give the pair credit though. They were both banging actresses. When Abby Harris had appeared at the flat in Shepherd's Bush he'd actually believed that she was panicking over her sister's whereabouts, and that she didn't know Jess was a stripper. As if. Huh. Of course, the reality was she was finding out what they knew about her. Baxter snorted in annoyance, causing his driver to glance his way.

'Keep your eyes on the road,' he ordered, his irritation at being duped by the sisters transferring itself in an instant to his subordinate.

They drove in silence to the address given by Matt Green, the Sat-Nav's clipped diction directing them the last few miles. When they arrived, there were half a dozen cars already outside the property and all the lights in the house were on full blast as various teams of specialist police took the place apart.

Baxter introduced himself to the senior police officer from Thames Valley Police present at the scene and asked to be updated on the situation.

'It wasn't just cannabis they were growing,' Inspector Middlemiss informed him. 'It looks as if there was a complete chemistry lab in the attic. Forensics are testing to see what it was they were making but my guess is they were producing E on an industrial scale too.'

Baxter whistled. 'Big operation.'

'Huge. Must have been worth hundreds of thousands to whoever was behind it.'

Behind them, a radio crackled noisily. The two men stopped and listened to the exchange between the police sergeant with the radio and the distant informant.

'That was an update from West Midlands Police,' said the sergeant. 'The three vans are still heading north on the M6.'

'Good. Let me know if there is a report of them leaving the motorway,' said Baxter. 'Looks as if our tip-off was right and they're heading for Scotland.' He thought for a moment. 'I wonder if either Morgan or the girls own any property north of the border?'

'I'll get someone onto that right away,' said Middlemiss.

Baxter stopped him from leaving. 'Is the girl we're after, Jess Dryden, in any of those vans?'

'Your bloke, Green, didn't say so. He's still here. I'll get him to come and talk to you.'

Baxter moved out of the main hall of the house and up the stairs. He was reminded of student digs he'd once occupied; everywhere he looked was mess and rubbish. There were clothes on the floors, drawers were half-open, cupboards unclosed; dirty plates and mugs littered flat surfaces and ashtrays overflowed. Whoever had been here had left in a hurry and only taken the bare minimum of their possessions. He was struck by the fact that although this house was owned by Dryden and Harris, there was no sign of them anywhere here. Not a sniff of anything female. Obviously they just provided the gaff, presumably for a share of the profits – although it was odd that Abby's address wasn't in a particularly nice area and Jess's rented flat was nothing to write home about, because even a small share in the profits would have been a considerable amount of dough. If they were earning loads from this drugs ring they were pretty discreet about how they spent it.

Baxter went back downstairs in search of a cup of black coffee. It was going to be a long night and caffeine was essential for getting through it. He'd just managed to scrounge a mug of instant when Green appeared, looking haggard and slightly unshaven; he was obviously under some strain and Baxter wondered when he'd last slept.

'You wanted me, sir? Only I'm due back on duty in a few hours and I've got to drive back into Town.'

'No, I want you here. Ring the duty sergeant and tell him I said so.' Green nodded. 'When did you last sleep?'

Matt looked at his watch. 'I got up about twenty-two hours ago.'

That explained why the man looked so shot. Still, he

was a healthy young chap and lack of sleep never killed anyone. 'Why did you decide to come over here?'

'I'm worried about Dryden, sir. And she brought me here a few weeks ago. She and her sister used to live here when they were kids but now they let the house out to tenants. I thought maybe she'd decided to bolt here because . . . Well, I think her life had gone a bit pear-shaped and this is somewhere familiar.'

'So did you see her?'

Matt shook his head. 'No, just the four blokes loading the vans.'

'Could you have missed her? It was pitch dark here, after all.'

'If she was travelling in the back of the vans when they left, I suppose I might have done, but why would she? There was plenty of space in the cabs.' Matt had a point there, thought Baxter. 'I really don't think she was here.'

'We'll find out when our friends north of the border nick them. Maybe she's travelling with Morgan.'

'You think she's involved then, do you, sir?'

'Frankly, yes. Don't you?'

'No,' said Green. 'No, I don't. I know she owns this house, but that's all. To be honest, sir, if she knew what was going on here, do you really think she'd have brought me over to show me?'

'Double bluff maybe.'

'Can I ask you something, sir?'

'Possibly.'

'Why didn't you nick Harris and Morgan earlier, if you knew what they were up to?'

'We wanted to find their cannabis farm. We were hoping one or other of them would lead us to it. If the Drugs Squad had known about this place, well, let's just say we'd have had this case wound up months back and your friend Jess would already be doing time as an accomplice.'

Jess nibbled on a stale ham sandwich which didn't taste quite right and watched the sky lighten and then the clouds scud across the sky outside her window. She didn't want a cloudy day. If it was overcast, she wouldn't be able to signal. It was imperative that the sun shone, but looking at the weather there seemed to be precious little chance of that. The thought that the one activity which gave her a spark of hope might be denied her almost made her cry.

'Get a grip,' she told herself angrily. She'd taken to talking to herself, just to hear a sound. The endless silence was awful. She'd seen an aircraft fly over the other day and she hadn't been able to hear a sound; no noise, no birdsong, nothing to break the endless monotony. So she talked out loud. 'A sign of madness,' she muttered. She put the rest of her sandwich back in the packet and got off the bed. It was too early for breakfast anyway.

She walked over to the window and stared glumly out. Once more all she could see were the waving tree-tops, dark in this half-light. There wasn't a sign of habitation; no lights, no smoke, no nothing. So where had that dog-walker and dog come from? Certainly not miles away; whoever it was hadn't looked any too steady on their pins – even with her crap eyes Jess had been able to see that. They definitely would not have been able to tramp miles, so somewhere down there was at least one house. She wished she knew where.

She coughed. A crumb had caught in her throat. It was just a tickle, but irritating all the same. She went and sipped some water. As she bent over the tap, her head went swimmy. She clutched the edge of the sink to steady herself. 'Scary,' she said. Why did she feel so shit?

Perhaps it was the lack of proper food. Maybe she'd lie down again for a minute or two. A diet of bought sandwiches and water was hardly the healthy option; no wonder she wasn't feeling on top form. She let her eyes close.

When Jess awoke it was obviously much later. There was a weak shadow cast by the cloud-obscured sun on her floor. She must have been asleep for quite a while. She still felt rough though, and weak. And she was so thirsty. She sat up and felt the room spin wildly. Ooh, not good. She leaned against the wall and waited for the sensation to stop. It was like being totally pissed but without the benefit of drink. Cold sweat broke out on her forehead and her ears began to ring. Shit, was she going to faint? She leaned forward and put her head between her knees before realising that that would only work if she was sitting on a chair and was getting her head lower than her torso. She flopped sideways back onto the mattress and waited for normality to return. Which it did slowly.

When the awful dizzy nausea stopped and she ceased to wonder if she was going to pass out, throw up or worse, crap herself, Jess rolled onto her back and decided that she really wasn't well. She'd never experienced malnourishment before so maybe this was how it manifested itself. Or maybe it was the fact that the sandwiches she was eating were way past their 'best before'. But not being well was not good in these circumstances, given that she was on her own and she had no idea when Miles might return.

She stared at the floor, at the shadow cast by the windowframe. The sky was obviously clearing; there was just a haze of cloud now. Maybe there was enough sun to catch the light on her makeshift mirror. She couldn't let an opportunity pass. She had to make the effort, no matter how shit it made her feel. Very slowly Jess sat up, then got on her hands and knees and finally to her feet. At least this time when she stood up she didn't think she was going to lose consciousness. Weakly, she tottered over to the window and leaned against the windowsill. She wished she had a chair to perch on. Standing up was so exhausting.

She began to move the plastic packet to and fro. This time she decided that even if she didn't know Morse code, if she made a pattern out of the light flashes, should anyone see them, they wouldn't think it was just some random trick of the light. At least the weather was hugely improved on what it had been up to earlier; the sun was shining quite strongly and the wind had almost dropped. Maybe it was enticing enough for someone to venture up the hill for a walk.

Alice Diamond watched the light flashing again from the house on the hill. There was definitely something going on up there, she thought as she paused in jointing a rabbit that Jim from the village had delivered to her earlier that morning. Flash, flash, flash, pause. Flash, flash, flash, pause. Very regular, very steady. This simply couldn't be a trick of the light or something catching the sunshine as it blew in the breeze. Besides, there was barely a breath of wind now.

She dusted the rabbit joints with flour and dropped them into the pan of oil sizzling on her ancient range. The smell of cooking meat wafted through her cottage, rousing Jumbo from his slumbers. He staggered into the kitchen on his elderly, arthriticky joints. Alice ignored him as he sat beside her gazing hopefully up at her with his rheumy eyes. She finished frying off the rabbit and added it to a large casserole half-full of chopped onions, carrots and potatoes, poured in a jug of stock, settled the lid on the pot and slammed it in the slow oven.

'There we go, Jumbo. That's our supper done.'

Jumbo looked disappointed. He'd been hoping that some of the rabbit might be destined for a snack there and then.

Alice returned to the window. Flash, flash, flash, pause. It was still there. Still regular, still weird. She walked over to the hook on the back of the door and picked off her pet's lead. Jumbo thumped his tail on the flagstone floor.

'Let's go up the hill again, boy. I want another look at that house. There's something rum going on there.'

Jumbo forgot about the rabbit. An extra walk seemed a far better offer.

33

In the kitchen of the old house in the Chilterns, Baxter sat on a chair, surrounded by hustle and bustle as policemen came and went, wrote reports, made hot drinks and organised carefully labelled evidence bags. He wondered about returning to his own police station but this was now the centre of the investigation and he wanted to be there when news that the Scottish police had apprehended the vans and their drivers came through.

He'd been told that Abigail Harris was now at Reading police station but that there was no sign of her husband and she was still protesting that she had no idea about either his whereabouts of that of her sister. Yeah, right. As soon as they got the rest of the gang the truth would come out, he was sure of that. Baxter looked at his watch again. It shouldn't be long now.

Right on cue, his mobile rang.

'The vans have been stopped, sir,' said the voice of one of his subordinates. 'Just heard it from the Fife Constabulary.'

'Good. And Morgan?'

There was a pause. 'He got away.'

Bugger. 'Presumably they're after him.'

'Oh yes, sir. They expect to apprehend him any time now.'

'Good.' That would have to do, he supposed. 'Get transport organised to bring the vans and their occupants down here for questioning as soon as possible. Was there a Miss Dryden amongst the passengers?'

'No, sir. Just four men. Apparently though, one is a relation of Miss Dryden's – her brother-in-law.'

No surprise there then, but what did surprise Baxter was the absence of Jess. He wondered where she'd got to. Presumably she was still in the country as it had been confirmed that she didn't possess a passport. Or, possibly it might be more correct to assume that she didn't possess a *genuine* passport. 'Let me know what time to expect the arrival of the detainees.'

'Very good, sir.'

'Goodbye.'

The connection was severed. It wasn't good news about Morgan but it was presumably only a matter of time before the Fife police nicked him too. That just left Dryden. But the net was closing, he thought with satisfaction.

Jess slumped against the windowframe as she flickered the plastic packet to and fro. She tried to focus her thoughts on the unseen house that she knew must be situated somewhere in the trees which spread in an unbroken green, undulating carpet that fell away down the hillside. That old person lived down there, Jess just knew it. Them and their fat Labrador. *Look at the light, look at the light*, she implored the stranger in an attempt at thought transference. But the area of grassland that stood between the house and the woods remained empty of any visible living creature.

She returned to sending telepathic thoughts to the old person but her arm was aching and her legs were starting to feel wobbly. She made a few more flashes with her old sandwich wrapper and then returned to her bed for a rest. Who was she kidding, it was useless. Desultorily, Jess nibbled on the last piece of sandwich – God, it tasted rank – but it didn't seem to give her any strength and it also did nothing to allay her pangs of hunger.

When, she wondered, was Miles going to appear with more food for her? It had been a day and a half now. Water alone wasn't going to keep her going for much longer and no one knew where she was. If something had happened to Miles, she was doomed. Which was a scary and sobering thought and one which drove her to her feet again and back to the window.

Shit! The dog-walker had come back with their doddery dog but they were walking away. Jess had missed them. Frantically she hammered on the window with one hand and tried to signal using the other but the old buffer plodded steadily on, along the path that skirted the edge of what had been the garden. Panic, frustration, impotence and sheer desperation swirled around in Jess making her feel even iller than before. In fact, she suddenly began to feel really bad. She leaned heavily on the windowsill as her stomach churned and her head whirled. A muck sweat broke out all over her body but she wasn't hot – far from it, she felt shivery and really weird. She shut her eyes and waited for the awful sensations to ease. Maybe, she thought, eating that last bit of sandwich had been a really unwise move.

When she next looked out of the window the old person had stopped and was turning around. Jess could just make out the fact that the person was wearing a skirt. It was a woman. Jess willed her with every fibre to look at her. The dog was snuffling in the bushes yards behind. Through the double glazing Jess could see her call to it but the dog was far too interested in whatever had caught its attention to respond. The woman called again and shook the lead in irritation and impatience. Jess became even more manic and frantic, yelling and shouting even though she was fairly sure that no sound would penetrate the barrier the triple glazing presented.

'Look up here!' she screamed. 'Look at me!' Her shouts brought on another series of stomach cramps and nausea but she found the strength from somewhere to keep on waving and banging on the windows and directed every ounce of her will into a beam of thought to get the lady to look upwards.

She did. Her eyes met Jess's. She dropped the lead and Jess could see her hand fly to her face.

'Help!' screamed Jess. 'Help me!'

The woman stood transfixed, staring at her as if Jess was something out of a horror movie, someone to be afraid of, not a young woman in desperate need of help.

The fat old dog ambled over to her and the woman picked up the lead and clipped it on. And then she turned and, as fast as she was able, she made off.

To get away?

To get help?

Jess collapsed on her bed. Suddenly she began to retch but with so little in her stomach, nothing came up. She could feel her muscles cramping with the effort and her ribs aching more than ever. She lay back, sweating, sore and feeling dreadful.

Was help going to come, or was the old woman so frightened she was going to pretend it was just something her imagination had cooked up? Jess knew that if nothing happened before sunset then she might as well abandon all hope.

Tears of desperation and fear rolled down her cheeks. She curled up, turned her face to the wall and tried not to think about what might come out of the encounter. What if it came to nothing? And then she began to feel even worse.

*

Baxter's eyes slowly closed as he and his driver sped along the M40 towards London in their unmarked car. He'd been up half the night and was shattered, and he needed some rest before he began questioning the four suspects who were also heading for the capital down a different motorway. Just forty winks now and he'd feel a lot fresher.

His mobile rang. Wearily he opened his eyes and pulled his phone from his jacket pocket. 'Yes?' he said.

'Sir, this is Constable Dixon, from the Fife Constabulary. I'm accompanying Mr Gavin Harris.'

'And?' What did the man want, a medal?

'He's very agitated. He says he's worried about his sister-in-law, a Miss Jess Dryden.'

Baxter was wide-awake. He sat up straighter in his seat. 'What about her?'

'He thinks her life might be in danger.'

'Why?'

'Apparently she's being detained against her will by Miles Morgan.'

'Where?'

'That's the problem, he doesn't know.'

'Hasn't he any idea? Any idea at all?'

There was a brief pause. 'He says no.'

'Okay. Let me know if he comes up with anything that might be of use.'

Baxter severed the call then after a moment or two's thought he tapped in some numbers. As soon as the phone was answered at the other end he gave orders for search warrants to be obtained for the club, Morgan's flat and Harris's house. 'And find out everything you can about Morgan,' he concluded. '*Everything.*'

He relaxed back in his seat. If Morgan was holding Jess against her will, maybe she wasn't the scheming little cow he had her down as, after all. Maybe she was another victim of this gang – just as much as the poor bloody addicts on the Windmill Estate,

Alice felt quite shaky when she got back to her cottage, and even though she was hot and out of breath she didn't make herself a cup of tea, which was what she really wanted, but went straight to the phone. Feeling extremely nervous, she lifted the receiver and dialled 999 carefully.

'Emergency, which service?' answered a calm female voice.

'I don't rightly know,' said Alice.

'Can you tell me the nature of the emergency?'

'I don't rightly know that either.'

'Can I ask why you are ringing this number then?'

'There's a woman trapped in a house.'

'And is she in any immediate danger?'

'I don't know, but she was calling for help.'

'Can I have the address of the property?'

Alice gave it to her.

'And the postcode?'

'I dunno. But it's only about half a mile from my house.' She told the operator what her code was.

'And you're sure she's trapped.'

Alice explained about the state of the property. 'It's been locked up for weeks, by the looks of things. And the girl looked to be in a right state.'

'Thank you,' said the operator. 'I'll get someone to look into it.' Then she took Alice's details before ending the call.

'I hope I've done the right thing,' she said to Jumbo, who was wondering where his post-afternoon-walk supper was. She pushed the kettle across the range and onto the hot plate. She could have that cuppa now and maybe a bit of supper.

Alice was finishing off her helping of rabbit casserole and Jumbo was chasing a bowl of gravy and vegetables around the kitchen floor, trying to get the last elusive morsels out of the corners of his plate when she heard the two-tones.

'Hear that, Jumbo? They've come to rescue that poor maid.' Alice wasn't a nosy soul, nor was she a busybody, but she felt that she had a personal interest in this event so she took down Jumbo's lead and headed for the door. Jumbo was surprised at the offer of yet another walk and was torn between the delicious flavours still lingering in his bowl and going out. After a moment's hesitation he padded across the kitchen to Alice.

The pair ambled up the lane towards the footpath that led to the back of the house. The siren had ceased its scream through the sultry evening air although Alice could hear the sound of men shouting commands at each other and the grumble of a large engine left idling. By the time she got to the back of the house she picked up the sound of another siren approaching. As she rounded the corner of the big house she saw an ambulance screech to a halt on the weed-ridden gravel. The security fencing that surrounded the property had been breached and there was a fire engine, a police car already in attendance and all manner of men in uniform. One of them was directing the ambulance crew into the house.

Feeling bold, Alice made her way over to one of the policemen.

'Is she all right?' she asked.

'Sorry, madam, I can't tell you. The medics are with her now. And I suggest you move along. There's nothing to see.'

'But I'm the one who called for help,' Alice insisted.

'Oh, that's different. Can I ask how you found her?'

'I saw her at the window. She looked real desperate. Frightened, like.'

'She's a poorly lady. But we'll take care of her.'

Alice hung around with the tacit agreement from the kindly policeman until the paramedics reappeared carrying a stretcher between them. She could see the thin figure of the girl under a pale blue blanket, a mask strapped to her face.

'Is she going to be all right?' she asked. 'I dialled 999,' she added, having learned this was the key to information.

'She's pretty sick but she should be fine physically in a day or so.'

'Who would lock a poor wee mite up like that? It's criminal.'

'It certainly is,' replied the ambulanceman as he and the other paramedic loaded the stretcher into the van. 'I should think the police will want to take a statement from you in due course.'

Half an hour later, Alice was back in her own place giving a statement over a cup of tea to a couple of policemen whose youth worried her.

'And you said you saw a man here yesterday?' one asked.

Alice nodded.

'Can you describe him?'

'I only caught a glimpse of him. He was driving a shiny black car.'

'Would you know the make or model?'

'It was a Merc. My late husband always wanted one, but we never got better than a Ford Cortina. And before you ask me, I haven't a clue what the registration was.' Alice had watched enough episodes of *Midsomer Murders* to be aware that the police always wanted to know that.

'If we showed you a picture of the driver, would you recognise him?'

'Don't rightly know. Maybe.'

One of the policemen laboriously wrote out Alice's statement, got her to check and sign it and then they left her in peace.

'Well, that was a bit of excitement, weren't it, Jumbo?' But Jumbo, shattered from his second unexpected walk, was out for the count on the rug in front of the range.

It took Jess a while to orientate herself. She certainly wasn't in that awful flat. After she had exchanged that look with the old woman walking her dog she'd felt so dizzy and weak from the exertion of standing by the window that she'd returned to her bed where she'd been hideously sick until finally, wrung out and exhausted, sleep had overwhelmed her. A commotion had woven its way into her dreams – restless, troubled dreams – and she'd some vague half-waking, half-sleeping recollection of men bending over her and then another of being carried away from the skanky mattress. And now she appeared to be in a proper bed with clean white sheets. But where?

She shifted her gaze from the unexpected bedding to look further afield, and saw there was another similar bed opposite, but to either side of her were drab, patterned curtains. What the . . . And there was noise and bustle. She was no longer alone, but where on earth was she? She shut her eyes again while she tried to make sense of things. When she reopened them she could see someone in a nurse's uniform. Hospital? Except that possibility raised more questions than it answered. Although it was too hard to try to work out any answers at the moment.

'Hey,' said a voice she recognised. 'Welcome back.'

Jess turned her head towards the sound. It was then

she noticed not only her sister sitting patiently beside her bed but also the drip in her arm.

'Abby,' she tried to say, but her voice came out a croak.

'You had us worried. No one knew where you were.'

Jess tried to smile at her but she was so thirsty her mouth seemed gummed shut with her lips stuck fast to her teeth.

'Water,' she managed to say.

Abby found a cup with a drinking spout and helped her sister to drink. Jess drained it.

'Better?'

Jess smiled gratefully and nodded.

'How are you feeling?' asked Abby.

'Shit.'

'Not surprising considering what you've been through, to say nothing of having food poisoning on top of everything else.'

Jess sighed. She'd known at the time she oughtn't to have had that last ham sandwich. Lucky for her she'd made contact with the old dog-walker when she had. She didn't like to think what might have happened to her if she'd been left there much longer. 'So where am I now?'

'Hospital – the Royal Surrey in Guildford, to be precise. And as soon as they've got you sorted out the police want to have a word with you,' said Abby.

Jess nodded again. 'About Miles?'

'Miles, the club, your abduction and the fact that Gavin and Miles had a full-on drugs factory set up in our house.'

'What?!' Jess lay against the pillows feeling shell-shocked. Bloody hell. But then she could feel all sorts of things clicking into place in her brain, starting with the real reason why Gavin had been so against her moving into the place when she'd been broke, the job at Shoq, Miles's interest in her, the fact he'd known stuff about

Abby . . . She shut her eyes as she considered how she'd been manipulated, first by Gavin and Miles and then by the police. She lay still for some minutes, trying to come to terms with everything. Eventually she opened her eyes again. Abby was still there.

'The police . . . have they had a word with you?'

'Several. In fact, they got pretty heavy. They refused to believe that Miles's and Gavin's connection was a big surprise to me, or that I knew nothing about what was going on. I think they began to believe me when it became obvious that I'd been kept so much in the dark I didn't even know what my own sister did for a living. It was pretty grim, I can tell you.'

'I'm sorry,' said Jess feeling suddenly tearful. 'It's all my fault.'

Abby leaned forward and gave her little sister a big hug. 'Don't you take the blame for this. It's certainly not your fault. If anything, it's mine, I'm the one who brought Gavin into our lives.'

'But you didn't know what a git he was.'

'But you sussed it and I didn't believe you. If only I'd taken more of an interest in Gran's house. If only I hadn't let Gav run it for us.' Abby sighed. 'No wonder he was always so cagey about the tenants and kept dissuading us from visiting the place.'

'Except that time recently.' Jess thought back to their visit to the house and the texts she'd heard ping back and forth. 'But I think Gav made sure there was nothing for us to see before we got there.'

'Well, he would, wouldn't he. So we just saw our house and presumably everything else was up in the attic.'

'Behind the locked door.'

Abby nodded. 'Which wasn't there to safeguard Gran's last bits of furniture.'

'How could we have been so blind?' Jess thought back to the other clues; the fact that the house had been rewired without their knowledge, presumably to support the lights the plants needed, the fact that Gav had suggested she should work at Shoq, that Miles had known Abby was vegetarian, that Gavin and Miles were both so keen that she and Abby should keep renting the house out for years longer. She snorted. 'God, I'm stupid as well as blind.'

'Miles and Gav have been as thick as thieves since uni apparently,' said Abby gloomily. 'The police think that as soon as Gav found out about our house, he and Miles had it marked as a nice safe place to set up their drugs factory. I mean,' and here she gave a hollow laugh, 'owned by a retired Oxford academic and his quiet wife and then inherited by their two granddaughters – we were hardly the types that anyone local would suspect of being involved in a multi-million-pound criminal operation. So he made a play for me, pretended he loved me, when all along it was the house he wanted.' Abby's eyes filled with tears that spilled down her face.

'Oh Abby, you poor thing. You must feel so hurt.'

'And foolish.' Abby choked back a sob. 'I thought he really loved me. I thought he cared about all the things I cared about, and after we were married, when . . . when he changed, I thought it was because . . . because . . .' the sobs were coming thick and fast now, 'because he had responsibilities and couldn't do the campaigning. But he never really cared, he just pretended he did so I'd fall for him.'

Jess reached out and held her sister's hand. 'He never deserved you. I never understood his attraction for you.'

'Because he was edgy, because he seemed so glamorous, because he always had money.'

'Drug money?' asked Jess gently.

'Probably, but I didn't know it then. I was just so desperate for someone to look after me for a change and he seemed to care about everything I did. Also, I was terrified that I'd wind up in Gran's house, mouldering away, and marrying Gav seemed a way out. And I was just . . . flattered, I suppose.'

'Flattery is very seductive,' said Jess, thinking about all the boring blokes she'd flattered shamelessly at Shoq; the fat businessmen and the self-obsessed celebrities she'd spent time with, telling them how wonderful they were to get them to drop a couple of hundred quid for a private dance. Jess knew all about the power of flattery.

Abby's sobs subsided. She took a tissue from the box by the bed and blew her nose. 'I hope the police throw away the key when they lock him up,' she said bitterly.

'Definitely. And the one to Miles's cell too.'

'And talking of Miles – why did you never tell me you were a lap-dancer?'

'Pole-dancer.'

'Lap, pole, what's the difference? Nor that you're a copper.'

Abby was back to being the superior older sister, thought Jess. But in a way she was pleased. Abby being vulnerable and tearful was more upsetting than her being judgemental and bossy. Jess didn't have the energy to go into the details about her secret life. 'I didn't think you'd approve,' was all she said.

'Dead right. And Gran would have had a fit if she'd known about the dancing.'

'Well, Gran didn't. And I needed the money.'

Just then, a man in a suit approached the bed. Jess's heart sank. 'Inspector Baxter,' she said, feeling suddenly even more overwhelmingly tired. Out of the corner of her eye, she could see Abby glowering at him; the fact that she'd discovered that her own sister was employed by the police hadn't endeared her to the boys in blue any.

'Jess, how are you feeling?' asked Baxter.

'Too ill to talk to you,' interjected Abby before Jess could say a word. Abby being bossy had its advantages, thought Jess gratefully.

'Jess?'

'Tired,' she admitted. 'Wiped out.'

'I just need you to confirm a couple of details. Then I'll get out of your hair because you've got another visitor waiting to see you.'

Jess sighed. Knowing her luck it would be someone like Dodds or McCausland. Hadn't she done enough for them? Shit, it was thanks to them she was in hospital. 'Fire away,' she said, with as much good grace as she could muster – which wasn't a lot.

'I just need you to confirm that it was Miles Morgan who abducted you and who held you against your will.'

Jess nodded. 'Yes.'

'Did he have any accomplices?'

'Tom the bouncer from Shoq,' she said. 'And I suspect Carrie knew something was up. I don't know how involved she was with Miles.'

'You might like to know that because of you they decided to move their operation to a place in Scotland,' Baxter informed her. 'We caught most of the gang, including your brother-in-law, at a service station in Fife. We then raided Shoq a few hours ago.'

'So you've arrested Miles,' said Jess hopefully.

'We've got Tom and Carrie. Miles seems to have done a runner.'

'Oh.'

'I've no doubt we'll get him in due course.'

Jess yawned. She felt shattered again.

'I'll leave you in peace,' said Baxter. 'We can do

statements later. You're a lucky lady. If it hadn't been for a tip-off about a woman trapped in a house, you might still be there. A bit of luck really.'

'You mean that without *luck* you flat-foots would still be looking for my sister,' said Abby angrily. Her earlier wobble was obviously now over.

'I wouldn't put it as strongly as that,' said Baxter.

Abby glowered again. She patently didn't agree.

'We were investigating all of Morgan's business interests, so we'd have found it. And Jess,' he added.

'Eventually,' muttered Abby.

'Sooner rather than later,' countered Baxter.

Abby wasn't going to give way. 'As I said, she'd still be there. In fact, considering how poorly she was when Surrey Police got the tip-off, she might have been dead before you lot pitched up.'

'Well, she isn't,' said a voice from the other side of the patterned curtain.

Jess recognised the voice with a shock. Her heart flick-flacked. My God, Matt. Then she remembered the awfulness of their parting; the appalling row, the accusations. And her spirits sank and she felt as if the life was being drained out of her. She couldn't go through that again. She didn't have the energy. She turned her head away from Matt.

'Miss Dryden is tired,' said an officious nurse, who bustled up, chart in hand. She plucked an electronic thermometer from a holder above the bed. 'That's quite enough visitors for the present.' She brandished the instrument at Jess and inserted it in her ear. After several seconds the thermometer bleeped and the nurse wrote the reading down. When Jess turned her head back her three visitors were being shooed out of the ward. Gratefully she shut her eyes.

She was awoken to have various pills doled out to her

which she washed down with a glass of water. After she'd taken them she realised she was feeling quite remarkably better. It was amazing what care, water and a few antibiotics could do. However, feeling better and being well enough to get up were two different things, she discovered, and apart from anything else, she only had her hospital pyjamas to wear. She attracted the attention of a passing nurse and asked if there was any chance of being allowed to shower and wash her hair.

'That's always a good sign, when our patients want to spruce themselves up a bit. I'll ask the Sister but I'm sure there won't be a problem.'

Half an hour later Jess was free of her intravenous drip and was luxuriating under a jet of deliciously warm water. She wasn't deemed well enough to stand up in the shower so she was having to sit on a drop-down plastic seat but Jess didn't care as she lathered shampoo into her hair and got rid of the grease and grime of a week.

'Are you all right in there?' The nurse checked through the closed door.

'Just fantastic,' Jess called back.

'There's a hair-drier on the counter out here for you when you've done.'

Jess rinsed all the soap out of her hair and revelled in the sensation of being truly clean for the first time in days. Then she wrapped her hair up in a towel, dried her body on another one and climbed back into her pyjamas. She looked at herself in a mirror and was quite shocked at how scraggy she was. A few packs of sandwiches over five days of captivity probably wasn't an ideal diet. And add food poisoning to the malnutrition and you had a fairly dodgy combo. But she reckoned it would be quite pleasant putting the weight back on again. Bacon butties! Bring them on!

She towelled her hair vigorously and then switched on

the dryer. After a few minutes her natural curls were restored to a bounce and shine that she knew had been lacking for days. Feeling refreshed and much better she left the bathroom area of the ward and returned to her bed.

A bunch of roses lay on her locker.

Jess sat down on her bed and automatically scanned the stems for an envelope containing the name of the sender. There it was. A little white square tucked in amongst the dark green glossy leaves.

Sorry, said the card. That was it. No name, no reason for the apology. Nothing.

So . . . Sorry from Miles for kidnapping her? Sorry from Abby for inflicting Gavin on her? Sorry from Matt for thinking she'd lied to him? Sorry from the Met for getting her into this mess? No, she could dismiss that idea right away. The Met say sorry? Unlikely.

She held the bunch of roses and continued to wonder exactly who might have sent them, and apart from Abby, she decided she didn't really care. Seeing Abby by her bed when she woke up had made her realise that she did love her sister. Oh, she could still be difficult and prickly, but there was a whole lot of truth in the old cliché about blood being thicker than water. They might have wildly differing opinions on the subject of food, farming and what was important in life but, when the chips were down, Jess knew that they would always be there for one another.

Actually, that was where she wanted to be right now – with Abby. Hospital might be the place the medical profession would recommend, but what Jess wanted was her sister, a bowl of veg soup, to be snuggled up on a sofa watching something mindless on the box, and to feel safe. Surely if she was well enough to take a shower, she was well enough for Abby to take her home.

She made her way through the ward to the nurses' station at the end.

'Is it possible for someone to get hold of my sister?' she asked with her sweetest smile.

'I expect so. But can we help?'

'I don't think so. I really need to talk to my sis. If you remember, I was brought in here with nothing but the clothes on my back – and I don't even know where they are now. I haven't even got the price of a cup of tea on me.'

'No,' said the nurse. 'Of course. I'll get your sister for you. Have a seat while I ring her.'

Jess, despite her bravado and her decision to ship out, sank gratefully onto the saggy seat beside the desk and watched the nurse look up the number and then dial Abby's mobile.

'Hang on a sec,' she said as she passed the phone to Jess.

Jess took the receiver and gave the nurse a pointed stare. She wanted a bit of privacy for the call. The nurse moved away and began shuffling some papers in a filing cabinet.

'Abby, it's me. Are you staying in Guildford?'

'Hi, sis. Yes, I'm in a B and B around the corner from the hospital.'

'Good. Can you do me a big favour?'

'It depends what it is.'

'Can you buy me some clothes: pants, a bra, maybe a pair of jeans and a top – size eight? I'll pay you back once I manage to get reunited with my handbag.'

'I can do that.'

'And bring them to the hospital this evening?'

'Sure.'

'See you at visiting time.'

'Okay, sis. See you then.'

Jess replaced the receiver. 'Thanks,' she called to the nurse. 'By the way, did you see who sent me the flowers?'

'A young man. I think he's the one who visited you this morning.'

Matt.

35

Jess returned to her bed and grabbed her roses, then she pushed them, heads first, into the bin by her locker. Matt could shove his roses. And his apology. She still felt completely and utterly betrayed by him, and she hurt more than she could ever have imagined. He hadn't believed her, he didn't trust her, he didn't love her and she never wanted to see him again. She didn't ask herself why a man who apparently felt like that about her would want to send flowers; she wasn't going to waste the brain cells thinking about it.

But in the previous days she'd thought about him a very great deal: she'd imagined him riding to her rescue like some latterday St George; she'd imagined him combing the countryside for a trace of her; having sleepless nights wracked with worry – and then she'd remember how they'd parted, the hideous final scene just before he stormed out and slammed the door. And then she'd felt so lost and bereft because even though there was no logical reason for him to be her saviour, her subconscious still hoped that he might be.

Lying on the less than clean mattress she'd known that whatever had been between them – and it had seemed so wonderful at the time – was all in the past, and she had forced herself to face up to the fact that her romantic dreams were dust at her feet. She recalled the words he'd used, the lack of trust he'd shown, and as she thought about it, it just seemed to demonstrate that that was what he'd always thought about her. He'd been prepared to turn a blind eye to her job in exchange for a place to sleep and a lot of sex, until something had convinced him he'd made a catastrophic error of judgement. How could he? How could he choose to believe some random office gossip rather than the word of a girl he'd professed to really care about?

So now she lay on her hospital bed, propped up against the pillows, and listened to the radio through her headphones so her memories wouldn't betray her and thwart her determination to eradicate him from her life. But somehow, whatever music came on the radio there seemed to be something in it that reminded her of him, and before the afternoon tea came around tears were sliding down her face.

She was still feeling wretched and empty when Abby arrived in the early hours of the evening.

'Here's the stuff you wanted,' said Abby, plonking a big carrier bag on the bed, 'although I can't see why on earth you're in such a hurry. They won't be letting you out for a couple of days yet.'

'They will.'

'What?'

'I want out of here. I'm going to discharge myself and they can't stop me.'

'Don't be more stupid than you can help, Jess,' said Abby.

But Jess had got out of her bed and was busy pulling the curtains round her cubicle. 'I'm not being stupid,' she said, hauling off her pyjamas. 'I've made my mind up.'

'But you can't leave here. Where will you go? How will you get there?'

Jess, stark naked, rummaged in the bag for underwear.

She found a pair of knickers and pulled them on. 'We,' she said firmly, 'are going back to your place, in a taxi.' She pulled a new bra out of the bag and began to put that on too.

'But my room at the B and B is only a single.'

'Not there. Your place. Your home.'

Abby was silent for a second or two as she took this on board. 'In a taxi?'

Jess nodded. 'And you'll have to pay. I'll transfer some money from my bank to yours to pay you back when I get to a computer. You may have noticed that I haven't anything in the world at the moment apart from what you've just brought me. Until I get hold of my bag, which I suppose is still at the night-club or with the police, I've no cash, cards or keys.' She sat on the bed and pulled on a pair of jeans, then stood up and zipped them up. The waistband gaped. 'Are these a size eight?' she asked. Abby nodded. 'Blimey, I have lost weight.'

'Which is why you should stay here.'

'Why? Won't you feed me if I come back with you?'

'No. I mean yes, of course I will.'

'So?' Jess heaved a deep sigh, then went on: 'Look, I've had a rotten time but I want creature comforts, not nursing. I've been scared shitless and I now want to be somewhere where I feel safe. I want my family – and I'm afraid, Abby, that as there isn't anyone else, you're it.'

'But don't you need counselling or something?'

Jess rolled her eyes. 'Maybe, but I'm prepared to take a risk. I suspect that time, some nice food, a glass or two of wine and a few decent nights' sleep will do me a power of good. And if they don't – well, I can try something else. Maybe even counselling – eventually.'

Abby didn't look convinced.

Jess finished dressing, shoved the tags and labels from

her new clothes in the bin on top of the roses and pulled back the curtains to the cubicle.

'Let's go,' she said.

Abby was staring at the roses. 'Surplus to requirements?'

'Correct,' replied Jess shortly.

'You didn't think someone else on the ward might want them?'

'If they knew where they'd come from they wouldn't.'

When Jess walked to the nurses' station and announced her plans to discharge herself, naturally the staff were against it. Jess needed another twenty-four hours in hospital to get over what she'd been through, they said, and they did their best to try to convince her to stay. However, Jess was determined and after several minutes of fairly intense discussion the nurses relented, produced the relevant forms for signature and Jess was on her way.

'We'll have to go back to my room to get my case,' said Abby as they left the hospital, but Jess didn't appear to be listening. She was staring at a figure emerging from a cab about ten yards ahead of them.

'I'll grab that cab,' said Abby, misinterpreting Jess's interest. But her sister clutched her arm, held her fast, hissed, 'Shush!' with some vehemence into her ear and then yanked her behind the car park ticket-vending machine.

'What the f . . . ?' said Abby.

'Shush.'

Abby stared at her sister as if she'd taken leave of her senses.

'That's Matt,' whispered Jess.

'And?'

'He visited me this morning. You were there.'

'Oh,' said Abby vaguely. 'The one who came with that inspector chappie.'

'The very same.'

'So don't you want to see him?'

Considering Abby had exhorted her not to be more stupid than she could help some thirty minutes earlier, Jess thought that Abby was setting a pretty fine example of exactly how to do just that. 'Er, no.'

'Why?'

'I'll tell you later. Long story.'

It was nearly ten when Abby let them both into her little terraced house.

'I can't believe the extravagance,' she grumbled, putting her credit card and her keys back in her bag.

'I said I'll pay you back just as soon as I can get on the net and access my bank account.'

'But seventy pounds!'

'You'll get it all back, with interest. And I'll pay your B and B bill and any other expenses.' Jess went into the living room and flopped into a chair. 'But right now I'm feeling really beat, so let's not argue.' She smiled at her sister.

'Actually, you don't look fantastic. You shouldn't have discharged yourself,' Abby fretted.

'I'll be fine. Nothing a nice cup of tea won't put right.'

'Sit there and I'll make you one. Don't want you passing out on me. But when I come back, I want you to tell me exactly what's been going on in your life recently. All about being a policewoman and all about the dancing. Deal?'

'Deal.'

They had given up on tea and were onto wine by the time Jess finished recounting what she'd been up to, her stint with the police, the dancing and her involvement with the Drugs Squad which left Abby wide-eyed and stunned. Then it was Abby's turn to supply the details she'd been told about Gavin and Miles and their involvement with each other. Putting the various pieces together, the sisters managed to make quite a lot of sense of the whole affair.

'I can't believe you didn't know what Gav was doing.' Jess scratched her head in disbelief.

'I trusted him, Jess.'

'I suppose you did. You never noticed that he had lots of dosh. I mean, if this organisation was as big as I was led to believe, they must have been minting it.'

'If he did have loads of cash it never came this way.'

'What, none of it?'

'None.'

'Like the rent money,' said Jess gloomily. 'And as it was involved in the whole drugs ring thing, I expect we can kiss goodbye to it. We should have had thousands put away in our name.' She sighed. 'Oh well, no use bitching about it. Back to the drawing board, I suppose.'

'We could just flog the place. Get rid of it, unmodernised.'

'Yeah. Miles and Gav have sort of spoiled it for us now, haven't they?'

'I feel like that. And I need to think about cash now. I've got no money coming in and I want to divorce Gav. Obviously I'll have to get a job and sack the voluntary stuff because the mortgage on this place won't pay itself.'

Jess felt sorry for her big sister. Abby had always been so sure she was right, always so sensible, and now it had all gone so terribly wrong.

'I can help you out for a bit,' said Jess.

'But you're out of work too, I should imagine. I can't see that club carrying on now the boss is in jail.'

'I wouldn't want to work there anyway. But I've got savings. And I don't think I'm going to have the police crawling all over my bank accounts and freezing my assets. My money is all legit.'

Abby snorted. 'Legit? From stripping?'

'Let's not argue about my choice of career, hey?'

Abby sighed. 'You're right. Sorry.'

Blimey, thought Jess. An apology, from Abby. A wave of tiredness engulfed her and she yawned. 'I think, if you don't mind, I'm going to hit the hay. We can talk some more in the morning.'

Abby yawned in sympathy and agreed. They abandoned their mugs and glasses in the sitting room and both went upstairs. Jess remembered the last time she'd been to bed in this house, when she and Abby had fought over their gran's house, and how poisonous the atmosphere had been that time.

'Night, sis,' she said, leaning over to Abby and giving her a peck on the cheek.

'Night, Jess,' said Abby, as she responded with a hug.

As Jess went into her room she was thankful that at least something good had come from this dreadful mess.

'How did you sleep last night?' asked Abby a week later as Jess appeared in her kitchen. 'Better?'

Jess nodded. 'I only woke a couple of times, which is an improvement on the last few nights, and I didn't feel as panicky as I did before.'

'That sounds encouraging.'

Jess decided not to mention the nightmares that still plagued her. Although physically she was fine, mentally the scars were still healing. If Abby got wind that things were still rocky at night she'd insist on carting her off to one of her mates for some sort of therapy. Jess thought she'd rather cope with the nightmares than have crystals waved in her face or have to sit in a circle, hold hands and chant 'ohmmm'.

Abby moved around the tiny kitchen getting stuff out of cupboards, filling the kettle and preparing breakfast.

'I've got to go out again today,' she said as she dumped stuff on the table in the corner. 'Will you be all right on your own?'

'I was yesterday.'

Abby stopped and looked at Jess as if checking for some criticism.

'I was *fine* yesterday,' Jess emphasised. 'Honest. I know I was a prisoner for just a matter of days but I'm still finding it weird to be free. God knows how people like hostages manage when they've been banged up for months. I really like just being able to go into the garden or switch on a radio, and I enjoy the peace now that silence isn't scary. Does that make sense?'

'Yeah, sort of. I suppose you have to have been through it to really understand where you're coming from.' Abby continued putting the breakfast things out.

The kettle clicked off having come to the boil and Jess made the tea. Then they both sat at the table and tucked into their tea and muesli.

'So have you any plans for today?' asked Abby.

'Not really. But there's something I've got to do tomorrow.' Jess looked up at Abby to gauge her reaction.

'Oh yes. Something nice?'

'I need to go up to London.'

Silence. Then, 'Why?'

'The police have got my handbag so I need to collect it and I also need to sort out my flat. God know what horrors are lurking in my fridge, plus I ought to pick up some more clothes. Ultimately I suppose I ought to get rid of the place.'

'I'll come with you.'

'No, really.'

'It's no trouble.'

Jess took a breath. 'I'd rather you didn't.'

Abby looked hurt by the rejection. 'I see.'

Jess dithered for a moment or two about coming clean for the other reason for her trip to London. If things between her and her sister were to continue to move forward, she'd have to start being absolutely truthful. 'When you were out shopping yesterday I had Inspector Baxter on the phone.'

'And?' The note of suspicion was unmistakable.

'And nothing. I've got to go and make a statement.'

'Can't they come to you?'

'They offered, but I decided that what with everything else I need to do I might as well kill several birds with one stone. He told me that Gavin, Miles and the rest of the gang have all been up in court and have been refused bail.'

'That's one good thing.' Abby shuddered. 'And to think I once shared a bed with Gavin. Why didn't I see what a bastard he really was?' Her voice trembled; his duplicity still hurt terribly.

'Oh, Abby.'

Abby sniffed and squared her shoulders as if to brush off her moment of weakness. 'Yeah, I know – pathetic, aren't I?'

'No, of course you're not.'

'I've always been so sure of myself, so convinced I knew best. I knew you'd never liked Gav but I paid no attention.'

'He scared me once,' Jess finally admitted. 'At Gran's.'

'You never said.'

'I did, you didn't listen. You and Gav were so loved up you didn't believe me.'

'Tell me again.'

Jess told her about finding Gav snooping around the house on his very first visit, how he'd sworn at her and she'd thought he was going to hit her.

'You're joking.'

'Afraid not. I suppose that's why I never really took to him.'

'Not surprised.' Abby sighed. 'Maybe if I'd paid attention, none of this would have happened.'

'Maybe, maybe not.' Jess shrugged. 'Who's to say?'

'And you're sure you're happy to go up to Town on your own?'

'I think I'll cope. I've got to get back into the saddle sometime soon.'

*

Jess felt a brief surge of panic when she got off the train at the London terminus. All the people! But she tightened her grip on her handbag (borrowed from Abby and containing money also borrowed from Abby, plus her ticket and not a lot else), and, concentrating on keeping her breathing regular, made her way to the ticket barrier and then headed for the Tube.

Once on the Underground, she looked about at her fellow passengers and was reassured to see that no one was taking the least bit of interest in her. No one was looking at her and no one stood too close; she was in a little anonymous bubble, just like the other hundreds of previous times when she'd travelled this way. It was oddly reassuring. She even found herself relaxing enough to pick up a discarded free newspaper and reacquaint herself with the gossip columns, as Abby didn't believe in taking a paper, saying it was a waste of resources. So engrossed was she in the shenanigans within the world of celebrities that she almost missed her stop. As she chucked the paper back onto the seat and scrambled out of the doors just before they slammed shut, Jess felt that she had begun to really move forward and put her horrific experience behind her. She knew she still had a way to go, but at least she'd made a start.

However, as she approached the police station she realised that there was a real chance that she might run into Matt, a thought that made her stomach lurch with apprehension. She didn't want a scene – certainly not in such a public place – but she had made her mind up that she couldn't have anything more to do with him. It was all just too painful.

Nervously, she walked up the front steps of the police station. The reception area was almost empty apart from a couple of people sitting on the plastic seating and looking bored stiff. The desk sergeant looked up as she came in.

'Hi, Jess. Good to see you again. How are you?'

'Okay. You know . . .'

'Bad do,' he muttered, looking uncomfortable.

Jess remembered that he was of the old-fashioned school of men who ran a mile from anything emotional or touchy-feely. If she was going to launch into a description of her psychological state or angsts he really wouldn't want to know.

'Yeah,' she said quietly. 'Anyway, I've got to see the boss and do the paperwork.'

She punched the code into the keypad by the door into the business side of the station and let herself in.

'Jess,' shrieked Sally, coming out of the locker room. 'Oh my God! How are you? You missed my wedding. I mean, I know you didn't intend to,' she gave a little laugh, 'but you not being there and people being worried about you . . . Well, it put a bit of a dampener on things. Anyway, despite that we managed to have a fantastic day and my dress was to die for . . .'

'Oh good,' said Jess weakly. She'd forgotten all about the wedding. Should she feel sorry that being kidnapped had nearly messed things up for Sally? Er, no. But she tried to look contrite if only to shut the woman up. 'So why aren't you and Simon away on your honeymoon?'

'We're going next month. You know, when we can both get leave because it was a bit of a rush but even so it was a fantastic day, and you dipped out by not being there. I'll have to show you the pictures and—'

'Some other time,' Jess interrupted hurriedly. 'I've got to see the boss. Mustn't keep him waiting.' She escaped towards the stairs and sanctuary.

It seemed to take hours to write her statement and give Inspector Baxter all the information he wanted about the kidnap. Eventually she was free to go, and feeling exhausted she took a bus over to her flat. But at least she now had her own bag and her flat keys back, and once she got into her home she could begin to sort her life out again. She needed to do that, no matter how knackered she felt.

When the lift stopped at her floor she was aware of a pleasant smell as the doors slid apart. She vaguely wondered if someone had been using an upmarket air freshener on the landing as she inserted her key in the lock. As she pushed open the door and bent to pick up the pile of post on her hall floor, she noticed that the scent was considerably stronger in here. Puzzled, she looked up and saw that her sitting room was filled with roses. Vases and vases of them on every surface.

What the . . . ?

'Surprise,' said Matt, coming out of the kitchen.

Jess sagged. She felt absolutely wrung out, and he was the last person, she realised, that she could cope with seeing.

37

'I'm sorry, Jess, I really am.'

'How did you know I was here? What are you doing in my flat?'

'I heard on the station grapevine that you were coming in today to give Baxter a statement. I assumed you'd come here, so I got here first – let myself in with that set of keys you gave me. I need to talk to you, Jess, to tell you I was wrong, to ask you to forgive me.'

Jess turned to go. She couldn't deal with this now. She was too vulnerable and the hurt was too raw.

'Don't go,' Matt called but Jess fled, slamming the front door behind her.

She took the three steps from her door to the lift and pressed the button angrily. How dare he come to her flat? Her flat, where the last time they'd been together he'd virtually called her a hooker and had stormed out taking her heart along with his clothes.

As she pressed the call button again, she heard the door to her flat open.

'Jess. How can I make it up to you?'

'You can't,' she told him. 'It's over. *You* said so.'

The light signalling which floor the lift had reached flashed at the one below. Jess hit the button a third time.

'I was wrong.'

'Some mistake,' said Jess icily. 'No!' she snapped as

she saw that the lift was going down to the ground floor, leaving her stranded with Matt. Stuff this. She tried to shoulder past him and head for the stairs but Matt caught her arm and held her.

'Let me go,' she snarled. 'I've had enough of being someone's prisoner.'

Matt dropped her arm hurriedly. 'I'm sorry, but please hear me out, Jess.'

'Why? Why should I?' She could feel the tears welling up and tried to blink them back. 'I asked the same of you a while back and you didn't give me that luxury.' The tears spilled over and trickled down her face. Jess ignored them. 'You just accused me of turning tricks for half the Met Police and then stormed out, if I remember rightly.'

Matt looked ashen. 'And I was wrong. So wrong. Why didn't you tell me what you'd got mixed up in?'

'Because I was frightened you wouldn't like it. How right I was,' she added bitterly. 'I was scared that you'd go ballistic if you knew what a lowlife I was working for, but when Dodds and McCausland asked me to get closer to him, to help put him away, I was stuck between a rock and a hard place. They were going to get heavy if I said no to them, and make sure Miles knew what I did with my weekends. I loved being a Special but I needed the money from dancing. What was I supposed to do?' Her voice had got suspiciously shrill as her emotions welled up.

'I wouldn't have gone ballistic. I'd have been worried, yes, I'd have been scared for you – but I would have supported you.'

'So why did you think I was getting paid for sex?'

Matt recounted the conversation he'd overheard and Jess listened, first stunned, then puzzled – and then the penny dropped.

'I'd got Dodds out of a tricky spot, Matt. I gave him a

reason to be at the club even though he didn't look a bit like one of our regular punters, and Miles bought it. Dodds was telling McCausland I was good at thinking on my feet, not good at performing on my back.'

As she said this the lift door opened and a startled neighbour who only caught the last bit of the sentence scuttled past and raced into her own flat.

'We can't talk here,' snapped Jess. She got her key out again and ushered Matt back into her flat. 'So you thought flowers would make it all better,' she said, throwing her bag onto a chair.

'I didn't know what else to do. I've never got anything quite so wrong before. How do you apologise for a fuck-up as big as mine?'

Jess shrugged. 'I don't think you can,' she said quietly.

'Oh.'

'And the flowers haven't really helped.'

'Oh,' said Matt again. 'Don't you like roses? I kind of assumed you'd left my roses at the hospital because you'd discharged yourself. I went back to try to apologise to you but I'd just missed you. The nurses said they'd advised you to stay but you wouldn't.'

'I thought you'd come back and I didn't want to face you.'

Matt sighed. 'I'm sorry. I really am. I don't know how to convince you just *how* sorry I am, *how* awful I feel.'

Jess eyed him, assessing just how contrite he was. 'Look, these roses,' she waved a hand at them, 'they're lovely but I came back here to start clearing the place out. As soon as I've got rid of any perishables, cleaned up and packed some clothes I'm going back to my sister's for the foreseeable future.'

'You needn't worry about the fridge. I've sorted it out for you.'

'You what?'

'I couldn't have you coming home to rancid milk, so I decide to clear it out. I forgot to give you my key back so I thought the least I could do was make myself useful.'

It was Jess's turn to say 'Oh.' Tears spilled again, this time triggered by his thoughtfulness, but she dismissed her weakness angrily as still being in a state after her recent ordeal.

'I took your dresses to the cleaners too.'

'That wasn't necessary. It's not like I'm ever going to need those again.' She knew she sounded brutal but tough. She hadn't asked him to rush around clearing up after her, had she?

'So you've given up dancing.'

'I can't see Shoq opening again, can you?'

'So what about your big plans to earn enough to buy the house in the country?'

'I've given up on those too.' Although why she was telling Matt this stuff defeated her. It wasn't as if any of it concerned him any more.

'That's a shame, it's a lovely place.'

'Correction, *was* a lovely place. I've gone right off it. I don't like the associations it's got any more.'

'But if you did it up, cleared out all the grot, did the garden, modernised it, gave it a coat of paint, it would be fantastic. I mean, the kitchen alone—'

'What do you know about the kitchen? You've never set foot in the place.'

'But I have. After you disappeared, I went looking for you. I went to the club and Nadine said you'd gone missing. She said Laura and some of the girls were really worried about you. Well, that made several of us. I don't know why, but I thought you might have bolted off to your gran's house.'

'You thought I might have high-tailed it out there to warn the gang.'

'No. I really, *really* didn't think you were involved in what Miles and Gavin were up to. Come on, if you had been, would you have taken me over to see the place?'

'It could have been a double bluff.'

Matt raised an eyebrow. 'I'm sorry, Jess, no disrespect but you're just not devious enough for that sort of thing.' Jess almost found herself smiling but managed to stop herself. 'You didn't have a clue what was going on in that house, did you?' Jess shook her head. 'And as for being the sort of double agent who can carry off subterfuge without turning a hair – I saw exactly how scared you were when Sally spotted you working at the club. You weren't scared because she'd found out what your day job was, you were scared because the day job was about to associate you with the police. You don't do double bluff, Jess. You're absolutely not cut out for a life of double-dealing and plotting. Unlike those scrotes in the Drugs Squad.'

'I can't say I was thrilled when you guys rocked up, no,' Jess conceded.

'Anyway, I went out to the house, got there in the middle of the night and found all hell breaking loose; vans parked outside, lights on, blokes scurrying around like blue-arsed flies and pot plants everywhere. And I mean *pot* plants. And then I remembered you telling me about the mothballs, and I should have made the connection.'

Jess looked askance.

'It's what growers and heavy users use to cover the smell of cannabis. Which convinced me you were innocent. There's no way you'd have let slip something like that to me if you'd known how significant it was.'

'Well, lucky old me,' said Jess.

'But you so nearly weren't. I mean, with Miles trying

to bugger off out of the country and you in that house in the middle of nowhere, we might not have found you until . . .' he paused.

'It was too late,' she finished for him calmly.

A silence descended between them. Then Jess said, 'So you went looking for me.'

Matt nodded. 'I was so worried. And I blamed myself for a whole heap of it because I should have looked after you better than that. The things you really love you take care of, right? Only I didn't.'

Jess didn't know what to say.

'Jess . . .'

'Yes?'

'I fucked up so badly. I made so many mistakes but the instant you were out of my life I realised how much I wanted you back in. Remember that old Joni Mitchell song?'

'Yes.'

'She was so right. I only knew how much you meant to me when you'd gone. Is there any way, any way at all you'd consider giving me a second chance?'

'Abby wouldn't like it. I've told you what she's like about the cops.'

'Sod Abby, it's you I'm asking.'

'I don't know, Matt . . .'

'Please. Just a chance.'

'I need to think.'

Matt moved towards the door. 'Yes, of course. Take as long as you like. I understand.'

Jess watched him open the door. 'Thanks for the roses. They're lovely. Over the top but lovely.'

Matt smiled at her and left.

Jess went over to her sofa and sat down. So he *had* tried to ride to her rescue, except that unlike Sleeping Beauty's admirer he'd fetched up at the wrong location, hacked his way through the wrong forest and gone to the foot of the wrong tower. But the thought had been there. And if he hadn't made that effort, the gang wouldn't have been nicked and the little old lady who had seen her signals might just have been dismissed as a daft old bag when she'd rung the police with her worries. So all in all Matt was probably, almost single-handedly responsible for her discovery.

But did that make up for everything? Well, it made up for a fair bit. And he wouldn't have done it if he hadn't still had feelings for her.

Jess stood up again and went into her bedroom. All her dresses were hanging up, all beautifully cleaned, just as he'd said. She went into the kitchen and had a look in the fridge. Pristine, just as he'd promised, and empty apart from a bottle of vintage champagne with a note pinned to it.

I love you, it said. *Forgive me?*

Jess found herself crying. 'And I love you, Matt Green,' she whispered. 'I love you too. Despite everything. I don't think I ever stopped. And I do forgive you, but can we ever trust each other again?'

'I expect Aunty Abby would like to see your picture. Shall we go and find her?'

The toddler with flaxen Shirley Temple curls grabbed the scribbled piece of paper in her pudgy fist, climbed off the kitchen chair and raced out into the garden. She trundled across the lawn behind her great-grandmother's old house to the enormous vegetable garden, her mother waddling along behind as fast as she could at almost eight months' pregnant.

'Abby, Abby,' called Jess. 'Felicity wants to show you something.'

Out from behind an immaculate row of runner beans which covered the tent of canes appeared Felicity's aunt.

'Aggy, Aggy,' squealed the little girl.

Her aunt swept her up and took the picture. 'My, that's wonderful,' she said. 'A real work of art.' She planted a kiss on the chubby cheek. 'How you feeling, sis?' she asked as Jess joined them.

'Knackered. I tried to get some kip this afternoon when Fliss had her rest but the sound of those bloody bulldozers kept me awake.'

'They've almost finished the foundations. Only a few more days to go, Patrick says, and then it'll be a bit more peaceful.'

'Hmm. I'll believe it when I see it.' And although Jess

was a bit cranky with lack of sleep and the late stages of pregnancy, she was amused to see Abby colour slightly when she mentioned the site manager. Jess said nothing but she wondered if anything was going to develop between the two of them. Over the last few weeks, since the building work on their land had really swung into action, she'd noticed Abby and Patrick's body language, when they were around each other, change quite markedly – and in a way that left no doubt, in Jess's mind, that there was some sort of attraction between them. And a jolly good thing too. She just hoped it would develop; Abby could do with a nice bloke in her life, and as far as Jess could see, Patrick was an extremely nice bloke – even down to sharing Abby's Green beliefs.

'Still,' continued Jess, suppressing a smile, 'I suppose if Patrick's in charge and he says they're almost there with the heavy machinery, then that's as good as a promise. Although sometimes I do wish we'd not started this until after I'd had the baby. I could really do without the noise and mess and everything.'

'But you don't want to do without the dosh.'

Jess grinned. The money from the sale of half the garden certainly was useful. She and Matt had put half of their share in trust for the kids and it had still left more than enough over for them to buy Abby's share of the old house and then completely remodernise it. It had been a win-win for both the sisters.

Felicity scrambled out of her aunt's arms and sat down on the grass to examine a daisy.

'Well,' said Abby, flexing her arms – Fliss was a solid little girl, 'we want to keep the developers cracking on because the sooner they finish, the sooner I can get out of your hair and move into my own little eco-friendly house.'

'It'll be funny having neighbours here, won't it?' said

Jess. 'I don't mean you, of course, I mean other people.'

'Quite nice, if you ask me. And let's face it, there won't be that many, although we've got to hope that some of the houses sell to families with kids. It'd be lovely for yours to have some friends to play with. And even with half the land gone, this garden is still almost too big for me to manage.'

Jess looked around her. 'You know, I can never remember the garden ever looking as tidy as this. Of course, it means it's crap for hide-and-seek.'

'Thanks a bunch,' said Abby. 'I don't know why I bother.'

'Because you like being self-sufficient.'

'And you don't like having organic veg grown on your doorstep?'

'It's okay.'

Abby gave her sister a friendly punch on the arm. 'And to think we nearly sold this place.'

'What a shame that would have been.'

'Matt was right; it wasn't as if anything dreadful had happened to either of us here. It was only the tenants and what Gav and Miles did that made it seem tainted.'

'By the way, we'll hear tomorrow if they're going to be allowed to appeal.'

'Do you think they will?' asked Abby.

'Matt reckons there's no chance.'

'Matt reckons there's no chance of what?' said a male voice behind them.

'Dadda,' squealed Fliss, abandoning her daisy and grabbing her father's legs.

Matt bent down and picked her up, swirling her high into the air till she shrieked and yelled.

'You'll make her sick,' said Jess indulgently. 'The appeal – we were talking about the appeal.'

'Well,' said Matt, putting Fliss back on the ground and

straightening up again, 'what with wrongful imprison-
ment, drug dealing, fraud, extortion and all the other
things that came to light once Morgan got nicked . . . ?
Nah, his life term will almost certainly stay. Gav might get
a couple of years lopped off his sentence, but now you've
got the decree absolute you're home free. And I can't see
him coming sniffing around here again when he does
eventually get out. Even he wouldn't have the balls for
that. Not with you having a copper for a brother-in-law.'

'No,' said Abby, 'and I'm about to say something that I
never thought I would, but it's quite nice having a tame
copper around the place.'

Jess feigned a swoon. 'Blimey Abby, you're right.
You've gone soft. If you carry on like this you may even
come to the next social evening with us.'

'No. I'll babysit so you two can go but I draw the line
at that. There are limits. It's one thing being related to a
copper but quite another making friends with dozens.'

Jess laughed. 'You'll come round.'

Abby just gave her a hard stare. 'Hmmm.'

At that moment, Patrick approached, removing his
hard hat and wiping his forehead. Jess watched Abby fluff
up her hair with her fingers and pull her T-shirt down.
She wondered what Abby would say if she invited Patrick
round for a drink one evening? Maybe she should; after
all, Jess was sure there might be some aspects of the
development that they ought to discuss informally.

Fliss was tugging at her father's hand.

'I think we ought to take this young lady in and give
her her tea,' said Jess. 'You can lend a hand,' she told her
husband.

Leaving Abby and Patrick, the little family walked
back to the house. As they reached the back door Jess
stood on tiptoe and gave Matt a kiss.

'What's that for?'

'For being you, for persuading Abby and me to keep this place, for being the father of my children.'

'Is that all?'

'I think that's quite enough, don't you?'

'And do you think Patrick can supply some of that for Abby?'

'You've noticed too.'

'Bloody hell, Jess. I *am* a copper, I *am* supposed to be observant – but even a blind man could see there's something going on between them. And do you know what the good thing about it is?'

'No.'

'You like him.'

Jess nodded. 'Just like Abby likes you. Which makes playing happy families so much easier.'

You can buy any of these other
Little Black Dress titles from your
bookshop or *direct from the publisher*.

FREE P&P AND UK DELIVERY
(Overseas and Ireland £3.50 per book)

TO ORDER SIMPLY CALL THIS NUMBER

01235 400 414

or visit our website: www.headline.co.uk